TOEIC®
Listening and Reading Test
Official Test-Preparation Guide Vol. **8**

TOEIC® 聽力與閱讀測驗[1]於 1979 年首次推出，為英語教育測驗界帶來許多重大且正面的影響。40 多年來，TOEIC 系列測驗為評估工作場所和日常生活所需的英語溝通技能設立了標準。全球有超過 160 個國家、14,000 家企業或機構，認同 TOEIC 測驗能夠準確評估應試者是否具備在日常生活或工作中，有效地使用英語與他人交流的能力和技能。

作為全球最大的教育測驗機構之一，ETS® 非常重視試題研發的品質。TOEIC 測驗的每一道題目，都有至少一個被設定好的目標能力（Abilities Measured），聽力測驗和閱讀測驗分別測量五種不同的能力。從 TOEIC 聽力與閱讀測驗成績單中的 Abilities Measured 部分[2]，應試者可以看到自己在每項目標能力的答對比例，進而針對該項英語目標能力做專長發揮或是能力補強。

長期以來，台灣的教學環境習慣以一個量化的結果（分數）作為學習的終點，而較少關注產生結果的過程，或是結果所代表的意義。這就是第八冊《TOEIC® 聽力與閱讀測驗官方全真試題指南》的起源。有別於過去僅提供解析的官方指南，第八冊清楚地說明了每一道題目的目標能力，希望讓準備要參加 TOEIC 測驗的應試者，藉由了解目標能力，發揮並改善自己的強項與弱項，提升溝通實力，強化個人競爭力，循序漸進地達到期望的結果；而教學者也可以透過目標能力，設定合適的教學目標與教學內容，讓教學與學習的結果都更具有實質意義。

第八冊同樣提供兩套全真模擬試題，並將聽力與閱讀分開出版，在聚焦學習的同時獲得最佳成效。期盼教學者、學習者、應試者都能利用本書，在英語學習的路上持續邁進，運用在生活及工作當中，成為能使用英語溝通的國際人才。

TOEIC® 臺灣區總代理　忠欣股份有限公司 董事長

邵作俊 謹識

[1] TOEIC 全名為 Test of English for International Communication，
　TOEIC 系列測驗分為聽力與閱讀測驗及口說與寫作測驗。其中口說及寫作測驗可分開選擇。
[2] 可參閱本書 P.9 目標能力（Abilities Measured）說明。

　　本書收錄兩套 *TOEIC®* 聽力與閱讀測驗的閱讀全真試題，每套各有 100 道題目，和實際測驗相同。在練習全真試題之後，可根據第 86、87 頁提供的分數換算表、目標能力正答率計算方式及目標能力對應，獲得參考的結果。最後則提供題目中文翻譯、重點解析及各項目標能力說明。

題型範例

　　提供閱讀測驗試題範例以及應答說明，讓讀者理解 TOEIC 閱讀測驗各題型的測驗方式。

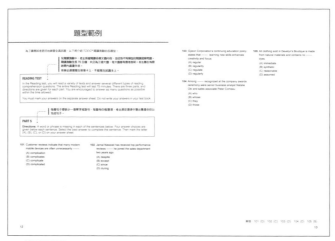

▲ 閱讀測驗

全真試題

　　共有兩套全真試題，內容與實際測驗相同，閱讀測驗有 100 題，可使用書中所附的模擬答案卡作答，並試著在 75 分鐘之限制時間內，完成所有題目。

▲ 全真試題

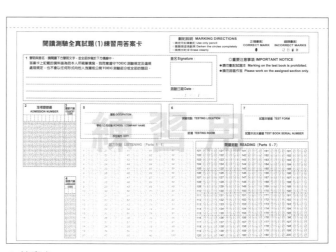

▲ 答案卡

分數及目標能力計算

　　測驗完畢後可依照第 83 頁開始的「試題解答與分數及目標能力計算」，計算出分數及目標能力正答率。需注意的是，本書所提供的分數換算方式僅適用於 *ETS®* 所提供的全真模擬試題，與實際測驗的成績計算方法不同，故本書獲得的分數為參考分數。

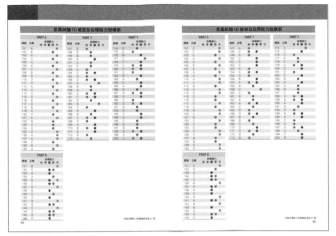

▲ 試題解答

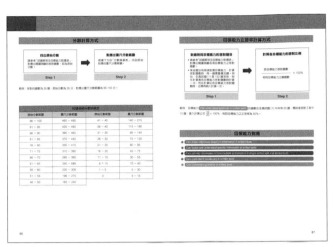

▲ 分數及目標能力計算

中文翻譯及目標能力解析

　　提供每一道題目的中文翻譯、詳盡解析，並標示出各題所要評量的目標能力及應試重點。

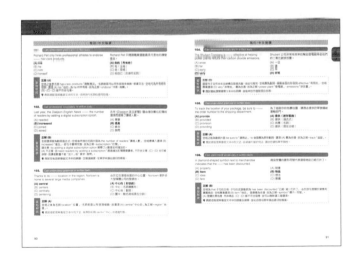

測驗簡介

　　TOEIC 聽力與閱讀測驗是 TOEIC Program 的一員，專為英語非母語人士測試英語聽力與閱讀能力。測驗內容主要是檢測職場情境或日常生活中所需的英語能力，考生不需具備特定專業知識或字彙。本項測驗的試題都經過一系列審查，排除不了解特定文化就無法理解的內容，以確保試題的公平性，適合全世界的考生受測。

測驗題型

　　測驗內容分成聽力（約 45 分鐘，100 題）和閱讀（75 分鐘，100 題）兩部分，各題型及題數如下表所示。

聽力測驗（Listening Section）測驗時間：約 45 分鐘		
大題	內容		題數
1	照片描述	Photographs	6
2	應答問題	Question-Response	25
3	簡短對話	Conversations	39（共 13 個題組，每題組有 3 題）
4	簡短獨白	Talks	30（共 10 個題組，每題組有 3 題）
總計			100

閱讀測驗（Reading Section）測驗時間：75 分鐘		
大題	內容		題數
5	句子填空	Incomplete Sentences	30
6	段落填空	Text Completion	16
7	單篇閱讀	Single Passages	29（共 10 個題組，每題組有 2～4 題）
	多篇閱讀	Multiple Passages	25（共 5 個題組，每題組有 5 題）
總計			100

成績單說明

　　成績單主要由三個項目所組成，包括（1）考生基本資訊及成績、（2）聽力測驗及閱讀測驗的能力論述說明、（3）目標能力的正答率。考生可藉由能力論述及目標能力正答率，了解所得分數代表的對應能力，以及自身英語能力的強弱項。

　姓名、出生年月日、測驗日期、成績

　聽力測驗及閱讀測驗之能力論述

　各項目標能力之正答率

分數計算

TOEIC 聽力與閱讀測驗分數是使用實驗驗證的統計等化程序（equating），將答對題數所得的原始分數（raw score）轉換成量尺分數（scaled score），答錯不倒扣。測驗本身沒有所謂的「通過」或「不通過」，而是將受測者的能力以聽力 5 ～ 495 分、閱讀 5 ～ 495 分、總分 10 ～ 990 分的分數來呈現。藉由換算程序，即使是不同次的測驗，所得出的分數意義是相同的。也就是說，某次測驗得分 550 分，和另外一次測驗得分 550 分，代表著相同的英語能力。

目標能力（Abilities Measured）

TOEIC 聽力與閱讀測驗在聽力及閱讀部份各有 5 項不同的目標能力：

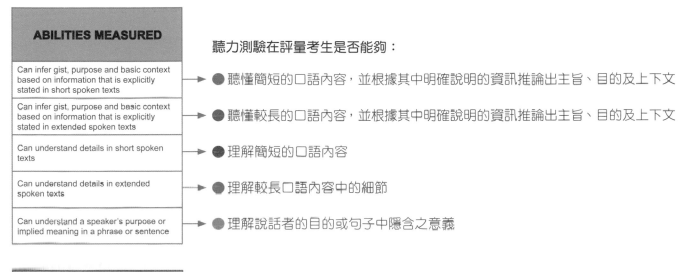

聽力測驗在評量考生是否能夠：

● 聽懂簡短的口語內容，並根據其中明確說明的資訊推論出主旨、目的及上下文

● 聽懂較長的口語內容，並根據其中明確說明的資訊推論出主旨、目的及上下文

● 理解簡短的口語內容

● 理解較長口語內容中的細節

● 理解說話者的目的或句子中隱含之意義

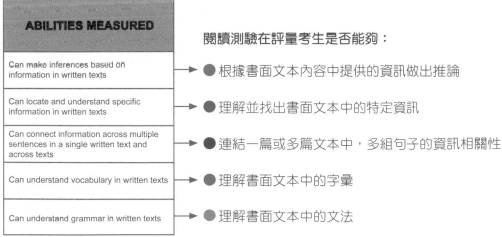

閱讀測驗在評量考生是否能夠：

● 根據書面文本內容中提供的資訊做出推論

● 理解並找出書面文本中的特定資訊

● 連結一篇或多篇文本中，多組句子的資訊相關性

● 理解書面文本中的字彙

● 理解書面文本中的文法

目標能力正答率

目標能力正答率是 TOEIC 聽力與閱讀測驗成績單中的一個項目，是由應試者在各項目標能力對應試題中的答對數量計算而來，在成績單上使用長條圖來呈現。假設某題本中，使用 20 道題目來評量考生某項目標能力，而考生答對了其中 11 題，則該目標能力之正答率為 55%。正答率之比例只能與參加同一次 TOEIC 聽力與閱讀測驗的考生進行比較，由於某些能力的問題數量相對較少，因此在比較時應謹慎。

能力論述

TOEIC 聽力測驗成績對應能力論述		
分數	強項	弱項
400	**簡短口語內容：** • 能從廣泛的詞彙中，推論出主旨、目的及基本的上下文。在對話內容不直接或難以預測時，也不影響其理解。 • 能夠理解內容細節，使用複雜的句子結構及困難字彙時，也不影響其理解。 **較長口語內容：** • 能夠推論出主旨、目的及上下文。即使不重複或不多加解釋時，也能理解其對話內容。 • 能夠連結不同資訊間的關聯性，並由解釋的方式理解其內容細節，在對話內容不重複或包含否定語句時，也不影響其理解。	• 僅在使用不常見或困難的文法及字彙時，才會出現問題。
300	**簡短口語內容：** • 能從廣泛的詞彙中，推論出主旨、目的及基本的上下文，特別是字彙程度不難的時候。 • 能夠理解並且使用簡單或中等程度字彙的口語內容細節。 **較長口語內容：** • 透過說話者重複或解釋，能夠推論出較長內容的主旨、目的以及基本的上下文。 • 當重點資訊出現在句首或句尾，並被重複說明的時候，能理解其內容細節。若訊息被稍加解釋，也能理解其細節。	**簡短口語內容：** • 若對話內容不直接、難以預測或使用困難字彙時，難以理解其主旨、目的或基本的上下文。 • 無法理解包含複雜的語法結構或者困難字彙的口語交流，亦無法理解包含否定結構的細節。 **較長口語內容：** • 當需要連結不同訊息，或使用困難字彙的時候，無法理解其主旨、目的或基本的上下文。 • 當訊息不重複或需要連結不同訊息時，無法理解其內容的細節。無法理解大多數需要透過解釋的內容或較困難的文法架構。
200	**簡短口語內容：** • 在簡短（一句話）描述的狀況下，能夠理解照片的主旨。 • 使用的字彙較簡單且只有少量必須理解的內容時，能理解簡短口語交流和照片描述中的細節。 **較長口語內容：** • 如果訊息被大量重複並使用簡單的字彙，有時候能推論出較長內容的主旨、目的及基本的上下文。 • 當被要求的資訊出現在句首或是句尾並與問題所使用的語言相同時，能夠理解其內容細節。	**簡短口語內容：** • 即使內容直接且沒有難以預測的訊息，仍無法理解其主旨、目的或基本的上下文。 • 當使用較困難的單字或複雜的文法結構時，無法理解其內容細節。無法理解包含否定結構的細節。 **較長口語內容：** • 當需要連結不同訊息，或使用困難字彙的時候，無法理解其主旨、目的或基本的上下文。 • 當被要求的訊息出現在文本中時，無法理解其細節，亦無法理解經過解釋的訊息或者困難的文法結構。

TOEIC 閱讀測驗成績對應能力論述

分數	強項	弱項
450	• 能夠推斷書面文本的主旨及目的，也能夠對細節做出推論。 • 能夠透過閱讀理解書面文本的含意，即使內容被經過解釋，也能理解真實訊息。 • 能夠連結同篇或是多篇文章中的不同訊息。 • 能夠理解廣泛的字彙，常用字少見的用法及片語的使用，也可以分辨相似詞之間的差異。 • 能夠理解有規則的文法架構，也可以理解困難、複雜或少見的句子結構。	• 在測驗的訊息特別密集或者牽涉到特別困難的字彙時，才會出現問題。
350	• 能夠推論書面文本的主旨及目的，也能夠對細節做出推論。 • 能夠透過閱讀理解書面文本的含意，即使內容被經過解釋，也能理解真實訊息。 • 即使使用較難的字彙或是文法，也能夠連結同篇文本中小範圍的資訊。 • 能理解中等程度的字彙，有時能藉由上下文理解困難的字彙、常用字少見的用法和片語的使用。 • 能夠理解有規則的文法結構，也可以理解困難、複雜或少見的句子架構。	• 無法將同篇文章內大範圍的訊息做連結。 • 無法完全理解困難的字彙、常用字少見的用法或是片語的使用。通常無法分辨出相似詞之間的差異。
250	• 能夠在有限的書面文本中做出簡單的推論。 • 當文本使用的語言與所需訊息相符時，可以找到真實訊息的正確答案。當答案是對文本訊息的簡單解釋時，有時可以回答關於事實的問題。 • 有時能連結單一或是兩個句子之間的訊息。 • 能夠理解簡單的字彙，有時候也能理解中等程度的字彙。 • 能夠理解常見或者具有規則的文法結構，即使在使用有難度的字彙或需要連結訊息時，仍能選出正確的文法選項。	• 無法理解需要透過解釋或者連結訊息所做出的推論。 • 使用困難的字彙解釋時，理解實際訊息的能力十分有限，需要依靠在文本中找出與問題相同的字詞來答題。 • 通常無法連結超過兩句的訊息。 • 無法理解困難的字彙、常用字少見的用法或是片語的使用，無法分辨出相似詞之間的差異。 • 無法理解更加困難、複雜或少見的文法架構。
150	• 當所需的閱讀量不多，且文本使用的語言與問題相同時，能夠找到正確的答案。 • 能夠理解簡單的字彙以及基本的慣用語。 • 在所需閱讀量不多時，能夠理解最常見並且具有規則的文法架構。	• 無法根據書面文本的訊息做出推論。 • 無法理解經過解釋的事實與訊息，必須依靠在文本中找出與問題相同的字詞來答題。 • 就算在單一句子裡，仍經常無法連結訊息。 • 能夠理解的字彙十分有限。 • 當使用較難的字彙或者需要連結訊息時，即使文法句構簡單亦無法理解。

題型範例

為了讓應試者更好地練習全真試題，以下將介紹 *TOEIC*® 閱讀測驗的各題型。

在閱讀測驗中，考生將會閱讀各類文體內容，並回答不同類型的閱讀理解問題。閱讀測驗全長 75 分鐘，共分為三個大題，每大題都有應考說明。考生應在有限時間內盡量作答。

答案必須填寫在答案卡上，不能寫在試題本上。

READING TEST

In the Reading test, you will read a variety of texts and answer several different types of reading comprehension questions. The entire Reading test will last 75 minutes. There are three parts, and directions are given for each part. You are encouraged to answer as many questions as possible within the time allowed.

You must mark your answers on the separate answer sheet. Do not write your answers in your test book.

每題句子都缺少一個單字或語句，每題有四個選項，考生須從選項中選出最適合的以完成句子。

PART 5

Directions: A word or phrase is missing in each of the sentences below. Four answer choices are given below each sentence. Select the best answer to complete the sentence. Then mark the letter (A), (B), (C), or (D) on your answer sheet.

101. Customer reviews indicate that many modern mobile devices are often unnecessarily ------- .

    (A) complication
    (B) complicates
    (C) complicate
    (D) complicated

102. Jamal Nawzad has received top performance reviews ------- he joined the sales department two years ago.

    (A) despite
    (B) except
    (C) since
    (D) during

103. Gyeon Corporation's continuing education policy states that ------- learning new skills enhances creativity and focus.
(A) regular
(B) regularity
(C) regulate
(D) regularly

104. Among ------- recognized at the company awards ceremony were senior business analyst Natalie Obi and sales associate Peter Comeau.
(A) who
(B) whose
(C) they
(D) those

105. All clothing sold in Develyn's Boutique is made from natural materials and contains no ------- dyes.
(A) immediate
(B) synthetic
(C) reasonable
(D) assumed

PART 6

Directions: Read the texts that follow. A word, phrase, or sentence is missing in parts of each text. Four answer choices for each question are given below the text. Select the best answer to complete the text. Then mark the letter (A), (B), (C), or (D) on your answer sheet.

Questions 131-134 refer to the following e-mail.

To: Project Leads

From: James Pak

Subject: Training Courses

To all Pak Designs project leaders:

In the coming weeks, we will be organizing several training sessions for ____131.____ employees. At Pak Designs, we believe that with the proper help and support from our senior project leaders, less experienced staff can quickly ____132.____ a deep understanding of the design process. ____133.____ , they can improve their ability to communicate effectively across divisions. When employees at all experience levels interact, every employee's competency level rises and the business overall benefits. For that reason, we are urging experienced project leaders to attend each one of the interactive seminars that will be held throughout the coming month. ____134.____ .

Thank you for your support.

James Pak

Pak Designs

131. (A) interest
    (B) interests
    (C) interested
    (D) interesting

132. (A) develop
    (B) raise
    (C) open
    (D) complete

133. (A) After all
    (B) For
    (C) Even so
    (D) At the same time

134. (A) Let me explain our plans for on-site staff training.
    (B) We hope that you will strongly consider joining us.
    (C) Today's training session will be postponed until Monday.
    (D) This is the first in a series of such lectures.

解答：131. (C)   132. (A)   133. (D)   134. (B)

PART 7

Directions: In this part you will read a selection of texts, such as magazine and newspaper articles, e-mails, and instant messages. Each text or set of texts is followed by several questions. Select the best answer for each question and mark the letter (A), (B), (C), or (D) on your answer sheet.

Questions 147-148 refer to the following advertisement.

Used Car For Sale. Six-year-old Carlisle Custom. Only one owner. Low mileage. Car used to commute short distances to town. Brakes and tires replaced six months ago. Struts replaced two weeks ago. Air conditioning works well, but heater takes a while to warm up. Brand new spare tire included. Priced to sell. Owner going overseas at the end of this month and must sell the car. Call Firoozeh Ghorbani at (848) 555-0132.

147. What is suggested about the car?

(A) It was recently repaired.
(B) It has had more than one owner.
(C) It is very fuel efficient.
(D) It has been on sale for six months.

148. According to the advertisement, why is Ms. Ghorbani selling her car?

(A) She cannot repair the car's temperature control.
(B) She finds it difficult to maintain.
(C) She would like to have a newer model.
(D) She is leaving for another country.

解答：147. (A)　148. (D)

Questions 149-151 refer to the following article.

On Monday, Salinas Products, a large food distributor based in Mexico City, announced its plans to acquire the Pablo's restaurant chain. Pablo Benavidez, the chain's owner, had been considering holding an auction for ownership of the chain. He ultimately made the decision to sell to Salinas without seeking other offers. According to inside sources, Salinas has agreed to keep the restaurant's name as part of the deal. Mr. Benavidez started the business 40 years ago right after finishing school. He opened a small food stand in his hometown of Cancún. Following that, he opened restaurants in Puerto Vallarta and Veracruz, and there are now over 50 Pablo's restaurants nationwide.

149. What is suggested about Mr. Benavidez?

(A) He has hired Salinas Products to distribute his products.
(B) He has agreed to sell his business to Salinas Products.
(C) He has recently been·hired as an employee of a school.
(D) He has been chosen to be the new president of Salinas Products.

150. According to the article, where is Mr. Benavidez from?

(A) Cancún
(B) Veracruz
(C) Mexico City
(D) Puerto Vallarta

151. What is indicated about the Pablo's restaurant chain?

(A) It was recently sold in an auction.
(B) It will soon change its name.
(C) It was founded 40 years ago.
(D) It operates in several countries.

解答：149. (B)　150. (A)　151. (C)

Questions 152-153 refer to the following text message chain.

> **SAM BACH** 11:59
> My first flight was delayed, so I missed my connection in Beijing.
>
> **SAM BACH** 12:00
> So now, I'm going to be on a flight arriving in Kansai at 18:00.
>
> **AKIRA OTANI** 12:05
> OK. Same airline?
>
> **SAM BACH** 12:06
> It's still Fly Right Airlines. It will be later in the day but still in time for our client meeting.
>
> **AKIRA OTANI** 12:06
> I'll confirm the arrival time. Do you have any checked bags?
>
> **SAM BACH** 12:10
> I do. Would you mind meeting me at the door after I go through customs?
>
> **AKIRA OTANI** 12:15
> Sure thing. Parking spots can be hard to find, but now I'll have extra time to drive around and look.
>
> **SAM BACH** 12:16
> Yes, sorry about that. See you then!
>
> | Send |

152. What is suggested about Mr. Bach?

(A) He has been to Kansai more than once.

(B) He currently works in Beijing.

(C) He is on a business trip.

(D) He works for Fly Right Airlines.

153. At 12:15, what does Mr. Otani mean when he writes, "Sure thing"?

(A) He has confirmed the arrival time of a flight.

(B) He is certain he will be able to find a parking place.

(C) He agrees to wait at the door near the customs area.

(D) He knows Mr. Bach must pass through customs.

解答：152. (C)　153. (C)

Questions 161-164 refer to the following information.

Notice Board SpaceAvailable to Community Groups

Mooringtown Library is pleased to invite local community groups to use the free advertising space on its new notice board, located outside the front entrance of the library. Space on the board is available for up to four weeks at a time.

Notices must be approved in advance at the library's front desk and must meet the following requirements. All content must be suitable for public display. The notice must be written or printed on standard-quality paper with dimensions of either 8.5 in x 11 in or 5.5 in x 8.5 in. The desired start and end date for display should be written in the front bottom right corner. — [1] —. Any notices that do not meet these requirements will not be considered and will be discarded.— [2] —.

— [3] —. Submissions are now being accepted at the Mooringtown Library front desk. Please have the actual notice, in the format in which you would like it to appear, with you when you arrive. Within one business day, you will receive a call confirming that your notice has been added to the board.— [4] —.

Mooringtown Library
www.mooringtownlib.co.au

---

161. What is indicated about advertising space on the Mooringtown Library notice board?

(A) It is available at no charge.
(B) It can be used for any length of time.
(C) It is open to all area businesses.
(D) It is intended mainly for sporting events.

162. What is NOT a stated requirement for a notice to be placed on the board?

(A) It must meet certain size requirements.
(B) It must be marked with posting dates.
(C) It must be reviewed beforehand.
(D) It must be signed by a librarian.

163. What should an advertiser bring to the library when making a submission?

(A) An outline of proposed content
(B) A final version of the notice
(C) A completed submission form
(D) A letter from an organization

164. In which of the positions marked [1], [2], [3], and [4] does the following sentence best belong?

"The name and telephone number of the person posting the notice must be clearly marked on the back."

(A) [1]
(B) [2]
(C) [3]
(D) [4]

解答：161. (A)　162. (D)　163. (B)　164. (A)

18

http://www.businessaudiopro.com

Business Audio Pro

Enhance Your Company's Image with a Professionally Recorded Telephone Greeting

A professional, personalized voicemail message creates an excellent first impression. **Business Audio Pro** meets your specifications to record a customized telephone greeting within three business days!

Services We Offer:

1. **Professional Voice Talent for Voicemail Messages** – We have numerous male and female voice actors with a wide range of tones, accents, and dialects. Visit businessaudiopro.com to hear examples of what each actor sounds like and choose the one that best suits your needs.
2. **On-Hold Messages** – We also create professional on-hold messages with pleasant music to enhance your customers' experience.
3. **Customized Script Writing** – Our experienced script writers can help you craft a personalized message that distinguishes you and your business.
4. **Multilingual Voice Production** – For those with a multilingual customer base, we offer services in a wide range of languages.

Send us an e-mail (inquiry@businessaudiopro.com) with your contact information and your specific needs. A representative will call you within 24 hours to discuss your project and provide a price estimate.

To:	inquiry@businessaudiopro.com
From:	j.annesly@anneslydata.com
Date:	June 25
Subject:	Request

I found your notice in the newspaper and wish to use your services for my data-processing and transcription business. I am looking specifically for a professionally recorded voicemail greeting intended for my clients, and I wonder if you would be available to write and record this for me, and how soon. Since I work with English- and Spanish-speaking clients, I would like the message to be recorded in both languages. Please reach out to me at my mobile phone between the hours of 10:00 A.M. and 5:00 P.M. I hope to hear from you soon.

Thank you,

Jody Annesly
Annesly Data
512-555-6879 (mobile)
342 Maymill Road, Fort Worth, TX 70609

176. According to the advertisement, why should customers visit the Business Audio Pro Web site?

(A) To hear voice samples
(B) To add a new phone number
(C) To submit a credit card payment
(D) To request recording equipment

177. What is suggested about Business Audio Pro?

(A) It fills orders once a week.
(B) It advertises in the newspaper.
(C) It specializes in data-processing services.
(D) It has recently expanded its business.

178. Who most likely is Ms. Annesly?

(A) An actor
(B) A script writer
(C) A sales associate
(D) A business owner

179. What service does Ms. Annesly NOT request from Business Audio Pro?

(A) Professional voice talent
(B) On-hold messages
(C) Customized script writing
(D) Multilingual voice production

180. What will Ms. Annesly most likely do within 24 hours?

(A) Meet with an actor
(B) Visit a recording studio
(C) Write a script
(D) Speak with a representative

解答：176. (A)　177. (B)　178. (D)　179. (B)　180. (D)

Sparky Paints, Inc.

Sparky Paints, Inc., makes it easy to select the right colors for your home. Browse through hundreds of colors on our Web site, www.sparkypaints.com. Select your top colors, and we'll send free samples right to your door. Our color samples are three times larger than typical samples found in home-improvement stores and come with self-adhesive backing, allowing you to adhere them to your walls so you can easily see how colors will coordinate in your home. When you're ready to begin painting, simply select your chosen colors online, and we'll ship the paint of your choice to arrive at your home within 3-5 business days, or within 2 business days for an additional expedited shipping fee.

*Actual colors may differ slightly from what appears on your monitor. For this reason, we recommend ordering several samples in similar shades.

---

http://www.sparkypaints.com/shoppingcart ▶

Sparky Paints, Inc.

Order Summary #3397		Customer: Arun Phan	
Item	**Size**	**Quantity**	**Price**
Caspian Blue SP 237	n/a	1	$0.00
Deep Sea Blue SP 298	n/a	1	$0.00
Stormy Blue SP 722	n/a	1	$0.00
Misty Gray SP 944	Gallon	2	$50.00

Tax (8 percent) $4.00
Expedited shipping $18.99
Total   **$72.99**

(Proceed to Checkout)

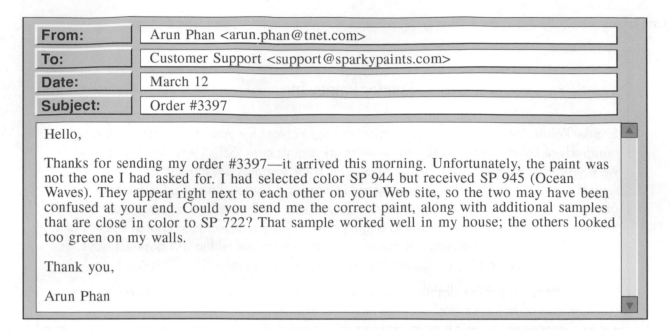

From:	Arun Phan <arun.phan@tnet.com>
To:	Customer Support <support@sparkypaints.com>
Date:	March 12
Subject:	Order #3397

Hello,

Thanks for sending my order #3397—it arrived this morning. Unfortunately, the paint was not the one I had asked for. I had selected color SP 944 but received SP 945 (Ocean Waves). They appear right next to each other on your Web site, so the two may have been confused at your end. Could you send me the correct paint, along with additional samples that are close in color to SP 722? That sample worked well in my house; the others looked too green on my walls.

Thank you,

Arun Phan

196. In the advertisement, the word "top" in paragraph 1, line 2, is closest in meaning to

(A) maximum
(B) favorite
(C) important
(D) upper

197. What are Sparky Paints customers advised to do?

(A) Apply an adhesive to color samples
(B) Visit a store to compare paint colors
(C) Adjust the color on their computer monitor
(D) Order samples of several similar colors

198. What is most likely true about order #3397 ?

(A) It arrived within two business days.
(B) It included an extra sample.
(C) It was shipped in February.
(D) It contained four gallons of paint.

199. Which color does Mr. Phan indicate that he likes?

(A) Caspian Blue
(B) Deep Sea Blue
(C) Stormy Blue
(D) Misty Gray

200. What problem does Mr. Phan mention in his e-mail?

(A) He received the wrong item.
(B) He was charged the wrong price.
(C) The delivery time was too long.
(D) The instructions were too confusing.

解答：196. (B)　197. (D)　198. (A)　199. (C)　200. (A)

閱讀測驗 全真試題(1)

In the Reading test, you will read a variety of texts and answer several different types of reading comprehension questions. The entire Reading test will last 75 minutes. There are three parts, and directions are given for each part. You are encouraged to answer as many questions as possible within the time allowed.

You must mark your answers on the separate answer sheet. Do not write your answers in your test book.

READING TEST

In the Reading test, you will read a variety of texts and answer several different types of reading comprehension questions. The entire Reading test will last 75 minutes. There are three parts, and directions are given for each part. You are encouraged to answer as many questions as possible within the time allowed.

You must mark your answers on the separate answer sheet. Do not write your answers in your test book.

PART 5

Directions: A word or phrase is missing in each of the sentences below. Four answer choices are given below each sentence. Select the best answer to complete the sentence. Then mark the letter (A), (B), (C), or (D) on your answer sheet.

101. Richard Pell only hires professional athletes to endorse ------- hair-care products.

(A) his
(B) he
(C) him
(D) himself

102. Last year, the *Daejeon English News* ------- the number of readers by adding a digital subscription option.

(A) needed
(B) increased
(C) joined
(D) asked

103. Thanks to its ------- location in the region, Nortown is home to several large media companies.

(A) central
(B) centers
(C) centrally
(D) centering

104. The Shubert Company is ------- effective at helping power plants reduce their carbon dioxide emissions.

(A) once
(B) far
(C) early
(D) very

105. To track the location of your package, be sure to ------- the order number to the shipping department.

(A) provide
(B) provided
(C) provision
(D) providing

106. A diamond-shaped symbol next to merchandise indicates that the ------- has been discounted.

(A) property
(B) item
(C) idea
(D) fare

107. Wilkes-Rogers customers who want more ------- to move around should try our new wireless headphone models.

(A) free
(B) freely
(C) freedom
(D) freed

108. The economic development summit will be held ------- the Xi'an Trade Tower on September 22.

(A) to
(B) at
(C) down
(D) of

109. If your job duties change often, ------- updating your résumé is recommended.

    (A) regular
    (B) regularly
    (C) regularity
    (D) regularized

110. ------- researchers at Starlight Toys finalize their data, they will share it with executive officers.

    (A) Why
    (B) Despite
    (C) Even
    (D) When

111. ------- necklace that is shipped from Gillis Designers is given a thorough quality check.

    (A) Whenever
    (B) Also
    (C) All
    (D) Each

112. The Ansan Science Museum averages ------- 2,000 visitors per month.

    (A) nearly
    (B) totally
    (C) relatively
    (D) fairly

113. Marketing employees should use the accounting department's watercooler while ------- is being replaced.

    (A) they
    (B) them
    (C) theirs
    (D) their

114. It is ------- for the audience to hold its applause until the speaker has finished.

    (A) enthusiastic
    (B) casual
    (C) exclusive
    (D) customary

115. Despite ------- that Legend Air would perform poorly with the entry of cheaper competition, it posted strong second-quarter earnings.

    (A) predicted
    (B) predictable
    (C) predicts
    (D) predictions

116. ------- the entire month of May, parking will be prohibited on Cole Avenue.

    (A) On
    (B) Throughout
    (C) Inside
    (D) Between

117. Main Street Restaurant offers a menu of ------- prepared lunch and dinner meals.

    (A) thought
    (B) thoughtfulness
    (C) thoughts
    (D) thoughtfully

118. Ms. Tsai was told that she would be contacted soon, ------- as early as next week.

    (A) sufficiently
    (B) possibly
    (C) sincerely
    (D) patiently

119. Videos of Korean pop music have become very popular ------- adolescents worldwide.

    (A) including
    (B) whereas
    (C) among
    (D) within

120. Rydell Law Group chose to lease the office space ------- the landlord offered a discount.

    (A) that
    (B) much as
    (C) no sooner
    (D) because

121. Hasin Fariz turned a study on the ------- effects of sleep into a best-selling book.

    (A) favorable
    (B) favor
    (C) favors
    (D) favorably

122. The Girard Botanical Archive has almost 300,000 plant -------, all neatly pressed onto archival paper.

    (A) authorities
    (B) specimens
    (C) founders
    (D) specifics

GO ON TO THE NEXT PAGE

123. Wynston Containers is ------- a yearly shutdown of its factory so that it can be evaluated for safety and efficiency.

(A) involving
(B) participating
(C) implementing
(D) producing

124. Clyden Bistro's ------- location is now occupied by Margie Sue's Bakery.

(A) recognized
(B) delayed
(C) responsible
(D) former

125. The ------- to review plans to replace the Tronton Bridge will be scheduled soon.

(A) heard
(B) hears
(C) hearing
(D) hear

126. ------- Amanda Simont finds a full-time job, she will open a savings account.

(A) As soon as
(B) Prior to
(C) In case of
(D) Not only

127. The grocery store ------- vegetables from out of town until local prices went down last month.

(A) is buying
(B) will be buying
(C) has been buying
(D) had been buying

128. If all the documentation is -------, a construction permit should take four weeks to process.

(A) too much
(B) over done
(C) in order
(D) on call

129. Chung-Li Medicine provides health care to people in ------- remote areas.

(A) geographer
(B) geographically
(C) geographic
(D) geography

130. ------- and cost factored equally in choosing Cantavox as our main supplier.

(A) Reliability
(B) Allowance
(C) Dependence
(D) Estimation

PART 6

Directions: Read the texts that follow. A word, phrase, or sentence is missing in parts of each text. Four answer choices for each question are given below the text. Select the best answer to complete the text. Then mark the letter (A), (B), (C), or (D) on your answer sheet.

Questions 131-134 refer to the following article.

CENTERVILLE—Luigi's, the Italian restaurant located in the Monmouth Hotel, ------- its doors next
131.
Saturday after ten years in business. Chef Giovanni Modica left the restaurant several weeks ago,

prompting rumors of a change. The space is going to be renovated this spring and then reopen with new

management and a new ------- according to Linda Hughes, spokesperson for the Monmouth Hotel. -------.
132.   **133.**

The restaurant's name, however, is ------- to be announced.
134.

131. (A) was closed
(B) will be closing
(C) closed
(D) to close

132. (A) address
(B) receipt
(C) supply
(D) menu

133. (A) Centerville has a diverse dining scene.
(B) Mexican cuisine will be the focus.
(C) Food costs have increased recently.
(D) There are other cafés on Main Street.

134. (A) yet
(B) really
(C) besides
(D) until

GO ON TO THE NEXT PAGE

To: Samuel Archerson <sarcherson@vona.co.uk>
From: James Darrers <jdarrers@sky.co.uk>
Date: 10 January
Subject: Cost Accountant position

Dear Mr. Archerson,

Thank you for taking the time to meet with me today. I ------- our conversation, and I remain very interested
                                                        135.
in the position of cost accountant. I would welcome the opportunity to return for the third and final round of

------- .
136.

I am confident my years of accounting experience would benefit your firm. As discussed, over the last ten

years, I have helped many companies save a ------- amount of money. I am especially adept at analysing
                                            137.
the day-to-day operations of a business and helping to determine more cost-effective methods.

I checked regarding your question about a potential start date. ------- . I hope to hear from you in the near
                                                                138.
future.

Sincerely,

James Darrers

---

135. (A) enjoy
     (B) enjoyed
     (C) enjoying
     (D) will enjoy

136. (A) revisions
     (B) promotions
     (C) interviews
     (D) receptions

137. (A) substance
     (B) substantiate
     (C) substantially
     (D) substantial

138. (A) I have four additional questions to ask you.
     (B) I would be able to begin during the first
         week of February.
     (C) I am confident I have the potential for this
         position.
     (D) Thank you for the offer of employment.

Questions 139-142 refer to the following article.

SYDNEY (5 January)—Olney Technology announced yesterday that its smart irrigation system is now available to commercial clients. The system is designed to dispense the proper amount of water to every plant on a farm. It works by measuring the amount of water in soil ------- the rates of evaporation and the
139.
amount of water used by every plant. ------- . All of this data is continuously analysed to determine the
140.
most effective watering schedules. ------- anticipate that the system will reduce the average farm's water
141.
usage by 20 percent. They also believe it will ------- crop damage. By constantly monitoring soil conditions
142.
and adjusting watering schedules, the system ensures that crops are not over- or underwatered.

---

139. (A) since
(B) while
(C) as well as
(D) as long as

140. (A) Weather forecasts are also taken into account.
(B) Olney also offers a mobile phone app to track crop growth.
(C) Larger irrigation systems can even spread plant food.
(D) Installation times vary based on farm location.

141. (A) Developed
(B) Developers
(C) Developing
(D) Developments

142. (A) detect
(B) prevent
(C) treat
(D) assess

GO ON TO THE NEXT PAGE

Questions 143-146 refer to the following article.

SHIRESBERRY (February 15)—The second annual Shiresberry Film Festival begins on April 18 and ------- for
143.

five weeks. This year's offerings will not be limited to entries from North America and Europe. We will also be

presenting ------- from Asia and South America. And everyone's favorite feature from last year's festival will be
144.

back: directors and screenwriters will hold question-and-answer sessions after their films' initial screening. Make

sure you do not miss this ------- event. Tickets always sell out quickly. ------- . Shiresberry Film Club members
145.   146

can now purchase priority tickets. Visit the Shiresberry Theater box office or www.shiresberrytheater.com.

143. (A) run
(B) has run
(C) will run
(D) ran

144. (A) movies
(B) clothing
(C) food
(D) books

145. (A) political
(B) popular
(C) practical
(D) preliminary

146. (A) The awards will be presented by Hunter
Johns.
(B) Renovations to the space are nearly
complete.
(C) The later offerings were an even bigger
success.
(D) Sales are open to the general public on
March 3.

PART 7

Directions: In this part you will read a selection of texts, such as magazine and newspaper articles, e-mails, and instant messages. Each text or set of texts is followed by several questions. Select the best answer for each question and mark the letter (A), (B), (C), or (D) on your answer sheet.

Questions 147-148 refer to the following advertisement.

Sedwick Electronics Hiring Event

March 2, 10 A.M.–5 P.M.
22 Myer Street, Hanover, PA 17331

Sedwick Electronics is opening a new manufacturing facility in Hanover, Pennsylvania, and we need to fill many positions. We offer a wonderful work environment and great benefits to our employees.

Come to the event and hear from employees from our Lancaster facility about their experience, learn about the open positions, and speak with our recruiters. No RSVP is necessary. Bring copies of your résumé.

---

147. For whom is the advertisement intended?

(A) Recruiters
(B) Job seekers
(C) Local business owners
(D) Current Sedwick Electronics employees

148. What is stated about Sedwick Electronics?

(A) It is moving its headquarters.
(B) It offers a training program for new employees.
(C) It requires employees to wear uniforms.
(D) It will have more than one location.

GO ON TO THE NEXT PAGE

Aguni Plumbing Supply Returns

Beginning March 1 at all Aguni Plumbing Supply locations, customers will be able to come to our stores to return purchases made online. For a complete refund, the return must be made within 30 days of purchase and must be accompanied by a receipt. In addition, the merchandise must be returned in the original packaging, and all components must be included. After 30 days, refunds will be limited to in-store credit only. Defective items may be exchanged for the same item only.

149. What will happen on March 1 ?

(A) A shipment will be returned.
(B) A new policy will go into effect.
(C) A promotional sale will take place.
(D) A customer survey will be published.

150. What is NOT a requirement for a complete refund?

(A) The return must be made at the original purchase location.
(B) The return must be made within a certain time frame.
(C) The item must be returned with all its components.
(D) The item must be returned in the original packaging.

Peter,

Here is my tentative schedule for Monday. Please check with these colleagues to confirm. Ani has arranged everything for my stay in sunny Samirabad—I certainly will not miss the weather here! My speech for the Samirabad Awards Banquet is nearly finalized. I will return to the office on Thursday, 15 February. If possible, please avoid making any appointments for the end of the week as I plan to focus on the Zoldanas Project when I return.

Sonya

Schedule for Sonya Barlow Monday, 12 February	
8:30 A.M.	Breakfast with Evan Wong, Human Resources
9:45 A.M.	Phone conference financial update, Nasreen Akhtar
10:30 A.M.	Status of technology upgrades, Aaliyah Taffe
11:15 A.M.	New facilities proposal meeting, Mitch Carr
12:30 P.M.	Leave for airport
4:52 P.M.	Flight departs

151. What will Ms. Barlow do in Samirabad?

(A) Take a vacation
(B) Conduct a training session
(C) Attend a special dinner
(D) Meet an important client

152. Who will likely discuss a new Idea?

(A) Mr. Wong
(B) Ms. Akhtar
(C) Ms. Taffe
(D) Mr. Carr

GO ON TO THE NEXT PAGE

TEST 1

Questions 153-154 refer to the following text-message chain.

Javier Palomo [2:04 P.M.]
Are you still at the farm? I haven't made a shelter for the new tractor yet, and rain has been forecast for today.

Conrad Genet [2:06 P.M.]
I'm still here. It looks like it might rain any minute.

Javier Palomo [2:07 P.M.]
Can you find a tarp to cover it?

Conrad Genet [2:12 P.M.]
I couldn't find a spare one in the shed. There is a large black tarp covering the hay bales, though.

Javier Palomo [2:13 P.M.]
That one needs to stay there. Could you search the barn?

Conrad Genet [2:17 P.M.]
OK, I found a tarp, but it's quite dirty.

Javier Palomo [2:18 P.M.]
That's fine. I'd rather clean the tractor than let it get drenched by the rain.

Conrad Genet [2:19 P.M.]
Okay.

153. What does Mr. Palomo ask Mr. Genet to do?

(A) Protect a piece of equipment
(B) Check the weather forecast
(C) Put some tools in the shed
(D) Move some hay bales

154. At 2:18 P.M., what does Mr. Palomo most likely mean when he writes, "That's fine"?

(A) He is pleased that the tractor is clean.
(B) He wants Mr. Genet to search the barn.
(C) He is not concerned about the dirt.
(D) He does not need Mr. Genet to work late.

Subway Sound to be Upgraded

BOSTON (April 1)—The public address systems at selected subway stations are scheduled to be refurbished, the Transit Authority announced this week. The systems are used to make announcements to commuters both on the platforms and in the stations.

Local commuters welcomed the news, although for some it was long overdue.

"It can be pretty difficult to understand the announcements at some of the stations I use most frequently," said Ian Miller, who has taken the subway to work nearly every week for the past eighteen years. "I had heard the reports about it on TV, and all I can say is that it is about time!"

Some of the systems currently in use are more than 30 years old. Worn-out speakers, wiring, microphones, and amplifiers will be replaced with new, more reliable devices. The work should be completed in October and cost more than $11 million.

Boston's subway system came together in stages over the course of several years. The foundational component of the system's Green Line first opened on Tremont Street in the late 1890s. It was the first of its kind in the United States.

155. What is the purpose of the article?

(A) To clarify where subway riders can locate information
(B) To describe improvements at some subway stations
(C) To announce the creation of a new subway line
(D) To explain why subway schedules will be revised

156. How does Mr. Miller feel about the plans?

(A) He expects the project to fail.
(B) He is concerned about the cost.
(C) He believes the work is unnecessary.
(D) He has been waiting for the changes.

157. The word "stages" in paragraph 5, line 2, is closest in meaning to

(A) steps
(B) scenes
(C) train cars
(D) platforms

GO ON TO THE NEXT PAGE

Questions 158-160 refer to the following Web page.

---

http://www.thesailboatfactory.fr/English/aboutus ▼

Enzo Moreau, Founder

Enzo Moreau has always loved the sea, but he has not always been the shipbuilder he is known as today. — [1] —. A civil engineer in the early years, he took a consultant position in Marseille almost a decade ago in order to be closer to the ocean. — [2] —. Mr. Moreau soon found himself devoting nearly all of his free time to his passion—sailing. Taking a chance, he made yet another change: he used his life savings to start his own sailboat-restoration company, the Sailboat Factory. — [3] —. The company did so well in its first year that Mr. Moreau decided to share his success by giving back to the community. — [4] —. He has also written a number of articles about sailboat restoration for leading industry journals.

---

158. What was Mr. Moreau's first profession?

(A) Writer
(B) Engineer
(C) Shipbuilder
(D) Consultant

159. What is indicated about Mr. Moreau?

(A) He is a business owner.
(B) He plans to retire soon.
(C) He won a community award.
(D) He grew up close to the ocean.

160. In which of the positions marked [1], [2], [3], and [4] does the following sentence best belong?

"He began offering sailing lessons at a nearby lake after hours, for example."

(A) [1]
(B) [2]
(C) [3]
(D) [4]

Questions 161-163 refer to the following e-mail.

```
═══════════════════════ *E-mail* ═══════════════════════

   From:        Simona Westwood

   To:          Undisclosed recipients

   Date:        3 June

   Subject:     Safety representative
```

As a follow-up to the contract agreement of 25 May between Roserburg City Hall (Sponsor) and Thore Construction (Subcontractor), a meeting was held on 2 June to discuss the selection of a safety representative based on the safety requirements and procedures noted in the contract agreement. Pierre Deparis was appointed as the safety representative for the project at Thore Construction's expense. Thore Construction has confirmed that Mr. Deparis is fully qualified and has completed the 30-hour Safety Requirements and Procedures Training Course.

Mr. Deparis will provide a certificate of training to City Hall prior to beginning work on-site. Thore Construction cannot delegate responsibility for project safety to third parties. This means that Mr. Deparis may not be substituted and will stay on-site until the completion of the project.

Simona Westwood

---

161. What was the purpose of the meeting?

(A) To revise a list of safety requirements
(B) To discuss a proposed construction site
(C) To fill a position for a project
(D) To sign a final agreement

162. What will Mr. Deparis do before construction begins?

(A) Estimate expenses
(B) Contact his substitutes
(C) Advertise an open position
(D) Present proof of qualifications

163. The word "stay" in paragraph 2, line 3, is closest in meaning to

(A) delay
(B) remain
(C) wait
(D) reside

GO ON TO THE NEXT PAGE

E-Commerce Opening Doors for African Fashion Industry

ADDIS ABABA (6 May)—Africa's role as a consumer of fashion has been on the rise in recent years. This trend is largely due to the emergence of e-commerce, which provides Africans the opportunity to buy clothing from retailers with no physical presence on the continent.

Perhaps more importantly, though, the growth of e-commerce is enabling small-scale African designers to also become *producers* of fashion, as they showcase their collections to consumers worldwide. African shopping Web sites like Jumjum and Longa are making the work of African designers available for purchase not just throughout the continent, but also as far away as London and New York. — [1] —.

"African designers are finally gaining visibility," says Mazaa Absher, founder of Abbi Sportscore, Africa's fastest-growing athletic footwear company. "We have always had terrific design and production capacity here on the continent, but it was hard getting it out into the world. Now we are generating more sales online than we are in our stores." — [2] —.

Even as Ms. Absher has transformed her company into an international powerhouse, she continues to highlight the advantages of manufacturing its products in her home city of Nazret. — [3] —. Africa's strong textile sector and innovative designs combine tradition and wearability, and this formula is allowing companies like hers to set their sights beyond the continent.

"As more cities in Ethiopia—and all over Africa—improve their manufacturing capacity, it will become easier to reach the rest of the world," says Ms. Absher. — [4] —.

164. What is the main topic of the article?

(A) New trends in marketing athletic footwear
(B) Increased competition in the African clothing market
(C) Recent growth in the African fashion industry
(D) The largest clothing companies in Africa

165. What is indicated about Abbi Sportscore?

(A) It sells its products only online.
(B) It manufactures its shoes in Nazret.
(C) It will be moving its main offices soon.
(D) It was the first shoe company in Ethiopia.

166. What is suggested about the Jumjum and Longa Web sites?

(A) They sell only handcrafted goods.
(B) They receive orders from around the world.
(C) They offer free shipping to London and New York.
(D) They are planning to open retail stores.

167. In which of the positions marked [1], [2], [3], and [4] does the following sentence best belong?

"The city boasts four garment factories, with a fifth scheduled to be built this year in nearby Wonji."

(A) [1]
(B) [2]
(C) [3]
(D) [4]

Questions 168-171 refer to the following text-message chain.

Gary Park (10:23 A.M.)
I e-mailed you the cover design for our September issue a few minutes ago. Did you receive it?

Jill Riley (10:26 A.M.)
Yes, but is this the latest version? I thought we agreed that the background color should be lighter so the article titles are more visible.

Gary Park (10:28 A.M.)
I forgot—sorry about that! I'm just now sending the file with the most recent version.

Jill Riley (10:30 A.M.)
Opening it now… That's more like it. I'll forward it to Graphics and request a sample printout.

Jill Riley (10:35 A.M.)
Good morning, Mr. Ojeda. Our new cover design is ready. When do you think you'll have a chance to work on it?

Frank Ojeda (10:38 A.M.)
Send it to me now. I'll have a print copy ready for your approval after lunch.

168. Where do the people most likely work?

(A) At a bookstore
(B) At a public library
(C) At a television studio
(D) At a magazine publisher

169. Why does Mr. Park apologize?

(A) He sent the wrong file.
(B) He used an old e-mail address.
(C) He missed a project deadline.
(D) He lost an important document.

170. At 10:30 A.M., what does Ms. Riley most likely mean when she writes, "That's more like it"?

(A) The budget is more reasonable.
(B) The color looks better.
(C) The story is more interesting.
(D) The schedule is more realistic.

171. What will Mr. Ojeda do by the afternoon?

(A) Approve a marketing plan
(B) Produce a sample
(C) Repair a printer
(D) Make copies of an agreement

GO ON TO THE NEXT PAGE

Thredquest Outfitters

WESTAN (March 6)—Thredquest Outfitters announced yesterday that it is the new sponsor of the Westan Panthers Basketball Team. The company officially replaced Marliner Sports on March 2. According to information from the Marliner Sports Web site, its longtime sponsorship agreement expired at the end of last season and was not renewed. Marliner Sports has since closed down its activewear division to focus on outdoor recreational equipment.

Under the new sponsorship agreement, Thredquest Outfitters will pay for the official game balls and nets, according to an e-mail from the company's marketing director, Marta Hsu. The company will also provide the players' jerseys, shorts, and court shoes. "Transportation and lodging costs associated with out-of-town games will remain the team's responsibility and are largely covered by ticket sales," said the team's coach, Pedro Cardenas.

Mr. Cardenas, along with the team's business manager and the facilities and equipment manager, helped negotiate the terms of the new sponsorship agreement. Mr. Cardenas studied athletic training at Halston University and worked for several competitive basketball teams in the region, advising on injury prevention and providing treatment. Then, he joined the Panthers as the coach. "We are looking forward to a long and fruitful relationship with Thredquest Outfitters," he said.

172. What is the article about?

(A) A new basketball coach
(B) A change in a team's supporter
(C) A company's marketing plan
(D) An update to a team's schedule

173. What is true about Marliner Sports?

(A) It no longer sells athletic clothing.
(B) It will close an outlet in Westan.
(C) It is now owned by Mr. Cardenas.
(D) It has merged with Thredquest Outfitters.

174. What part of the Westan Panthers' budget is funded by audience attendance at games?

(A) Basketball equipment
(B) Uniforms
(C) Footwear
(D) Team travel

175. What most likely was Mr. Cardenas' previous job?

(A) Marketing director
(B) Business manager
(C) Facilities and equipment manager
(D) Sports trainer

GO ON TO THE NEXT PAGE

To:	riedewald@parasur.net.sr
From:	client_services@mhf.ca
Date:	April 2, 12:21 P.M.
Subject:	Your feedback

Dear Mr. Riedewald,

Thank you for filling out the McMann Home Furnishings (MHF) survey. To show our appreciation, we have added reward points to your account. They can be applied to the purchase of products offered online as well as those offered in our retail stores. Clearance items and those priced $15.00 and above may not be purchased using credits.

To use your reward points for an online purchase, select the items you would like to purchase and then check out. At the bottom of the page, select "Apply credits." The value of the applied credits will appear on your order receipt as a special discount.

If you would prefer to use reward points at one of our retail locations, you can do so by logging in to your account on our Web site. Go to the My Rewards page, and then select "Print as a coupon." The coupon will have a bar code that can be scanned at the store's checkout counter.

Sincerely,

Client Services, McMann Home Furnishings

Online Order #1157
McMann Home Furnishings Store
March 19, 11:31 A.M.

Hand-Painted Picture Frame
Quantity: 1
Price: 10.00
Special Discount: -10.00

Sailboat Ceramic Mug
Quantity: 4
Price: 40.00
Clearance Discount: -20.00

Floral Blanket
Quantity: 1
Price: 25.00

Photo Album
Quantity: 1
Price: 34.00
Seasonal Item Discount: -17.00

Item total: 62.00
Shipping: Free
Total: 62.00

176. According to the e-mail, how did Mr. Riedewald receive reward points?

  (A) He won an online contest.
  (B) He participated in a customer survey.
  (C) He spent a certain amount of money.
  (D) He returned an item.

177. In the e-mail, the phrase "filling out" in paragraph 1, line 1, is closest in meaning to

  (A) emptying
  (B) supplying
  (C) completing
  (D) expanding

178. How can customers apply their reward points in an MHF retail store?

  (A) By entering their account number
  (B) By entering their phone number
  (C) By scanning a coupon's bar code
  (D) By going to the Client Services Department

179. According to the receipt, what is true about Mr. Riedewald?

  (A) He paid for delivery of the items.
  (B) He purchased the items in the evening.
  (C) He paid over $70 for all items combined.
  (D) He purchased only one item at regular price.

180. What item did Mr. Riedewald most likely purchase using reward credits?

  (A) The picture frame
  (B) The ceramic mug
  (C) The floral blanket
  (D) The photo album

GO ON TO THE NEXT PAGE

To:	All Staff
From:	Cassandra Clausen, Office Manager
Date:	February 17
Re:	Second quarter travel schedule

The staff's travel schedule for the second quarter is now posted online. These months tend to be our busiest, so it is important that you keep the schedule updated. To avoid confusion, please include travel, whether domestic or international, only after it has been approved by a department supervisor. Do not forget that any travel exceeding ten consecutive business days is considered long-term and requires additional approval from the division head.

Also, please note that there will likely be a few days of overlap in the travel dates of department supervisors during this quarter. For instance, Tessa Alexander has just been invited to lead several workshops in Seoul. Her dates are not yet confirmed, but her trip is expected to be at the same time as Natasha Danilchenko's trip to Denver. Bear in mind that any date-sensitive documents or approvals requiring the signature of a department supervisor should be acquired ahead of your departure.

Let me know if you encounter difficulty viewing or editing the schedule. Have a fantastic second quarter.

Best,

Cassandra

Garcia Architecture Group—Travel Schedule, April-June
Important Reminders
— Requests for long-term travel should be directed to Laura Garcia.
— This is a schedule of conferences and trade events requiring off-site travel. Please send information regarding sick leave and vacation time to Devon Taylor at Human Resources for entry into a separate calendar.

Dates	Name	Event, Location
April 3–8	Natasha Danilchenko	Symposium on Modern City Structure, Denver
April 22–27	Tania Schultz	Safety in Factory Design Workshop, Tokyo
May 1–10	Gil Shaw	International Urban Architecture, Singapore
May 1–10	Natasha Danilchenko	International Urban Architecture, Singapore
June 7–12	Dionne O'Donnell	Reflections in Architecture Exposition, Ottawa

181. What is the purpose of the e-mail?

    (A) To invite employees to attend an event
    (B) To request feedback on a recent meeting
    (C) To encourage participation in conferences
    (D) To announce the availability of an online document

182. Why most likely are Ms. Alexander's travel plans not included on the schedule?

    (A) Her travel dates fall within the third quarter.
    (B) The schedule lists only confirmed travel.
    (C) The schedule is limited to domestic travel.
    (D) She missed the deadline for travel approval.

183. Why are employees asked to contact Ms. Taylor?

    (A) To inform her of absences
    (B) To request approval for long-term travel
    (C) To report updates to their contact information
    (D) To seek advice on presenting at trade shows

184. What is Ms. Garcia's job title?

    (A) Office Manager
    (B) Department Supervisor
    (C) Division Head
    (D) Head of Human Resources

185. When will Ms. Alexander most likely be traveling?

    (A) April 3–8
    (B) April 22–27
    (C) May 1–10
    (D) June 7–12

GO ON TO THE NEXT PAGE

FOR IMMEDIATE RELEASE

New Leader at Hilsun

Vancouver (21 June)—Hilsun Media Company has selected Diana Silva as its new Chief Executive Officer. After graduating with a master's degree in business administration from Vardia University, Ms. Silva joined Cordha Networks, where she earned a reputation as a skilled negotiator. She presided over the merger of Cordha and Renar Universal five years ago. She has worked for Cordha for ten years, the last three as Vice President of Sales.

Ms. Silva replaces Gregor Zuev, who announced his departure last year. After an extensive search, Ms. Silva was the board's unanimous choice for CEO. She will begin her new position in August.

To:	All staff
From:	Alex Briard
Subject:	CEO announcement
Date:	21 June

Dear Colleagues,

As you know, we, the board of directors here at Hilsun Media have been searching for a new CEO. As of today, we can officially announce that Diana Silva has been selected for the position, and we are thrilled she will be joining us.

At this time, we do not anticipate changes in departmental leadership, nor do we foresee new policies regarding promotions. Naturally, Ms. Silva may elect to revise both over time, but she has expressed her confidence in the assignments and policies as they currently stand.

Ms. Silva will be welcomed with a luncheon in her honor on her first day. The tentative location for it is Tenley Hall. You can expect to see messages asking about menu preferences, scheduling, and special activities over the next few weeks.

All my best,

Alex Briard

To:	Diana Silva
From:	Alton Hague
Subject:	News
Date:	23 June

I just heard the news about your new position, and I am so pleased for you. You have been wonderful to work with these past several years. The sales division in particular will miss your energy and leadership. I hope that we can continue to stay in touch and, with luck, work together in the future.

Best,

Alton

---

186. What does the press release indicate about Ms. Silva?

(A) She used to work for Renar Universal.
(B) She was in charge of uniting two companies.
(C) She recently graduated from university.
(D) She hired Mr. Zuev at Cordha Networks.

187. Who most likely is Mr. Briard?

(A) A department manager
(B) A member of Hilsun's board
(C) Ms. Silva's assistant
(D) Ms. Silva's former supervisor

188. What is suggested about the luncheon for Ms. Silva?

(A) It will take place in August.
(B) It will be held at a local restaurant.
(C) The menu has been finalized.
(D) The company hosts it annually.

189. Why did Mr. Hague write the e-mail to Ms. Silva?

(A) To extend a job offer
(B) To schedule an appointment
(C) To offer his congratulations
(D) To discuss travel plans

190. Where does Mr. Hague most likely work?

(A) At Hilsun Media
(B) At Vardia University
(C) At Renar Universal
(D) At Cordha Networks

GO ON TO THE NEXT PAGE

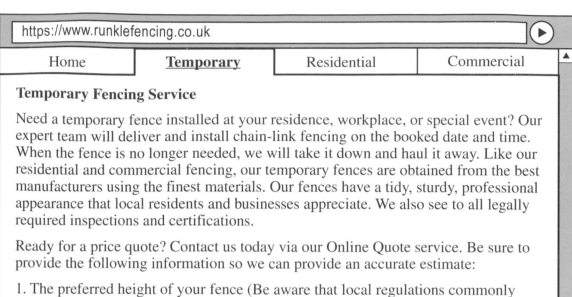

https://www.runklefencing.co.uk

| Home | **Temporary** | Residential | Commercial |

Temporary Fencing Service

Need a temporary fence installed at your residence, workplace, or special event? Our expert team will deliver and install chain-link fencing on the booked date and time. When the fence is no longer needed, we will take it down and haul it away. Like our residential and commercial fencing, our temporary fences are obtained from the best manufacturers using the finest materials. Our fences have a tidy, sturdy, professional appearance that local residents and businesses appreciate. We also see to all legally required inspections and certifications.

Ready for a price quote? Contact us today via our Online Quote service. Be sure to provide the following information so we can provide an accurate estimate:

1. The preferred height of your fence (Be aware that local regulations commonly allow a maximum height of three metres.)
2. The perimeter of the area you need to enclose
3. The number of gated entrances needed
4. The number of days the fence needs to be up

Name: Marguerite Carhart   **Phone:** (0117) 555-9102
Installation Address: 438 Stretford Way, Bristol BS5 7TB
E-mail: mcarhart@stockporteventcentre.co.uk
Today's date: 8 August

Fence Details:

I need a temporary three-metre-tall fence installed around the Stockport Event Centre within the next two weeks. This is to prevent the public from entering while we make renovations from 18 to 30 August. Two gates are needed so that workers and vehicles may enter and leave the location.

To:	mcarhart@stockporteventcentre.co.uk
From:	hmontalbo@runklefencing.co.uk
Date:	9 August
Subject:	Quote Number 080817
Attachment:	📎 fencequote_mcarhart

Dear Ms. Carhart,

Thank you for your enquiry. Please see the attached estimate for the work you requested. Note that the price of delivery is included at no further charge unless a rush order—one providing less than three weeks' notice—is required. This is a rough estimate based on the information you provided. If you ring us at (0117) 555-2938 and provide us with a missing detail, I can give you a more accurate quote.

You might also consider including a plastic curtain with your order. This would be wrapped around and fastened to the fence, hiding the construction site from the view of pedestrians. If this interests you, we can include it in the revised quote.

Best Regards,

Howard Montalbo

191. What does the Web site indicate about fences taller than three meters?

(A) They are made of plastic.
(B) They are usually prohibited by law.
(C) They require special transportation.
(D) They must be ordered directly from the manufacturer.

192. According to the form, why does Ms. Carhart need a temporary fence installed?

(A) To mark a property line
(B) To draw attention to an exhibit
(C) To control a crowd at a special event
(D) To limit public access to a work site

193. What information does Ms. Carhart fail to give about the fence she needs?

(A) The height of the fence to be erected
(B) The dates when the fence is needed
(C) The perimeter of the area to be enclosed
(D) The number of entrances needed

194. What is implied about Ms. Carhart's fence project?

(A) There will be a charge for delivery.
(B) The project involves work at several job sites.
(C) Extra workers must be hired to install the fence.
(D) Inspectors must first approve the project.

195. Why does Mr. Montalbo recommend adding a curtain?

(A) It would act as a noise barrier.
(B) It would help keep in dust.
(C) It would serve as a visual screen.
(D) It would improve safety conditions.

GO ON TO THE NEXT PAGE

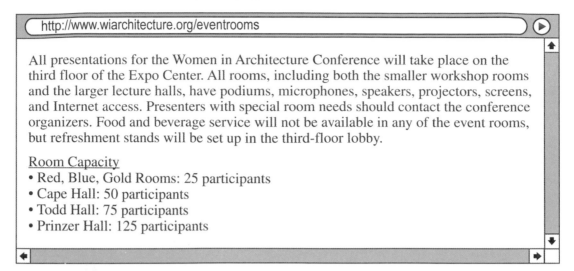

http://www.wiarchitecture.org/eventrooms

All presentations for the Women in Architecture Conference will take place on the third floor of the Expo Center. All rooms, including both the smaller workshop rooms and the larger lecture halls, have podiums, microphones, speakers, projectors, screens, and Internet access. Presenters with special room needs should contact the conference organizers. Food and beverage service will not be available in any of the event rooms, but refreshment stands will be set up in the third-floor lobby.

Room Capacity
• Red, Blue, Gold Rooms: 25 participants
• Cape Hall: 50 participants
• Todd Hall: 75 participants
• Prinzer Hall: 125 participants

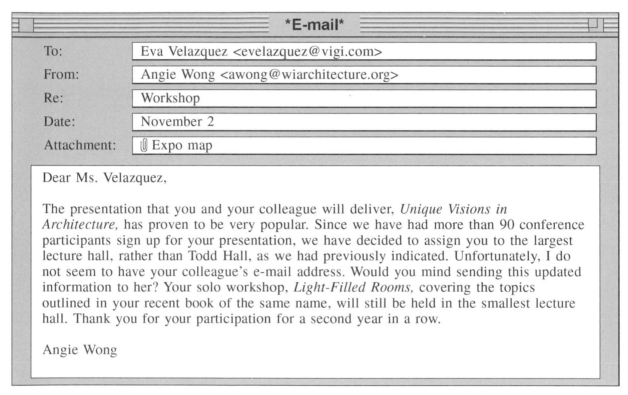

E-mail

To:	Eva Velazquez <evelazquez@vigi.com>
From:	Angie Wong <awong@wiarchitecture.org>
Re:	Workshop
Date:	November 2
Attachment:	📎 Expo map

Dear Ms. Velazquez,

The presentation that you and your colleague will deliver, *Unique Visions in Architecture,* has proven to be very popular. Since we have had more than 90 conference participants sign up for your presentation, we have decided to assign you to the largest lecture hall, rather than Todd Hall, as we had previously indicated. Unfortunately, I do not seem to have your colleague's e-mail address. Would you mind sending this updated information to her? Your solo workshop, *Light-Filled Rooms,* covering the topics outlined in your recent book of the same name, will still be held in the smallest lecture hall. Thank you for your participation for a second year in a row.

Angie Wong

```
╔═══════════════════════════════════════════════════════════════╗
║                         *E-mail*                              ║
╠═══════════════════════════════════════════════════════════════╣
```

To:	Amalia Harris <aharris@vigi.com>
From:	Eva Velazquez <evelazquez@vigi.com>
Re:	Workshop
Date:	November 2
Attachment:	📎 Expo map

Hello Amalia,

Please see the forwarded message and the attached map Ms. Wong sent to me this morning. It looks like we have been upgraded to a larger room due to the popularity of our presentation—great news! It might be a good idea if we get together next week to go through our presentation and finalize the agenda and the handouts we have chosen to distribute. Let me know what time might work for you.

Thanks,

Eva

196. According to the Web page, what is unavailable in the event rooms?

(A) Podiums
(B) Projectors
(C) Internet
(D) Catering

197. What is suggested in the first e-mail about Ms. Velazquez?

(A) She prefers to present in smaller rooms.
(B) She has published a book.
(C) She is a conference organizer.
(D) She has not presented at this conference before.

198. Where will the presentation *Unique Visions in Architecture* be given?

(A) In the Blue Room
(B) In Cape Hall
(C) In Todd Hall
(D) In Prinzer Hall

199. What does Ms. Wong ask Ms. Velazquez to do?

(A) Forward an e-mail
(B) Register for an event
(C) Confirm her payment details
(D) Provide biographical details

200. Who most likely is Ms. Harris?

(A) Ms. Velazquez's classmate
(B) Ms. Wong's editor
(C) Ms. Velazquez's work colleague
(D) Ms. Wong's assistant

Stop! This is the end of the test. If you finish before time is called, you may go back to Parts 5, 6, and 7 and check your work.

NO TEST MATERIAL ON THIS PAGE

閱讀測驗 全真試題 (2)

In the Reading test, you will read a variety of texts and answer several different types of reading comprehension questions. The entire Reading test will last 75 minutes. There are three parts, and directions are given for each part. You are encouraged to answer as many questions as possible within the time allowed.

You must mark your answers on the separate answer sheet. Do not write your answers in your test book.

READING TEST

In the Reading test, you will read a variety of texts and answer several different types of reading comprehension questions. The entire Reading test will last 75 minutes. There are three parts, and directions are given for each part. You are encouraged to answer as many questions as possible within the time allowed.

You must mark your answers on the separate answer sheet. Do not write your answers in your test book.

PART 5

Directions: A word or phrase is missing in each of the sentences below. Four answer choices are given below each sentence. Select the best answer to complete the sentence. Then mark the letter (A), (B), (C), or (D) on your answer sheet.

101. The coaches are ------- that the Gremon Soccer Club will win tomorrow night.

(A) hope
(B) hopes
(C) hopeful
(D) hopefully

102. Mr. Hodges ------- that volunteers sign up to assist with the Hannock River cleanup by Friday.

(A) requesting
(B) to be requested
(C) requests
(D) to request

103. The office's copy machine will be out of service until ------- notice.

(A) extra
(B) temporary
(C) further
(D) ongoing

104. If ------- are not satisfied with an item, return it for a full refund within 30 days of purchase.

(A) you
(B) your
(C) yours
(D) yourself

105. Our most recent survey was sent to clients just last week, ------- it is too soon to send another one.

(A) when
(B) since
(C) so
(D) finally

106. Guests were ------- with the table decorations for the company banquet.

(A) impressive
(B) impressed
(C) impressing
(D) impressively

107. After a 10 percent increase in delivery costs last year, management decided to look for a new paper -------.

(A) officer
(B) supplier
(C) finder
(D) starter

108. Inclement weather was ------- responsible for the low turnout at Saturday's Exton Music Festival.

(A) largely
(B) large
(C) largest
(D) larger

109. The location of next month's online gaming forum is yet to be -------.

(A) concluded
(B) prevented
(C) invited
(D) decided

110. The annual report has been posted online,
------- the director's office has not yet received
a printed copy.

(A) but
(B) why
(C) with
(D) once

111. Tomorrow at ------- 12:15 P.M., the mayor will
break ground at the site of the new courthouse.

(A) precise
(B) precision
(C) precisely
(D) preciseness

112. Compri Tech, Inc., was able to increase its
profits ------- making its processes more
efficient.

(A) around
(B) by
(C) to
(D) for

113. An online module will be provided for those
------- cannot attend the training session.

(A) who
(B) what
(C) when
(D) where

114. Before the updated design can go into -------,
it must be approved by management.

(A) product
(B) producer
(C) productive
(D) production

115. Ms. Valdez' sales numbers are good ------- for
her to be considered for the employee-of-the-
month award.

(A) forward
(B) even
(C) ahead
(D) enough

116. Mr. Nigam was ------- retirement when his boss
asked him to be the head of security at the new
facility.

(A) under
(B) ahead of
(C) nearby
(D) close to

117. Milante Shoes ------- altered the firm's
marketing strategy after a recent economic
shift.

(A) quick
(B) quickest
(C) quickly
(D) quicken

118. The Auto Tools Manufacturing Convention will
begin with an informal ------- on Friday evening.

(A) destination
(B) section
(C) reception
(D) invention

119. The Rockton Restaurant chain employs
standardized practices to ensure a -------
customer experience.

(A) consist
(B) consistent
(C) consisting
(D) consistently

120. The third-shift lead position ------- available and
can be applied for in person at the warehouse.

(A) to become
(B) had to become
(C) has become
(D) becoming

121. As our regular provider did not have the desks
we needed in stock, we ordered from a local
store -------.

(A) namely
(B) instead
(C) otherwise
(D) though

122. Aaron Park's new book features photographs of
homes designed and built by the homeowners
-------.

(A) itself
(B) himself
(C) themselves
(D) ourselves

123. Kieu Tech Services ------- to build three more
data centers in southern Vietnam in the next
two years.

(A) refers
(B) delivers
(C) intends
(D) indicates

GO ON TO THE NEXT PAGE

124. ------- our public relations manager, Ms. Ghazarian has just been appointed vice president of media relations.

(A) Sincerely
(B) Immediately
(C) Solely
(D) Formerly

125. The Dubai Physicians Group believes that ongoing ------- between researchers and practitioners is essential.

(A) collaborate
(B) collaborated
(C) collaboration
(D) collaborates

126. All Hershel Industries employees must have a valid ID card ------- enter the building.

(A) in order to
(B) as long as
(C) regarding
(D) always

127. Hotels and universities are ------- to recycle their used mattresses through the city's recycling program.

(A) systematic
(B) eligible
(C) familiar
(D) successful

128. Kovox Ltd. aims to optimize quality ------- reducing the impact on the environment.

(A) which
(B) while
(C) because
(D) unless

129. ------- the potential success of a product is often done through market research.

(A) Calculate
(B) Calculation
(C) Calculating
(D) Calculated

130. Despite initial ------- over the size of the venue, the Westover Fashion Show was a great success.

(A) critical
(B) criticize
(C) critically
(D) criticism

PART 6

Directions: Read the texts that follow. A word, phrase, or sentence is missing in parts of each text. Four answer choices for each question are given below the text. Select the best answer to complete the text. Then mark the letter (A), (B), (C), or (D) on your answer sheet.

Questions 131-134 refer to the following letter.

Dear PGD Account Holder,

PGD Bank strives ------- the highest levels of client security and service. This applies not only to online-
131.
and telephone-based services, but also to our brick-and-mortar locations. Our three branch offices have

proudly been a part of the community ------- a combined total of 40 years.
132.

To assist you even better in the future, our Smithville branch will be temporarily closed for renovations July

8–22. ------- . In the meantime, our other two regional branches in Pine Grove and Bradford will maintain
133.

normal business ------- . We value your feedback and will respond to any concerns that you may have as
134.

soon as possible.

Sincerely,

Edwin Chen, Operations Manager
PGD Bank

131. (A) to provide
(B) provided
(C) providing
(D) to be provided

132. (A) except
(B) amid
(C) near
(D) for

133. (A) Unfortunately, services will be limited.
(B) We thank you for trusting in PGD Bank over these years.
(C) We apologize for any inconvenience this may cause.
(D) Traffic on the boulevard has increased lately.

134. (A) investments
(B) hiring
(C) hours
(D) interests

GO ON TO THE NEXT PAGE

Questions 135-138 refer to the following letter.

August 29

Greene & Lauer Logistics
2334 Hoyt Street
Boston, MA 02121

Dear Hiring Manager:

I am pleased to be writing this letter of recommendation for Mr. Nobuo Omoto. He ------- as an intern
135.
for our Finance Department. During this time, Mr. Omoto worked on a variety of tasks, from ------- data
136.
for budget reports to reviewing files ahead of our annual audit. Mr. Omoto quickly mastered our regular

procedures, and he routinely made suggestions for making our workflow processes more efficient. In fact,

some of these ------- have since been incorporated into the department's everyday operations.
137.

I strongly recommend Mr. Omoto for any entry-level position in the financial services industry. ------- . If I
138.
can be of any further assistance, please do not hesitate to contact me at the above address or by e-mail at

ojimenez@greenelauer.com.

Sincerely,

Oscar Jimenez
Financial Officer

---

135. (A) networked
(B) applied
(C) served
(D) followed

136. (A) gathers
(B) gathering
(C) having gathered
(D) gathered

137. (A) instruments
(B) changes
(C) events
(D) resources

138. (A) He will be a great asset to your
organization.
(B) He will be completing his internship very
soon.
(C) I hope to work with Mr. Omoto one day.
(D) Please send your application to me directly.

To: Mason Wu <mwu@wustudios.co.nz>
From: Trent Tuiloma <ttuiloma@canterburyairport.co.nz>
Subject: Canterbury Airport project
Date: Monday, 2 July

Dear Mr. Wu,

Thank you for agreeing to consult on the Canterbury Airport redesign project. ------- . As a result, I am
                                                                            139.
particularly eager to hear your ideas about upgrading our main terminal.

Can we meet this week? There are a number of ------- restaurants near my office. If you are available this
                                              140.
Friday, we could meet at Celia's Café on Cumberland Street. I would also like a few of my colleagues to

------- us. They would appreciate ------- ways to enhance the airport user's experience.
141.   **142.**

I look forward to hearing from you soon.

Sincerely,

Trent Tuiloma
Chairman, Canterbury Airport Redesign Team

139. (A) I can meet you when you arrive.
(B) Scheduling flights can be quite tricky.
(C) I have long admired your work on regional
airports.
(D) There are several dining options at the
airport.

140. (A) excel
(B) excellent
(C) excellently
(D) excelled

141. (A) join
(B) pay
(C) remind
(D) defend

142. (A) to discuss
(B) discussing
(C) discuss
(D) discussed

GO ON TO THE NEXT PAGE

Questions 143-146 refer to the following e-mail.

To: anna.goldstein@mail.com
From: jhlee@lindstromuniversity.co.uk
Subject: Executive Management Certificate
Date: 10 February

Dear Anna,

On behalf of Lindstrom University, I am writing to welcome you to the Executive Management Certificate program.

As a member of the incoming class, you ------- in an intensive yearlong online curriculum. While the majority of
                                      143.
the training takes place via online classes, the program begins with a three-day ------- workshop to be held on
                                                                                  144.
the campus of Lindstrom University from 25 to 27 May.

Prior to the session, you will have access to course materials as well as some preliminary assignments. These

assignments must be completed ------- the training in May. We will use this work as a starting point for the
                              145.
workshop. ------- .
          146.

Many congratulations, Anna. We look forward to seeing you in May.

Ju Hae Lee
Dean of Admission, Lindstrom University

143. (A) participated
     (B) will be participating
     (C) have participated
     (D) have been participating

144. (A) introduce
     (B) introducing
     (C) introductory
     (D) introductorily

145. (A) before
     (B) behind
     (C) despite
     (D) throughout

146. (A) You performed very well in your interview.
     (B) Your application stood out to the faculty.
     (C) Thank you for attending all of the preliminary sessions.
     (D) We expect students to give each assignment careful attention.

PART 7

Directions: In this part you will read a selection of texts, such as magazine and newspaper articles, e-mails, and instant messages. Each text or set of texts is followed by several questions. Select the best answer for each question and mark the letter (A), (B), (C), or (D) on your answer sheet.

Questions 147-148 refer to the following coupon.

AMS

Encounters with Science and Technology
$3 OFF

$3 off the price of one admission

Present this coupon at AMS and receive $3 off one general admission ticket. Limit one per household. Coupon cannot be combined with any other offers, including group rates and senior discount tickets. Valid for all permanent exhibits and galleries (not valid for featured exhibits or planetarium).

Regular hours: Tue–Sun, 9 a.m.–5 p.m.
Summer hours (June 12–September 5):
Open every day 9 a.m.–7 p.m.

---

147. What most likely is AMS?

(A) A museum
(B) A repair facility
(C) An electronics store
(D) An energy provider

148. What happens at AMS during the summer?

(A) It closes earlier.
(B) It opens at a later time.
(C) It is open an extra day.
(D) It is closed for special events.

GO ON TO THE NEXT PAGE

Questions 149-150 refer to the following e-mail.

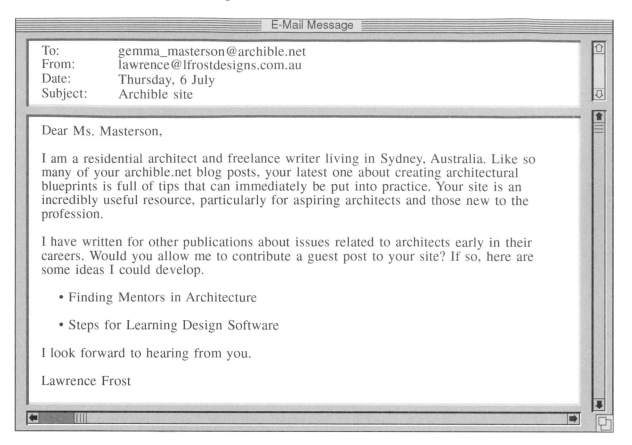

149. What does Mr. Frost suggest he likes about archible.net?

(A) Its informative content
(B) Its interactive features
(C) Its directory of architects
(D) Its collection of drawing tools

150. What does Mr. Frost list in the e-mail?

(A) Articles he published on his own site
(B) Posts by Ms. Masterson that he enjoyed
(C) Problems he noticed on the Web site
(D) Topics that he would like to write about

Springfield Community School
Computer Courses

Internet Safety

This course teaches students everything they need to navigate the Web safely.

Course ID	Class Time	Instructor	Room
249800: 01	Tuesday 5:30–7:30 P.M.	Patrick McCann	211
249800: 02	Saturday 1:00–3:00 P.M.	Nora Farid	166

Spreadsheet Basics

This course teaches the basics of online spreadsheets. Students will learn how to create effective charts for calculating and analyzing data clearly and easily.

Course ID	Class Time	Instructor	Room
225810: 01	Thursday 5:30–8:30 P.M.	Remi Sanders	118
225810: 02	Sunday 1:00–4:00 P.M.	Nora Farid	315

151. Why would people enroll in the course taught by Ms. Sanders?

(A) To practice designing Web sites
(B) To improve their Internet searches
(C) To get tips on creating spreadsheets
(D) To learn how to advertise on the Internet

152. What is indicated about Ms. Farid?

(A) She also teaches children.
(B) She is Ms. Sanders' supervisor.
(C) She teaches twice a week.
(D) She used to work as a data analyst.

GO ON TO THE NEXT PAGE

Sally Witham (4:47 P.M.)
Hi Wakiko. I just finished up here at the Kyoto store. I'll be on the train that arrives in Tokyo at 11:35 tomorrow morning. How should I get to your location?

Wakiko Ohara (4:48 P.M.)
I'll have an associate pick you up at the station. How do things look in Kyoto?

Sally Witham (4:49 P.M.)
The Kyoto store is doing a great job. It has everything that we at the home office are looking for. Athletic shoes and sandals are displayed according to specifications, and sales associates are friendly and knowledgeable.

Wakiko Ohara (4:51 P.M.)
You should like things here, too. Do you want to begin your visit after lunch, say at 2:00?

Sally Witham (4:52 P.M.)
Sounds good. See you tomorrow.

153. Why did Ms. Witham contact Ms. Ohara?

(A) To review sales figures
(B) To arrange a store visit
(C) To discuss employee performance reviews
(D) To determine the most convenient train to take

154. At 4:51 P.M., what does Ms. Ohara most likely mean when she writes, "You should like things here, too"?

(A) The Tokyo store is being run according to corporate policy.
(B) Ms. Witham will find the athletic shoes she needs.
(C) Ms. Ohara's associate is always punctual.
(D) The Tokyo store is located next to a popular restaurant.

TEST 2

GO ON TO THE NEXT PAGE

Structure: Blaine River Drawbridge	Location: Ridgeline Highway, KM 147
Main span material: Steel girder	Owner: State Highway Agency
Age of structure: 30 years	Report completed by: Vivian Tulio
	Date: October 17

Notes:
The bridge is overall structurally sound. Inform Department of Transportation about small cracks in asphalt.

Bridge component	Rating	Key to ratings
Support elements	4	1 Failed; immediate closure required
Towers	4	2 Deteriorated; may fail soon
Road surface	3	3 Shows deterioration but still functions within acceptable parameters
Drainage features	4	4 Shows minor wear
Safety barriers	5	5 New condition
Sidewalk or walkway	6	6 Not applicable

155. What did Ms. Tulio most likely do?

(A) Make repairs
(B) Hire a contractor
(C) Perform an inspection
(D) Authorize a construction plan

156. What part of the structure is in most need of maintenance?

(A) The support elements
(B) The road surface
(C) The drainage features
(D) The safety barriers

157. What is probably true about the Blaine River Drawbridge?

(A) It was not designed for pedestrian use.
(B) It will be closed for the month of October.
(C) It does not have the required signage.
(D) It is the oldest bridge on the Ridgeline Highway.

Alma Poised for Growth

This month has seen a huge jump in sales of Condor PX brand wheat seed in Argentina. Last year, across much of this nation, there were above-average temperatures and below-average rainfall, causing fields to yield sharply less wheat overall. But despite the adverse weather conditions, Condor PX wheat did comparatively well.

Condor PX was bred by Alma Seed Company in Brazil. Although Alma has been selling Condor PX through its Argentinian distributors for several years, it was slow to catch on until now. Investors also have taken notice of Alma's rapidly improving fortunes.

158. According to the article, what is one condition that affected wheat harvests?

(A) Excessive rain
(B) Unusually warm weather
(C) A shortage of wheat seeds
(D) A loss of wheat fields

159. The word "yield" in paragraph 1, line 5, is closest in meaning to

(A) allow
(B) fail
(C) follow
(D) produce

160. According to the article, what did Alma Seed Company do?

(A) Relocate to Argentina
(B) Purchase Condor PX
(C) Develop a type of wheat
(D) Invest in a new company

GO ON TO THE NEXT PAGE

To:	All Staff
From:	Selene Hong
Date:	March 25
Subject:	Reminder

Dear Staff,

I would like to draw your attention to several new procedures regarding business trip expense reports. — [1] —. Beginning next month, business-related dining receipts must be accompanied by a listing of each dinner attendee. Also, please make sure that you do not include receipts for any non-work-related items or activities with your report. — [2] —. Finally, note that our accounting software will now automatically calculate for you the total to be reimbursed. You need only to upload images of your receipts for the software to do this.

I will be happy to respond to your questions. — [3] —. However, I will be flying to Tokyo this Friday to meet clients, so I will not be checking e-mail that day. — [4] —.

Sincerely,

Selene Hong
Assistant Director, Human Resources Department
Datoric Systems

161. What is indicated about Datoric Systems?

(A) It has increased the spending amount allowed for business dinners.
(B) It will adopt new procedures for filing travel expense reports.
(C) It has office locations in several countries.
(D) It plans to hold a company celebration.

162. Why is the accounting software mentioned?

(A) To highlight a special capability it has
(B) To encourage staff to install it
(C) To help employees log on to it
(D) To point out that it will be replaced

163. In which of the positions marked [1], [2], [3], and [4] does the following sentence best belong?

"Following these steps will enable us to quickly issue your reimbursement payment."

(A) [1]
(B) [2]
(C) [3]
(D) [4]

Questions 164-167 refer to the following text-message chain.

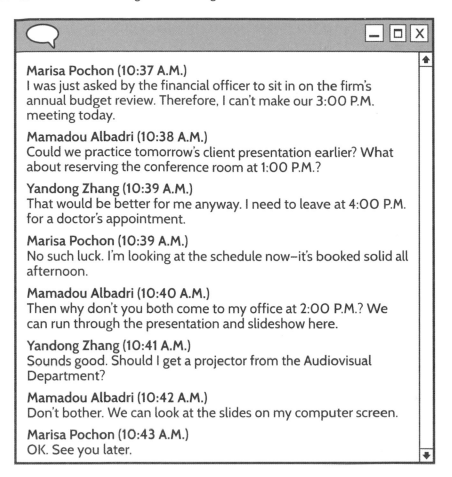

Marisa Pochon (10:37 A.M.)
I was just asked by the financial officer to sit in on the firm's annual budget review. Therefore, I can't make our 3:00 P.M. meeting today.

Mamadou Albadri (10:38 A.M.)
Could we practice tomorrow's client presentation earlier? What about reserving the conference room at 1:00 P.M.?

Yandong Zhang (10:39 A.M.)
That would be better for me anyway. I need to leave at 4:00 P.M. for a doctor's appointment.

Marisa Pochon (10:39 A.M.)
No such luck. I'm looking at the schedule now—it's booked solid all afternoon.

Mamadou Albadri (10:40 A.M.)
Then why don't you both come to my office at 2:00 P.M.? We can run through the presentation and slideshow here.

Yandong Zhang (10:41 A.M.)
Sounds good. Should I get a projector from the Audiovisual Department?

Mamadou Albadri (10:42 A.M.)
Don't bother. We can look at the slides on my computer screen.

Marisa Pochon (10:43 A.M.)
OK. See you later.

---

164. Why is Ms. Pochon unavailable at 3:00 P.M.?

(A) She has a phone call with important clients.
(B) She has to give a presentation.
(C) She has been asked to attend a meeting.
(D) She has a medical appointment.

165. Why does Mr. Albadri suggest using his office?

(A) Because it can accommodate a lot of people
(B) Because it is located near the finance office
(C) Because his audiovisual equipment has been upgraded
(D) Because the conference room is unavailable

166. At 10:42 A.M., what does Mr. Albadri most likely mean when he writes, "Don't bother"?

(A) He should not be disturbed this afternoon.
(B) Ms. Pochon should not reserve a room.
(C) Mr. Zhang does not have to come to a meeting.
(D) Mr. Zhang does not need to bring a projector.

167. When will the three people meet?

(A) At 1:00 P.M.
(B) At 2:00 P.M.
(C) At 3:00 P.M.
(D) At 4:00 P.M.

GO ON TO THE NEXT PAGE

Nairobi Daily Journal

2 April

Two supermarket chains are currently competing to be number one in Kenya. Both retailers, AT Mart and Duggan's, have announced that they are determined to place first with consumers. — [1] —.

In March, AT Mart, which is based in the United Kingdom, announced it was planning to launch its first store in Nairobi. — [2] —. It is one of the largest supermarket chains in the world. Duggan's, on the other hand, is not well-known outside of Africa, but it is South Africa's most dominant supermarket chain and has established a presence here. Now there are eight Duggan's stores in Kenya with a loyal customer base.

— [3] —. Some supermarket chains, such as Wentworth's, which is based in the United States, have not been willing to pay what they consider to be exorbitant leasing fees when their stores simply were not attracting a significant number of shoppers. As a result, Wentworth's closed all three of its stores after only two years in Kenya.

Duggan's, however, has an advantage. — [4] —. The company created its own real estate division, D Properties Ltd. This company has built four shopping complexes with Duggan's as the main tenant in each. Moreover, Duggan's has paid special attention to tailoring its product inventory to the local culture. It also has developed an effective supply-and-delivery system to service its famous on-site bakeries, butcher shops, and produce sections. AT Mart may have much wider name recognition, but it will need to be more innovative to compete against the popular Duggan's.

--**Susan Kotter, Staff Reporter**

168. What is the article mainly about?

(A) Business strategies that work well
(B) The competition within an industry
(C) Places to find bargains in Kenya
(D) The growth of new shopping malls

169. What is indicated about Wentworth's?

(A) It has a loyal customer base.
(B) Its branch stores were mostly in South Africa.
(C) Its business in Kenya was relatively short-lived.
(D) It is a family-owned enterprise.

170. What is NOT mentioned as an accomplishment of Duggan's?

(A) Establishing a real estate division
(B) Creating an efficient delivery system
(C) Setting up on-site bakeries
(D) Developing a global reputation

171. In which of the positions marked [1], [2], [3], and [4] does the following sentence best belong?

"Rents in desirable locations for supermarkets are often extremely high."

(A) [1]
(B) [2]
(C) [3]
(D) [4]

8 February

Ms. Mala Chelvi
60 Jalan Tun Razak
54200 Kuala Lumpur

Dear Ms. Chelvi,

We are delighted to inform you that you have been nominated as a finalist for the Small Business Challenge competition this year. Now in its fifth year, this competition is designed to highlight innovative products and services launched by young entrepreneurs. The Web application that you developed, which provides a means of matching charitable organizations with volunteers, earned one of the top scores from our panel of judges.

In the next round of the challenge, you will participate in a live presentation about your product before a panel of expert judges. The three people with the best presentations will receive one-time grants of MYR 10,000 each to invest in their businesses.

Please go to sbc.org/competition and submit an outline of your presentation, a brief video that clearly illustrates the use of your application, and a passport-sized photograph of yourself. You will also need to sign a consent form allowing us to use your name and photo, if needed, in promotional materials on our Web site. The deadline for submission of these materials is 10 March.

Best regards,

Felix Pang

Felix Pang
Chairperson, Small Business Challenge Committee

172. What is the purpose of the letter?

(A) To seek volunteers for an event
(B) To notify a contest finalist
(C) To sell business consultation services
(D) To offer a small-business loan

173. What does Ms. Chelvi most likely specialize in?

(A) Law
(B) Technology
(C) Finance
(D) Marketing

174. The word "illustrates" in paragraph 3, line 2, is closest in meaning to

(A) represents
(B) translates
(C) lightens
(D) decorates

175. What is Ms. Chelvi asked to do by March 10?

(A) Update a Web page design
(B) Give a presentation
(C) Sign a consent form
(D) Pay a fee

GO ON TO THE NEXT PAGE

Two Swan Press
72 Holywell Road, Edinburgh EH8 8PJ

4 December

Mr. Albert Morello
17 Peyton Avenue
Kingston 5
Jamaica, W.I.

Dear Mr. Morello:

Enclosed please find your royalty payment for *Understanding Our Oceans*. You should have recently received an e-mail that listed the sales figures and the royalties due to you for the print and electronic versions of your book.

We are proud to announce that Two Swan Press was given the Publisher of the Year Award by the UK Book Industry in October. We thank the authors who have worked with us since our founding five years ago.

All Two Swan Press authors are entitled to an author discount of 40 percent off any title on our Web site. Simply use the code AUX1417 for your discount.

If you have any questions at all, please do not hesitate to contact me.

Kind regards,

Sarah Wicklin

Sarah Wicklin

Encl.

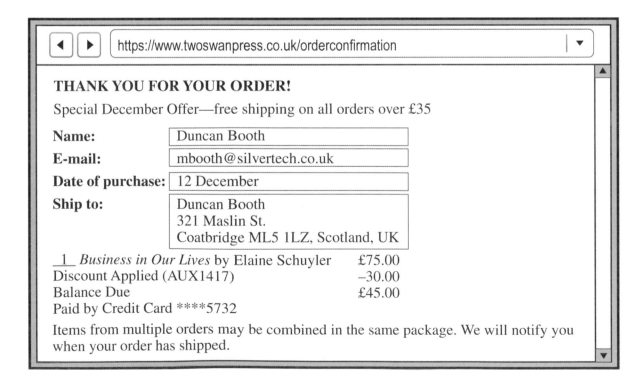

https://www.twoswanpress.co.uk/orderconfirmation

THANK YOU FOR YOUR ORDER!

Special December Offer—free shipping on all orders over £35

Name: Duncan Booth

E-mail: mbooth@silvertech.co.uk

Date of purchase: 12 December

Ship to: Duncan Booth
321 Maslin St.
Coatbridge ML5 1LZ, Scotland, UK

1 *Business in Our Lives* by Elaine Schuyler		£75.00
Discount Applied (AUX1417)		−30.00
Balance Due		£45.00

Paid by Credit Card ****5732

Items from multiple orders may be combined in the same package. We will notify you when your order has shipped.

176. What is a purpose of the letter?

(A) To ask Mr. Morello to write a book
(B) To explain an enclosed contract
(C) To notify Mr. Morello of a payment
(D) To describe an updated personnel policy

177. What was sent in a previous message to Mr. Morello?

(A) Incorrect contact information
(B) Detailed sales numbers
(C) A list of suggested changes
(D) A link to an electronic book

178. What does Ms. Wicklin mention about Two Swan Press?

(A) It moved to a new location in October.
(B) It has launched a new program for its fifth anniversary.
(C) It has won an industry award.
(D) It has decided to focus on scientific publications.

179. What is suggested about Mr. Booth?

(A) He is a Two Swan Press author.
(B) He wrote *Business in Our Lives*.
(C) He is an acquaintance of Mr. Morello.
(D) He has purchased items from Two Swan Press before.

180. What is indicated about the order?

(A) It has been delayed.
(B) It has not yet been paid.
(C) It contains multiple books.
(D) It includes free shipping.

GO ON TO THE NEXT PAGE

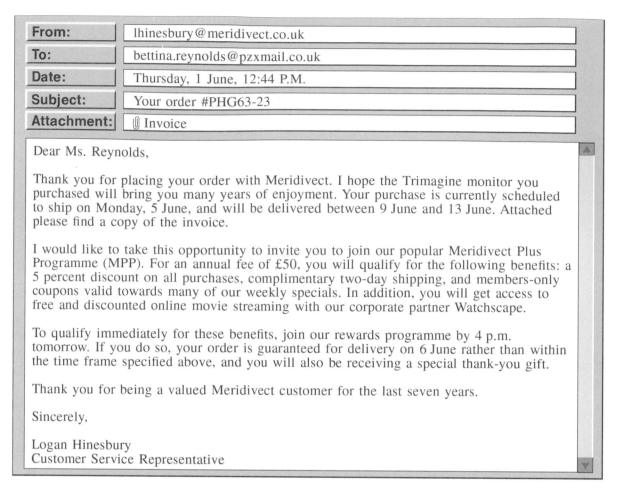

From:	lhinesbury@meridivect.co.uk
To:	bettina.reynolds@pzxmail.co.uk
Date:	Thursday, 1 June, 12:44 P.M.
Subject:	Your order #PHG63-23
Attachment:	📎 Invoice

Dear Ms. Reynolds,

Thank you for placing your order with Meridivect. I hope the Trimagine monitor you purchased will bring you many years of enjoyment. Your purchase is currently scheduled to ship on Monday, 5 June, and will be delivered between 9 June and 13 June. Attached please find a copy of the invoice.

I would like to take this opportunity to invite you to join our popular Meridivect Plus Programme (MPP). For an annual fee of £50, you will qualify for the following benefits: a 5 percent discount on all purchases, complimentary two-day shipping, and members-only coupons valid towards many of our weekly specials. In addition, you will get access to free and discounted online movie streaming with our corporate partner Watchscape.

To qualify immediately for these benefits, join our rewards programme by 4 p.m. tomorrow. If you do so, your order is guaranteed for delivery on 6 June rather than within the time frame specified above, and you will also be receiving a special thank-you gift.

Thank you for being a valued Meridivect customer for the last seven years.

Sincerely,

Logan Hinesbury
Customer Service Representative

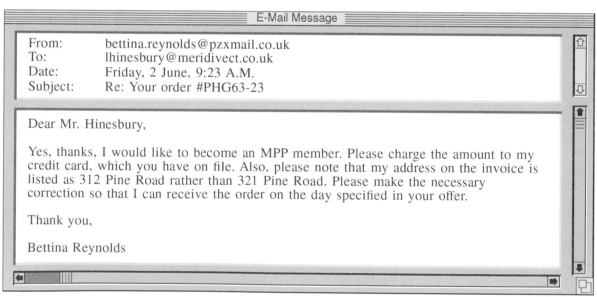

E-Mail Message

From:	bettina.reynolds@pzxmail.co.uk
To:	lhinesbury@meridivect.co.uk
Date:	Friday, 2 June, 9:23 A.M.
Subject:	Re: Your order #PHG63-23

Dear Mr. Hinesbury,

Yes, thanks, I would like to become an MPP member. Please charge the amount to my credit card, which you have on file. Also, please note that my address on the invoice is listed as 312 Pine Road rather than 321 Pine Road. Please make the necessary correction so that I can receive the order on the day specified in your offer.

Thank you,

Bettina Reynolds

181. What is one reason why the first e-mail was sent?

    (A) To announce a delay in delivery
    (B) To advertise a new product
    (C) To introduce a new service
    (D) To promote a special customer benefit

182. What is NOT mentioned as a feature of the Meridivect Plus Programme?

    (A) Membership with an online movie service
    (B) Free shipping on purchases
    (C) Access to an online music library
    (D) Discounts on merchandise

183. What is indicated about Ms. Reynolds?

    (A) She recently moved to a new address.
    (B) She has been a Meridivect customer for several years.
    (C) She is already a Watchscape customer.
    (D) She makes most of her purchases online.

184. When will Ms. Reynolds' order arrive?

    (A) On June 2
    (B) On June 6
    (C) On June 9
    (D) On June 13

185. What problem does Ms. Reynolds report?

    (A) She could not open the attached invoice.
    (B) She did not receive any coupons.
    (C) Her credit card has been canceled.
    (D) Her house number was listed incorrectly.

TEST 2

GO ON TO THE NEXT PAGE

To:	All Staff
From:	Personnel Department
Date:	June 20
Subject:	Mentoring Program
Attachment:	📎 Application

Employees who have been with Broadside Electronics for less than eighteen months are invited to apply to participate in a new mentoring program that will match a maximum of ten junior employees with long-term company veterans. The goal is that junior employees will sharpen corporate skills, better understand company culture, and develop a more focused career path. Mentees will be assigned to a mentor based strictly on their work assignment and professional interests. The pairs will meet at mutually convenient times throughout the year, from three to five hours per month.

To be considered for participation in this initiative, complete the attached application and return to Mentoring Program Director Tim Wrigley at t.wrigley@broadsideelec.com by July 1. Mr. Wrigley will send notification of his selections by July 15.

MENTORING PROGRAM APPLICATION

Name: <u>Cara Drummond</u>   Extension: <u>144</u>

Division: <u>Sales</u>

Professional areas of interest:
<u>I am most interested in learning about our markets abroad and developing my sales-presentation abilities for these international markets. I am also interested in general career guidance.</u>

Best workdays and times for meeting:
<u>Any weekday morning except Monday.</u>

The Broadside Company Newsletter

Mentoring Program Sees Results

Long-time employee and Vice President of Sales Alena Russo was intrigued when a Personnel Department director approached her about mentoring a less experienced employee under a program that began last year. She is glad to have accepted the assignment. "After working with Ms. Drummond, I am more satisfied with my own duties, because I know I have helped a professional who is just getting started. I only wish that I had had someone looking out for me in my early years," remarked Ms. Russo.

Ms. Drummond explains that she "needed pointers on how to make better sales pitches." She reports that her sales are up by 20 percent now. She better understands the opportunities Broadside Electronics has to offer and what is required to become a manager. "Thanks to Ms. Russo, I have been able to define my career goals, and I am a happier person when I arrive to work every day."

New mentorship pairs are now being formed. Interested parties should contact Tim Wrigley in the Personnel Department.

186. What does the e-mail indicate about the mentoring program?

   (A) It is popular industry-wide.
   (B) The number of participants is limited.
   (C) It is designed for staff in the sales division.
   (D) Participants must attend an orientation meeting.

187. How will the junior employees most likely be selected?

   (A) They will be chosen from a management-training group.
   (B) They will undergo competitive interviews.
   (C) They will be evaluated by Mr. Wrigley.
   (D) They will be recommended by a local business school.

188. What is suggested about Ms. Drummond?

   (A) She has worked at Broadside Electronics for less than eighteen months.
   (B) She has just transferred from another department.
   (C) She has received a positive annual review.
   (D) She has made many successful presentations abroad.

189. What is most likely true about Ms. Russo?

   (A) She is planning to retire soon.
   (B) She has international sales experience.
   (C) She has mentored many junior employees.
   (D) She recently joined the hiring team.

190. What benefit from the mentoring program have both Ms. Drummond and Ms. Russo enjoyed?

   (A) Increased job satisfaction
   (B) Quick promotions
   (C) Paycheck bonuses
   (D) Clearer career goals

GO ON TO THE NEXT PAGE

Bartowsky Manufacturing ◈

Production Trial-Run Schedule

Product: Guadiana Office Chair

Date	Activity
Sunday 8 July	• David Mateja arrives in Biłgoraj
Monday 9 July	• Preproduction setup of machinery • Calibrating and adjusting equipment to designated specifications
Tuesday 10 July	• Production and assembly of parts
Wednesday 11 July	• Durability tests (weight, resistance, and material quality)
Thursday 12 July	• David Mateja departs for Bratislava

From:	dmateja@nostilde.sk
To:	thammond@nostilde.it
Subject:	Guadiana trial run
Date:	13 July

Dear Ms. Hammond,

I have an update about the Guadiana trial run at Bartowsky Manufacturing. I am happy to report that the factory is capable of manufacturing the chairs per our design specifications, and the estimated production costs suggest that this would be a viable partnership.

On Monday, I supervised the calibration of the equipment, and the next day, during the trial run, I noticed that the paint that was used to coat the metal elements did not meet our specifications. They were recoated immediately with the correct paint after I pointed out the problem. There were no other issues. The chair was tested on Wednesday and passed all tests.

Today, I discussed our production schedule by telephone with Martin Havranec, explaining that our distribution policy requires that the chairs be available at all retail locations on the release date. He assured me that Bartowsky Manufacturing was prepared to make a significant investment in order to meet our deadline.

David Mateja

Polish Firm Wins Nostilde Contract

22 July–Bartowsky Manufacturing, based in Biłgoraj, Poland, has secured a contract to produce office chairs for the international furniture brand Nostilde.

Nostilde plans to deliver an estimated 200,000 chairs to all its stores in the European Union. This is the largest order in Bartowsky's history. In order to meet the demand, the company pledged to invest in additional equipment to increase the factory's production capacity.

"We've been contemplating a large-scale equipment purchase for a couple of years," explained Bartowsky Manufacturing president Martin Havranec. "We have the space and an available labour pool. Once the new equipment is in place, we will be able to put many skilled applicants to work immediately."

191. According to the schedule, what happened on July 9 ?

(A) Specifications were printed.
(B) Machines were adjusted.
(C) Personnel were trained.
(D) Quality was tested.

192. What does Mr. Mateja suggest about production costs?

(A) They will be confirmed by Mr. Havranec.
(B) They were difficult to negotiate.
(C) They have been revised.
(D) They are acceptable.

193. When did Mr. Mateja most likely request a change to meet specifications?

(A) On July 8
(B) On July 10
(C) On July 11
(D) On July 12

194. What was Mr. Mateja promised on July 13 ?

(A) That Bartowsky Manufacturing would purchase additional production equipment
(B) That expedited delivery would be available for some customers
(C) That production of the Nostilde chairs would start immediately
(D) That most materials would be sourced in Poland

195. What does Mr. Havranec suggest about Bartowsky Manufacturing?

(A) It has produced items for Nostilde before.
(B) It designed a chair exclusively for Nostilde.
(C) It will easily find qualified workers.
(D) It will repair a section of the factory.

GO ON TO THE NEXT PAGE

To:	Daniel Rodrigues Pereira
From:	Livia Romero
Subject:	Company outing
Date:	August 5

Hello Daniel,

I hope you are settling in well. I'm sure you have had a busy few weeks. Around this time of year, the office manager typically begins arranging our annual company outing. I think we mentioned this during your interview in June. Previously, we have done things like going to a concert and taking a local river cruise. The outing is always great for morale, and everyone looks forward to it.

This year, I think it would be a good idea to get tickets to a sporting event. I know that many staff members are fans of the San Jose Starlings baseball team. It should be an evening game when the team is playing at home. We have a budget of $600.00 this year. Looking at the ticket prices, it seems that will be just enough to get a ticket for every staff member.

I'm sure Elise can assist you with this; she has often helped organize the outings. Let me know if you have any questions.

Best,

Livia Romero
Director of Administration, Loftgren Consulting

Plan your next event with the San Jose Starlings!

Discounted tickets are available for groups of ten or more. The more tickets you buy, the more you save—perfect for family gatherings, company outings, or charity fund-raisers! Get perks such as free tickets for the organizer, discounts on food, and your group's name displayed on the scoreboard.

Group Ticket Pricing

10 tickets	$130.00
30 tickets	$360.00
50 tickets	$550.00
70 tickets	$700.00

Contact **grouptickets@sanjosestarlings.com** or call **408-555-0101** for more information.

San Jose Starlings August Schedule				
Date	**Day**	**Time**	**Opposing Team**	**Home or Away**
August 13	Sunday	1:05 P.M.	Aspen Monarchs	Home
August 15	Tuesday	7:05 P.M.	Aspen Monarchs	Home
August 19	Saturday	1:05 P.M.	Philipsburg Pinstripes	Away
August 22	Tuesday	7:05 P.M.	Philipsburg Pinstripes	Away
Purchase tickets online at **www.sanjosestarlings.com/tickets**.				

196. Why did Ms. Romero send the e-mail to Mr. Rodrigues Pereira?

(A) To tell him about an upcoming budget cut
(B) To invite him to a concert
(C) To introduce him to his new assistant
(D) To ask him to arrange an event

197. What does the e-mail imply about Mr. Rodrigues Pereira?

(A) He recently attended a San Jose Starlings game.
(B) He will be leaving in a few weeks to go on vacation.
(C) He is a professional party planner.
(D) He recently began working for Loftgren Consulting.

198. According to the flyer, what is a benefit of buying tickets as a group?

(A) Reduced ticket prices
(B) Free food
(C) Front-row seating
(D) T-shirts with the team's logo

199. How many employees does Loftgren Consulting most likely have?

(A) 10
(B) 30
(C) 50
(D) 70

200. On what date could Loftgren Consulting employees attend a game?

(A) August 13
(B) August 15
(C) August 19
(D) August 22

Stop! This is the end of the test. If you finish before time is called, you may go back to Parts 5, 6, and 7 and check your work.

NO TEST MATERIAL ON THIS PAGE

試題解答與
分數及目標能力計算

1. 本書所提供的分數換算方式，僅適用於 *ETS*® 所提供的全真模擬試題，與實際測驗的成績計算方法不同，故本書獲得的分數為參考分數。

2. 本書為《*TOEIC*® 聽力與閱讀測驗官方全真試題指南 Vol.8 閱讀篇》，僅能計算閱讀測驗之參考分數；若想了解聽力測驗之參考分數，請使用《*TOEIC*® 聽力與閱讀測驗官方全真試題指南 Vol.8 聽力篇》。

全真試題 (1) 解答及目標能力對應表

PART 5

題號	正解	目標能力①	②	③	④	⑤
101	A					●
102	B			●		
103	A					●
104	D			●		
105	A					●
106	B			●		
107	C					●
108	B			●		
109	B		●			
110	D					●
111	D					●
112	A			●		
113	C				●	
114	D			●		
115	D					●
116	B			●		
117	D					●
118	B		●			
119	C			●		
120	D			●		
121	A					●
122	B			●		
123	C			●		
124	D			●		
125	C					●
126	A					●
127	D					●
128	C			●		
129	B					●
130	A			●		

PART 6

題號	正解	目標能力①	②	③	④	⑤
131	B					●
132	D			●	●	
133	B			●		
134	A				●	
135	B			●		●
136	C			●		
137	D					●
138	B			●		
139	C				●	
140	A			●		
141	B					●
142	B			●	●	
143	C					●
144	A			●	●	
145	B			●	●	
146	D			●		

PART 7

題號	正解	目標能力①	②	③	④	⑤
147	B	●				
148	D		●			
149	B		●			
150	A			●		
151	C		●			
152	D		●			
153	A	●				
154	C	●	●			
155	B		●			
156	D	●	●			
157	A				●	
158	B		●			
159	A		●			
160	D	●	●			
161	C	●	●			
162	D		●			
163	B				●	
164	C	●				
165	B		●			
166	B		●			
167	C	●	●			
168	D	●				
169	A		●			
170	B	●	●			
171	B		●			
172	B	●				
173	A		●			

PART 7

題號	正解	目標能力①	②	③	④	⑤
174	D		●			
175	D	●				
176	B			●		
177	C				●	
178	C			●		
179	D	●		●		
180	A	●		●		
181	D	●				
182	B			●		
183	A		●			
184	C			●		
185	A			●		
186	B		●	●		
187	B	●		●		
188	A	●		●		
189	C	●				
190	D	●		●		
191	B			●		
192	D			●		
193	C			●		
194	A	●				
195	C			●		
196	D	●				
197	B			●		
198	D	●		●		
199	A	●				
200	C	●		●		

●●●●● 詳細目標能力對應請參考第 87 頁

全真試題 (2) 解答及目標能力對應表

PART 5

題號	正解	目標能力 ①	②	③	④	⑤
101	C					●
102	C					●
103	C				●	
104	A					●
105	C				●	
106	B				●	
107	B				●	
108	A					●
109	D				●	
110	A					●
111	C				●	
112	B			●		
113	A					●
114	D					●
115	D				●	
116	D				●	
117	C					●
118	C				●	
119	B					●
120	C					●
121	B				●	
122	C					●
123	C				●	
124	D				●	
125	C					●
126	A					●
127	B				●	
128	B				●	
129	C					●
130	D				●	

PART 6

題號	正解	目標能力 ①	②	③	④	⑤
131	A					●
132	D				●	
133	C			●		
134	C			●	●	
135	C			●	●	
136	B					●
137	B			●	●	
138	A			●		
139	C			●		
140	B					●
141	A			●	●	
142	B					●
143	B			●		
144	C					●
145	A			●	●	
146	D			●		

PART 7

題號	正解	目標能力 ①	②	③	④	⑤
147	A	●				
148	C	●		●		
149	A	●				
150	D			●		
151	C			●		
152	C			●		
153	B	●		●		
154	A	●		●		
155	C	●		●		
156	B			●		
157	A	●		●		
158	B		●			
159	D				●	
160	C	●				
161	B		●			
162	A		●			
163	A	●		●		
164	C		●			
165	D	●				
166	D	●		●		
167	B		●			
168	B	●				
169	C	●				
170	D			●		
171	C	●		●		
172	B		●			
173	B	●				

PART 7

題號	正解	目標能力 ①	②	③	④	⑤
174	A					●
175	C			●		
176	C	●				
177	B		●			
178	C		●			
179	A	●		●		
180	D			●		
181	D	●				
182	C			●		
183	B			●		
184	B			●		
185	D		●			
186	B			●		
187	C					
188	A	●		●		
189	B	●		●		
190	A			●		
191	B	●				
192	D	●				
193	B	●		●		
194	A			●		
195	C	●				
196	D	●				
197	D			●		
198	A		●			
199	C			●		
200	B			●		

●●●●● 詳細目標能力對應請參考第 87 頁

分數計算方式

<table>
<tr>
<td>

找出原始分數

請參考「試題解答及目標能力對應表」，對應出閱讀測驗的答對題數，即為原始分數。

Step 1
</td>
<td></td>
<td>

對應出量尺分數範圍

根據下方的「分數換算表」，找到原始對應的量尺分數範圍。

Step 2
</td>
</tr>
</table>

範例：答對的題數為 35 題，原始分數為 35 分，對應出量尺分數範圍為 95-145 分。

閱讀測驗分數換算表			
原始分數範圍	量尺分數範圍	原始分數範圍	量尺分數範圍
96 － 100	460 － 495	41 － 45	140 － 215
91 － 95	425 － 490	36 － 40	115 － 180
86 － 90	395 － 465	31 － 35	95 － 145
81 － 85	370 － 440	26 － 30	75 － 120
76 － 80	335 － 415	21 － 25	60 － 95
71 － 75	310 － 390	16 － 20	45 － 75
66 － 70	280 － 365	11 － 15	30 － 55
61 － 65	250 － 335	6 － 10	10 － 40
56 － 60	220 － 305	1 － 5	5 － 30
51 － 55	195 － 270	0	5 － 15
46 － 50	165 － 240		

目標能力正答率計算方式

對應相同目標能力的答對題目

- 請參考「試題解答及目標能力對應表」，對應出閱讀測驗各項目標能力之答對題數。
- 某些題目有兩項對應目標能力，計算答對題數時，同一題應重複加總。例如：全真試題(1)第132題答對，則在計算黃色目標能力答對題數時計算一次；而在計算紅色目標能力答對題數時，也需再納入計算一次。

Step 1

計算各目標能力的答對比例

$$\frac{\text{該目標能力答對題數}}{\text{相同目標能力之總題數}} \times 100\%$$

Step 2

範例：目標能力 的題數在全真試題 (1) 中共有 20 題，應試者答對了其中 10 題，套入計算公式 $\frac{10}{20}$ × 100%，則該目標能力之正答率為 50%。

目標能力對應

- Can make inferences based on information in written texts
- Can locate and understand specific information in written texts
- Can connect information across multiple sentences in a single written text and across texts
- Can understand vocabulary in written texts
- Can understand grammar in written texts

中文翻譯及
目標能力解析

題目/中文翻譯

101. Can understand grammar in written texts

Richard Pell only hires professional athletes to endorse ------- hair-care products.

(A) his
(B) he
(C) him
(D) himself

Richard Pell 只聘請職業運動員來代言他的護髮產品。

(A) 他的（所有格）
(B) 他（主格）
(C) 他（受格）
(D) 他自己（反身代名詞）

> **正解 (A)**
> 空格之後是名詞 hair-care products「護髮產品」，名詞前面可以用形容詞來修飾，根據文法，空格可為所有格形容詞，選項 (A) his「他的」為 he 的所有格，故為正解。endorse「代言、推薦」。
> (B)、(C)、(D) 皆不符合句意。
>
> 💡 應試者能理解書面文本的文法，並辨別代名詞的使用時機。

102. Can understand vocabulary in written texts

Last year, the *Daejeon English News* ------- the number of readers by adding a digital subscription option.

(A) needed
(B) increased
(C) joined
(D) asked

去年《Daejeon 英文新聞》藉由增加數位訂閱的選項而提高了讀者人數。

(A) 需要
(B) 提高
(C) 參加
(D) 詢問

> **正解 (B)**
> 全部選項皆為動詞過去式。空格後所接的名詞片語為 the number of readers「讀者人數」，空格應填入選項 (B) increased「增加」，使句子變得完整，故為正解。subscription「訂閱」。
> 請注意，by adding a digital subscription option 解釋了人數是如何增加的。
> (A) 不正確，因 need readers by adding a subscription「透過增加訂閱需要讀者」不符合文意；(C)、(D) 也可被排除，因讀者數量不能「加入」或「要求、詢問」。
>
> 💡 應試者能理解書面文本中的詞彙，並根據語意，從單字中選出適切的答案。

103. Can understand grammar in written texts

Thanks to its ------- location in the region, Nortown is home to several large media companies.

(A) central
(B) centers
(C) centrally
(D) centering

由於位在這個地區的中心位置，Nortown 是許多大型媒體公司的發源地。

(A) 中心的（形容詞）
(B) 中心（名詞複數形）
(C) 中心地（副詞）
(D) 置中（動名詞或現在分詞）

> **正解 (A)**
> 空格之後為名詞 location「位置」，名詞前面以形容詞修飾，故選項 (A) central「中心的」為正解。region「地區」。
>
> 💡 應試者能理解書面文本中的文法，能辨別 center「中心」的適當形態。

104.

Can understand vocabulary in written texts

The Shubert Company is ------- effective at helping power plants reduce their carbon dioxide emissions.

(A) once
(B) far
(C) early
(D) very

Shubert 公司非常有效率的幫助發電廠降低他們的二氧化碳排放量。

(A) 一旦
(B) 遠
(C) 早
(D) 非常

正解 (D)
重點解說
這個句子已符合文法結構且語意完整，由此可推知，空格應為副詞，修飾後面的形容詞 effective「有效的」，空格應填選項 (D) very「非常地」，最為合適，故為正解。power plant「發電廠」，emissions「排放量」。

💡 應試者能理解書面文本中的詞彙，並能辨別四個副詞的含意。

105.

Can understand grammar in written texts

To track the location of your package, be sure to ------- the order number to the shipping department.

(A) provide
(B) provided
(C) provision
(D) providing

為了追蹤你的包裹位置，請務必提供訂單號碼給運輸部門。

(A) 提供（原形動詞）
(B) 提供（過去式）
(C) 供應（名詞）
(D) 提供（現在分詞）

正解 (A)
重點解說
空格之前為動詞片語 be sure to「請務必」，to 後面應為原形動詞，選項 (A) 最為合適，故為正解。track「追蹤」。

💡 應試者能理解書面文本中的文法，並根據片語的用法，選出合適的單字詞性。

106.

Can understand vocabulary in written texts

A diamond-shaped symbol next to merchandise indicates that the ------ has been discounted.

(A) property
(B) item
(C) idea
(D) fare

商品旁邊的菱形符號代表這個物品已經打折了。

(A) 財產
(B) 物品
(C) 想法
(D) 票價

正解 (B)
重點解說
空格為 that 子句的主格，子句的述語動詞為 has been discounted「已經（被）打折了」，由於該句是關於銷售和購買商品，空格應填選項 (B) item「物品」，語意最為合適，故為正解。symbol「標示、符號」。
(A) 是關於房地產，而非商品；(C)、(D) 都不符合語意，故可以刪除這三個選項。

💡 應試者能理解書面文本中的詞彙及語意，並從四個名詞中選出適切的答案。

107. Can understand grammar in written texts

Wilkes-Rogers customers who want more ------- to move around should try our new wireless headphone models.

(A) free
(B) freely
(C) freedom
(D) freed

想要行動自如的 Wilkes-Rogers 顧客們，應該要試試我們的新款無線耳機。

(A) 自由的（形容詞）
(B) 自由地（副詞）
(C) 自由（名詞）
(D) 釋放（過去式動詞）

重點解說

正解 (C)

名詞子句中的動詞 want「想要」，後面須接名詞或不定詞。然而空格後面 to move around 也修飾空格，依照文法規則，空格內應填入名詞，故選項 (C) 為正解。want ＋名詞「想要某物」，want to ＋動詞「想要做某事」。wireless「無線的」。

💡 應試者能理解書面文本中的文法，能從名詞子句中找出動詞，並選出動詞 want「想要」後須接的單字詞性。

108. Can understand vocabulary in written texts

The economic development summit will be held ------- the Xi'an Trade Tower on September 22.

(A) to
(B) at
(C) down
(D) of

經濟發展高峰會將會在 9 月 22 日於 Xi'an 世貿大樓舉行。

(A) 到…
(B) 在…
(C) 在…下面
(D) …的

重點解說

正解 (B)

句子中主格為 the economic development summit「經濟發展高峰會」，述語動詞為 be held「被舉辦」，空格之後為地點 the Xi'an Trade Tower「Xi'an 世貿大樓」，因此空格應填入能接特定地點的介系詞，故選項 (B) 為正解。summit「高峰會」。

其他選項也為介系詞，但都不符合語意或文法。(A) to 表示位置的變化或差異，hold to 意思是「堅持」，不符合語意；(C) hold down 為「克制」的意思，也不符合語意；(D) 則既不符合語法也沒有意義。

💡 應試者能理解書面文本中的詞彙，並能分辨四個不同介系詞的使用時機。

109. Can understand grammar in written texts

If your job duties change often, ------- updating your résumé is recommended.

(A) regular
(B) regularly
(C) regularity
(D) regularized

如果你的工作職務經常更換，建議定期更新你的履歷。

(A) 定期的（形容詞）
(B) 定期地（副詞）
(C) 規律性（名詞）
(D) 使…規律（過去分詞）

重點解說

正解 (B)

以「If...」為首的假設語氣，這個句子已符合文法結構且語意完整，由此可推知，空格應為副詞，修飾 updating your résumé「更新你的履歷」，故選項 (B) 為正解。résumé「履歷」，recommend「推薦、建議」。

💡 應試者能理解並辨別 if 假設語氣的用法，在空格內填入對應詞性的單字。

110. Can understand vocabulary in written texts

------- researchers at Starlight Toys finalize their data, they will share it with executive officers.

(A) Why
(B) Despite
(C) Even
(D) When

當 Starlight 玩具公司的研究員完成他們的資料時，他們將會和行政主管分享。

(A) 為什麼
(B) 儘管
(C) 甚至
(D) 當

正解 (D)

重點解說

空格內需填入連接詞，連接兩個完整句子。選項 (D) when「當」語意最合適，故為正解。finalize「完成」，executive「行政主管」。

(A) why「為什麼」當連接詞時，通常會和 the reasons 做搭配；(B) despite「儘管」為介系詞，後面需加名詞，若要接一個完整句子，必須使用 despite the fact that...；(C) even「甚至」為副詞，用來強調特定的人事物，並不能當連接詞使用。

💡 應試者能理解書面文本中的詞彙，並能辨別四個單字的使用時機。

111. Can understand grammar in written texts

------- necklace that is shipped from Gillis Designers is given a thorough quality check.

(A) Whenever
(B) Also
(C) All
(D) Each

每一條經由 Gillis 設計公司寄出的項鍊都有經過徹底的品質檢查。

(A) 無論何時
(B) 也
(C) 所有的
(D) 每一個

正解 (D)

重點解說

此句子的主格為單數名詞 necklace「項鍊」，述語動詞為 is given「被給予」，為第三人稱單數動詞，選項 (D) each「每一個」為形容詞，強調的是整體中的個體，動詞要用單數，故為正解。quality「品質」。

(A) whenever「無論何時」為連接詞，連接兩個子句，不符合此題狀況；(B) also「也」為副詞，且語意不適切；(C) all「所有的」為形容詞，可置於可數或不可數名詞前面，用於三者或三者以上的人或事物，動詞應為複數。

💡 應試者能理解書面文本中的文法，且能辨別四個單字的用法。

112. Can understand vocabulary in written texts

The Ansan Science Museum averages ------- 2,000 visitors per month.

(A) nearly
(B) totally
(C) relatively
(D) fairly

Ansan 科學博物館平均每個月有接近 2,000 位遊客。

(A) 接近地
(B) 全部地
(C) 相當地
(D) 公平地

正解 (A)

重點解說

空格中就算不填入任何字，這個句子也符合文法及語意，由此可推知，空格應為副詞，修飾前面的動詞 average「平均」，故填入選項 (A) nearly「接近地」最為合適。

(B)、(C)、(D) 也為副詞，但意思皆不符合語意，無法正確完成句子。

💡 應試者能理解書面文本中的詞彙，也可以區分不同單字的含意。

113. Can understand grammar in written texts

Marketing employees should use the accounting department's watercooler while ------- is being replaced.

(A) they
(B) them
(C) theirs
(D) their

行銷部的員工應該在他們的飲水機被更換時使用會計部的飲水機。

(A) 他們（主格）
(B) 他們（受格）
(C) 他們的（所有格代名詞）
(D) 他們的（所有格）

正解 (C)

空格之後 is being replaced「現在正在被更換」為現在進行被動語態，填入選項 (C) theirs 所有格代名詞，指的是 their watercooler「他們的飲水機」，故為正解。accounting「會計」，watercooler「飲水機」。

(A) they 為主格，述語動詞須用複數 are；(B) them 為受詞，須放在動詞後面；(D) their 為所有格，後面須接名詞。

💡 應試者能理解書面文本中的文法，辨別人稱代名詞的使用時機。

114. Can understand vocabulary in written texts

It is ------- for the audience to hold its applause until the speaker has finished.

(A) enthusiastic
(B) casual
(C) exclusive
(D) customary

觀眾持續鼓掌直到講者結束是一種慣例。

(A) 熱情的
(B) 休閒的
(C) 獨有的
(D) 傳統的

正解 (D)

此句構為「It is adj to V」強調句，空格應填入形容詞，形容「觀眾鼓掌直到講者結束」這件事，空格應填入選項 (D) customary「傳統的、習慣的」最為合適。

(A) enthusiastic 無法形容後面的 hold its applause；(B) casual 不適用於此題情況，因句中提及觀眾、掌聲和演講者，為較正式的活動；(C) 不符合文意。

💡 應試者能理解書面文本中的詞彙，並能從四個形容詞中選出語意適切的答案。

115. Can understand grammar in written texts

Despite ------- that Legend Air would perform poorly with the entry of cheaper competition, it posted strong second-quarter earnings.

(A) predicted
(B) predictable
(C) predicts
(D) predictions

儘管預測 Legend 航空將隨著低價競爭的加入而表現不佳，它仍公布了強勁的第二季收益。

(A) 預測（過去分詞）
(B) 可預測的（形容詞）
(C) 預測（第三人稱單數現在式動詞）
(D) 預測（名詞）

正解 (D)

句首 Despite 為介系詞，因此後面要接名詞，唯選項 (D) 最為合適，故為正解。competition「競爭」，quarter「季度」，earnings「收益」。

(A) predicted 為 predict「預測」的過去式；(B) predictable 為形容詞；(C) predicts 為第三人稱單數現在式動詞。

💡 應試者能理解書面文本中的文法，並根據介系詞的用法，選出詞性正確的單字。

116.

------- the entire month of May, parking will be prohibited on Cole Avenue.

(A) On
(B) Throughout
(C) Inside
(D) Between

整個五月，Cole 大道將禁止停車。

(A) 在...之上
(B) 自始至終
(C) 在...裡面
(D) 在...之間

重點解說

正解 (B)
全部選項皆有介系詞的作用。空格後為名詞 the entire month of May「整個五月」，選項 (B) throughout「自始至終」表示一整個五月，最符合語意，故為正解。prohibit「禁止」。
(A) on ＋特定時間，例如：on Mother's day、on Friday；(C) inside 通常搭配地方使用；(D) between 的用法為 between A and B，通常 A、B 指的是兩個特定的地點、人事物或時間。

💡 應試者能理解書面文本中的詞彙，並能從四個不同介系詞選出適切的答案。

117.

Main Street Restaurant offers a menu of ------- prepared lunch and dinner meals.

(A) thought
(B) thoughtfulness
(C) thoughts
(D) thoughtfully

Main Street 餐廳提供精心準備的午餐和晚餐菜單。

(A) 想法（名詞形）
(B) 體貼（名詞）
(C) 想法（名詞形）
(D) 體貼地（副詞）

重點解說

正解 (D)
空格中就算不填入任何字，句子也符合文法及語意。因此空格應填入副詞，修飾後面名詞片語 prepared lunch and dinner meals，故選項 (D) thoughtfully 為正解。offer「提供」，menu「菜單」。
(A)、(B)、(C) 皆不是副詞，不符合整句文法，因此不合適。

💡 應試者能理解書面文本中的文法，並能辨別一個完整句子的結構，選出正確的詞性。

118.

Ms. Tsai was told that she would be contacted soon, ------- as early as next week.

(A) sufficiently
(B) possibly
(C) sincerely
(D) patiently

Tsai 小姐被告知很快會與她聯繫，最快可能在下周。

(A) 足夠地
(B) 可能地
(C) 誠摯地
(D) 有耐心地

重點解說

正解 (B)
空格中就算不填入任何字，句子也符合文法及語意。空格應填入副詞，修飾後面的 as early as next week，選項 (B) possibly 語意最為合適，故為正解。
(A)、(C)、(D) 雖皆為副詞，但因不符合語意，無法正確完成句子。

💡 應試者能理解書面文本中的詞彙，並能從四個副詞選出適切的答案。

題目／中文翻譯

119. Can understand grammar in written texts

Videos of Korean pop music have become very popular ------- adolescents worldwide.

(A) including
(B) whereas
(C) among
(D) within

韓國流行音樂影片已經在全世界的青少年之間變得非常熱門。

(A) 包含
(B) 然而
(C) 在...之中
(D) 在...之內

重點解說

正解 (C)

空格之後為名詞片語 adolescents worldwide「全世界的青少年」，當對象數量超過三個，且這些對象都是此群體中的一員時，介系詞應用 (C) among「在...之中」，故為正解。

(A) including 是用來帶出包含的事物，空格前並未提及含有範圍的事物；(B) whereas「然而」為連接詞，用於平衡對比的想法，不符合語意，句子也不完整；(D) within「在...之內」，用來描述某段時間或空間之內。

💡 應試者能理解書面文本中的文法，並從四個單字中選出最適切的答案。

120. Can understand vocabulary in written texts

Rydell Law Group chose to lease the office space ------- the landlord offered a discount.

(A) that
(B) much as
(C) no sooner
(D) because

因為房東提供了優惠，Rydell 法律集團決定租借辦公空間。

(A) 那
(B) 雖然
(C) 一...就...
(D) 因為

重點解說

正解 (D)

空格應填入連接詞，連接兩個子句，空格之後表示「房東提供了優惠」，填入選項 (D) because「因為」，結合後面的句子，提供了為何 Rydell 法律集團做此決定的原因，語意最為合適。lease「租借」。

(A) that 放在名詞後面為名詞子句，語意不合適；(B) much as「雖然、即使」為連接詞，填入格子裡，語意不合適；(C) no sooner 需搭配 than，為「一...就...」，表示某事緊接著另一件事發生，語意不合適。

💡 應試者能理解書面文本中的詞彙，並能從四個連接詞選出適切的答案。

121. Can understand grammar in written texts

Hasin Fariz turned a study on the ------- effects of sleep into a best-selling book.

(A) favorable
(B) favor
(C) favors
(D) favorably

Hasin Fariz 將一項關於睡眠有利影響的研究變成一本暢銷書。

(A) 有利的（形容詞）
(B) 恩惠、贊成（名詞）；偏袒、支持（動詞）
(C) 恩惠、贊成（名詞複數形）；偏袒、支持（第三人稱單數現在式動詞）
(D) 有利地（副詞）

重點解說

正解 (A)

空格之後為名詞 effects「影響」及 of sleep「睡眠的」，因此填入形容詞修飾最為適合，故選項 (A) favorable「有利的」為正解。best-selling「暢銷的」。

其他選項皆不能形容 effects，也不能正確完成句子。

💡 應試者能理解書面文本中的文法，並辨別單字 favor「偏愛」的各式詞性與對應用法。

122. Can understand vocabulary in written texts

The Girard Botanical Archive has almost 300,000 plant ------, all neatly pressed onto archival paper.

(A) authorities
(B) specimens
(C) founders
(D) specifics

Girard 植物圖鑑裡有將近 300,000 種植物標本，全部都整齊地壓在案卷紙上。

(A) 權威
(B) 標本
(C) 創始人
(D) 細節

正解 (B)

重點解說

全部選項皆為名詞。空格後表示「全部都整齊地壓在案卷紙上」，選項 (B) specimens「標本」，最符合語意，故為正解。archive「檔案」，neatly「整齊地」，archival paper「案卷紙」。
其他選項皆不能放置在紙上，所以皆不能正確地完成句子。

💡 應試者能理解書面文本中的詞彙，了解語意，並從四個名詞中選出答案。

123. Can understand vocabulary in written texts

Wynston Containers is ------ a yearly shutdown of its factory so that it can be evaluated for safety and efficiency.

(A) involving
(B) participating
(C) implementing
(D) producing

Wynston 貨櫃公司正在實施工廠年度停機，以便評估安全性和效能。

(A) 涉及
(B) 參與
(C) 實施
(D) 生產

正解 (C)

重點解說

空格前為 be 動詞 is，故空格應填入合適的現在分詞。空格後為名詞片語 a yearly shutdown，選項 (C) implementing「實施」，最符合語意，意即正在實施停工，故為正解。shutdown「暫時關閉」，evaluate「評估」，efficiency「效能」。
(A)、(D) 不符合語意；(B) 除了不符合語意，participate 後面通常需接介系詞 in。

💡 應試者能理解書面文本中的詞彙和語意，並從四個現在分詞中選出答案。

124. Can understand vocabulary in written texts

Clyden Bistro's ------ location is now occupied by Margie Sue's Bakery.

(A) recognized
(B) delayed
(C) responsible
(D) former

Clyden 小酒館原先的位置現在被 Margie Sue's 麵包店占據了。

(A) 公認的
(B) 延遲的
(C) 負責任的
(D) 原先的

正解 (D)

重點解說

空格之後為名詞 location，選項 (D) former「原先的」為形容詞，修飾名詞 location，最符合語意，故為正解。occupy「占據」。
其他選項皆沒有正確修飾 location 或沒有正確完成句子，故不合適。

💡 應試者能理解書面文本中的詞彙，了解語意，並從四個形容詞中選出答案。

125. Can understand grammar in written texts

The ------- to review plans to replace the Tronton Bridge will be scheduled soon.

(A) heard
(B) hears
(C) hearing
(D) hear

審查 Tronton 橋更換計畫的聽證會很快就會安排。

(A) 聽見（過去式動詞）
(B) 聽見（第三人稱單數現在式動詞）
(C) 聽證會（名詞或動詞的現在分詞形式）
(D) 聽見（現在式動詞）

正解 (C)

重點解說

空格為句子的主格，will be scheduled 為述語動詞，由於本句是有關審查橋梁更換計畫的事件，選項 (C) hearing「聽證會」為唯一符合句意的名詞，故為正解。review「審查」，replace「更換、取代」，schedule「安排」。
(A) heard 為 hear「聽見」的過去式動詞；(B) hears 為第三人稱單數現在式動詞；(D) hear 為現在式動詞。三個選項皆不能正確完成句子。

💡 應試者能理解書面文本中的文法，並辨別動詞 hear「聽見」的形態與用法。

126. Can understand grammar in written texts

------- Amanda Simont finds a full-time job, she will open a savings account.

(A) As soon as
(B) Prior to
(C) In case of
(D) Not only

Amanda Simont 一找到全職工作，她就會開一個儲蓄帳戶。

(A) 一...就...
(B) 在...之前
(C) 萬一
(D) 不只...

正解 (A)

重點解說

空格應填入連接詞，連接兩個子句，填入選項 (A) as soon as「一...就...」最為合適，因第二個子句中的動作將在第一個子句中的動作完成後，幾乎立即發生，故為正解。full-time「全職」，savings account「儲蓄帳戶」。
(B) prior to「在...之前」，後面接動名詞或名詞；(C) in case of「萬一」，要接動名詞或名詞；(D) not only「不只...」，通常搭配 but also 使用，not only 放在句首，需使用倒裝句型。選項 (B)、(C)、(D) 皆不符合句意。

💡 應試者能理解書面文本中的文法，辨別連接詞的使用方法與時機。

127. Can understand grammar in written texts

The grocery store ------- vegetables from out of town until local prices went down last month.

(A) is buying
(B) will be buying
(C) has been buying
(D) had been buying

這家雜貨店過去一直從外地購買蔬菜，直到上個月當地的價格下降為止。

(A) 購買（現在進行式）
(B) 購買（未來進行式）
(C) 購買（現在完成進行式）
(D) 購買（過去完成進行式）

正解 (D)

重點解說

空格前為名詞片語 the grocery store，空格後為名詞 vegetables，因此空格應填入適當的動詞型態，until「直到…為止」，指一直做某件事情直到某個時間點。由於在 until 子句中的動詞為過去式，所以主要子句的動詞應為過去完成進行式，故選項 (D) had been buying「過去一直購買」為正解。out of town「外地的」，go down「下降」。
(A)、(B)、(C) 的時態不符合句意。

💡 應試者能理解書面文本中的文法，並辨別動詞的不同時態與使用時機。

128. Can understand vocabulary in written texts

If all the documentation is -------, a construction permit should take four weeks to process.

(A) too much
(B) over done
(C) in order
(D) on call

如果所有的文件都準備就緒，施工許可應該需要四周來辦理。

(A) 太多
(B) 過多的
(C) 準備就緒
(D) 待命

 重點解說

正解 (C)
以「If...」為首的假設語氣，主格為 the documentation「文件」，述語動詞為 is，選項 (C) in order「準備就緒」表示文件的狀況，語意最為通順，故為正解。construction「施工、建設」，permit「許可」，process「辦理、過程」。

💡 應試者能理解書面文本中的詞彙，了解語意，並從四個詞彙選出答案。

129. Can understand grammar in written texts

Chung-Li Medicine provides health care to people in ------- remote areas.

(A) geographer
(B) geographically
(C) geographic
(D) geography

Chung-Li 醫藥為了偏遠地區的人們提供健康照護。

(A) 地理學家（名詞）
(B) 地理上地（副詞）
(C) 地理學的（形容詞）
(D) 地理學（名詞）

重點解說

正解 (B)
空格內不填入任何字，句子也很完整，因此空格應為副詞以修飾 remote「偏遠的」，故選項 (B) geographically「地理上地」為正解。

💡 應試者能理解書面文本中的文法，辨別 geography「地理」的不同形態與使用時機。

130. Can understand vocabulary in written texts

------- and cost factored equally in choosing Cantavox as our main supplier.

(A) Reliability
(B) Allowance
(C) Dependence
(D) Estimation

在選擇 Cantavox 作為我們的主要供應商時，誠信和成本是同等重要的考量因素。

(A) 誠信
(B) 零用金
(C) 依賴
(D) 估算

重點解說

正解 (A)
「＿＿和成本」為此句的主格，動詞為 factored...in「把 ... 納入重要因素」，選項 (A) reliability「誠信、可信賴」語意最為合適，故為正解。equally「同等地」，supplier「供應商」。

💡 應試者能理解書面文本中的詞彙，了解語意，並從四個名詞選出答案。

Questions 131-134 refer to the following article.

CENTERVILLE—Luigi's, the Italian restaurant located in the Monmouth Hotel, ------ its doors next Saturday
131.
after ten years in business. Chef Giovanni Modica left the restaurant several weeks ago, prompting rumors
of a change. The space is going to be renovated this spring and then reopen with new management and
a new ------ according to Linda Hughes, spokesperson for the Monmouth Hotel. ------ . The restaurant's
132. **133.**
name, however, is ------ to be announced.
134.

請參考下列報導，回答第 131 至 134 題。

CENTERVILLE －位於 Monmouth 旅館的義大利餐廳 Luigi's，在經營了十年之後將在下週六結束營業。主
廚 Giovanni Modica 在幾個星期前離開了餐廳，因而引發變動的傳聞。根據 Monmouth 旅館的發言人 Linda
Hughes 表示，這個空間在春天將會進行翻修，並以新的管理者及菜單重新出發，**＊而墨西哥料理將會是主打**。然
而，餐廳的名字尚未公布。

＊第 133 題插入句的翻譯

131. | Can understand grammar in written texts

(A) was closed   (A) 結束營業（被動式）
(B) will be closing   **(B) 結束營業（未來進行式）**
(C) closed   (C) 結束營業（過去式）
(D) to close   (D) 結束營業（to 不定詞）

重點解說	**正解 (B)** 從空格後面句子中的 next Saturday「下週六」得知結束營業的時間是下週，因此空格應填入未來式。此句強調 「將結束營業」，故 (B) will be closing 為正解。 💡 應試者能理解書面文本中的文法，選出正確的動詞時態。

132. | Can connect information across multiple sentences in a single written text and across texts
| Can understand vocabulary in written texts

(A) address   (A) 地址
(B) receipt   (B) 收據
(C) supply   (C) 補給品
(D) menu   **(D) 菜單**

重點解說	**正解 (D)** 空格之前的句子意思為「這個空間在春天將會進行翻修，並以新的管理者及____重新出發」，且文章最後提及新 餐廳的名字尚未公布，故選項 (D) 最符合語意。 (A) 因文章提及是在飯店裡的原空間開設新餐廳，故地址不會改變；(B)、(C) 雖與餐廳相關，但從前後文來看，選 項 (D) 語意最為適切。 💡 應試者能從相似的選項中，透過前後句子判斷最符合句意的答案。 💡 應試者能理解這篇報導的內容及其中所提到關於餐廳與經營相關的單字／慣用語。

133. Can connect information across multiple sentences in a single written text and across texts

(A) Centerville has a diverse dining scene.
(B) Mexican cuisine will be the focus.
(C) Food costs have increased recently.
(D) There are other cafés on Main Street.

(A) Centerville 有多樣的用餐環境。
(B) 墨西哥料理將會是主打。
(C) 最近食材成本上漲了。
(D) 在 Main 街上有其他咖啡廳。

重點解說

正解 (B)
選項 (B) 提到墨西哥料理，延續前一句新管理者及菜單，使文章更清楚呈現新餐廳的重點在於他的料理。其他選項皆不符合文意。cuisine「料理、菜餚」。
(A) diverse「多樣的」，dining「用餐」，scene「場景、圈子」；(C) increase「增加」，recently「最近」。

💡 應試者能理解這篇報導的內容，並從前後句子判斷最符合句意的答案。

134. Can understand vocabulary in written texts

(A) yet
(B) really
(C) besides
(D) until

(A) 尚未
(B) 真正地、非常
(C) 除了…之外還有
(D) 直到…

重點解說

正解 (A)
根據報導最後一個句子，新餐廳的名字仍未決定，因此空格應填入選項 (A) yet「尚未」。另外兩種說法是 It has yet to be announced 或 It has not yet been announced。
(B)、(C)、(D) 與前後句子語意不連貫。

💡 應試者能理解這篇報導中與餐廳及經營相關的單字／慣用語，以及常用字但較少見的意思或用法。

題目／中文翻譯

Questions 135-138 refer to the following e-mail.

To: Samuel Archerson <sarcherson@vona.co.uk>
From: James Darrers <jdarrers@sky.co.uk>
Date: 10 January
Subject: Cost Accountant position

Dear Mr. Archerson,

Thank you for taking the time to meet with me today. I ------- our conversation, ❶ and I remain very
                                                     135.
interested in the position of cost accountant. I would welcome the opportunity to return for the third and
final round of -------.
              136.

I am confident my years of accounting experience would benefit your firm. As discussed, over the last ten
years, I have helped many companies save a ------- amount of money. I am especially adept at analysing
                                           137.
the day-to-day operations of a business and helping to determine more cost-effective methods.

I checked regarding your question about a potential start date. -------. I hope to hear from you in the near future.
                                                               138.

Sincerely,

James Darrers

請參考以下電子郵件，回答第 135 至 138 題。

致：Samuel Archerson <sarcherson@vona.co.uk>
來自：James Darrers <jdarrers@sky.co.uk>
日期：1 月 10 日
主旨：成本會計職務

敬愛的 Archerson 先生，

非常感謝您今日抽空與我見面。我很享受我們的談話過程，而且我對於成本會計這個職務仍然很感興趣。很高興
有機會再來參與第三輪也是最後一輪的面試。

我有信心我多年的會計經驗會對貴公司有所助益。如我們討論的，過去十年間，我幫助許多公司節省大量資金。
我特別擅長分析企業的日常營運，並且協助決策更具成本效益的方法。

關於您提到何時可以開始工作，經確認，* 我可以在二月的第一週開始。期望不久後的將來能得到您的回覆。

James Darrers 敬上

*第138 題插入句的翻譯

135. Can connect information across multiple sentences in a single written text and across texts
          Can understand grammar in written texts

(A) enjoy	(A) 享受（現在式）
(B) enjoyed	**(B) 享受（過去式）**
(C) enjoying	(C) 享受（現在分詞）
(D) will enjoy	(D) 享受（未來式）

重點解說

正解 (B)
從第一句得知，寄信者與面試官今天已見過面，整封信也都強調此次會面是發生在過去，空格應填入過去式。
若兩人經常對談，(A) 也會是正解，但寫信者使用正式語氣及期望收到回覆，可看出他們不是一直有交談的關係。
💡 應試者能理解較長的信件，並將資訊連結得知信件主題。
💡 應試者能理解書面文本中的文法，選出正確的動詞時態。

136. Can connect information across multiple sentences in a single written text and across texts

Can understand vocabulary in written texts

(A) revisions
(B) promotions
(C) interviews
(D) receptions

(A) 修訂
(B) 促銷
(C) 面試
(D) 接待

重點解說

正解 (C)
根據❶可知，寄信者對 position of cost accountant「成本會計職務」很感興趣，由此得知這是一封求職相關的信件。空格前的句子寄信者表示他很高興擁有第三輪也是最後一輪的機會，故空格應填入選項 (C) interviews「面試」，上下文意才通順。

💡 應試者能透過前後句判斷最符合句意的答案。
💡 應試者能理解此篇書信的內容及與求職相關的詞彙。

137. Can understand grammar in written texts

(A) substance
(B) substantiate
(C) substantially
(D) substantial

(A) 物質（名詞）
(B) 證實（動詞）
(C) 相當多地（副詞）
(D) 相當多的（形容詞）

重點解說

正解 (D)
空格內不填入任何字，句子也很完整。因此空格應為修飾名詞 amount「數量」的形容詞，故選項 (D)substantial「相當多的」為正解。

💡 應試者能理解書面文本的文法，並辨別同一單字的不同詞性與使用時機。

138. Can connect information across multiple sentences in a single written text and across texts

(A) I have four additional questions to ask you.
(B) I would be able to begin during the first week of February.
(C) I am confident I have the potential for this position.
(D) Thank you for the offer of employment.

(A) 我還有四個問題請教您。
(B) 我可以在二月的第一週開始。
(C) 我相信我有潛力勝任這個職位。
(D) 感謝您提供的工作機會。

重點解說

正解 (B)
空格前的句子語意為「關於您提到何時可以開始工作」，可推知空格須填入選項 (B)，語意最為通順。
雖然 (A)、(C)、(D) 都是可能在求職電子郵件中表達的說法，但他們都不符合前後文意，故須排除。(A) additional「額外的」；(C) potential「潛力」；(D) employment「受雇」。

💡 應試者能透過前後句子去判斷最符合句意的答案。

Questions 139-142 refer to the following article.

SYDNEY (5 January)—Olney Technology announced yesterday that its smart irrigation system is now available to commercial clients. The system is designed to dispense the proper amount of water to every plant on a farm. It works by measuring ❶ the amount of water in soil ------- the rates of evaporation and
<u>139.</u>
the amount of water used by every plant. ------- All of this data is continuously analysed to determine the
<u>140.</u>
most effective watering schedules. ------- anticipate ❷ that the system will reduce the average farm's water
<u>141.</u>
usage by 20 percent. They also believe it will ------- crop damage. By constantly monitoring soil conditions
<u>142.</u>
and adjusting watering schedules, the system ensures that crops are not over- or underwatered.

請參考以下報導,回答第 139 至 142 題。

雪梨(1月5日)—Olney 科技昨天宣布其所屬的智慧灌溉系統現在可供商業客戶使用。該系統是為了讓農場上的每株植物分配到適量的水而設計,透過測量土壤中的水分,以及每株植物的蒸發率和用水量來進行。* **天氣預測也被列入考量。** 所有的數據都被持續分析以決定最有效的澆水時間表。開發者預計該系統將會減少 20% 的農場平均用水量,他們也相信此系統能避免農作物損害。藉由不斷地監測土壤狀況以及調整澆水時間表,該系統能確保農作物不會被過度澆水或是澆水不足。

*第 140 題插入句的翻譯

139. `Can understand vocabulary in written texts`

(A) since
(B) while
(C) as well as
(D) as long as

(A) 自從
(B) 當
(C) 和
(D) 只要

> **重點解說**
>
> **正解 (C)**
> 包含空格的句子意思是「它透過測量土壤中的水分____每株植物的蒸發率和用水量來進行」,由此得知 water in soil「土壤中的水分」、rates of evaporation「蒸發率」和 the amount of water「用水量」皆為測量的因素,故選項 (C) as well as「和」為正解。
>
> 💡 應試者能理解書面文本中的詞彙,了解文章內容,並從四個不同連接詞中,選出正確答案。

140.

(A) Weather forecasts are also taken into account.
(B) Olney also offers a mobile phone app to track crop growth.
(C) Larger irrigation systems can even spread plant food.
(D) Installation times vary based on farm location.

(A) 天氣預測也被列入考量。
(B) Olney 也提供一款手機應用程式來追蹤農作物成長。
(C) 較大型的灌溉系統甚至可以用來施肥。
(D) 安裝時間因農場位置而有所不同。

正解 (A)

空格後的句子表示「所有的數據都被持續分析以決定最有效的澆水時間表」，這邊的數據為❶所提到測量的水分、蒸發率和用水量。故空格應填入選項 (A)，上下文意通順自然。

數據中並沒有與 (B)、(C)、(D) 相關的資訊。(B) track「追蹤」；(C) irrigation「灌溉」；(D) installation「安裝」。

💡 應試者能透過段落中的前後句，判斷最符合句意的答案。

141.

(A) Developed
(B) Developers
(C) Developing
(D) Developments

(A) 開發（過去式）
(B) 開發者（名詞複數形）
(C) 開發（現在分詞）
(D) 發展（名詞複數形）

正解 (B)

空格為此句的主格，動詞為 anticipate「預期」，由此推斷主格為人或名詞，故選項 (B) developers「開發者」為正解。

雖然 (D) 也是名詞，但並不符合文意，故須排除。

💡 應試者能理解書面文本中的文法，根據上下文意辨別同一單字不同詞性的使用。

142.

(A) detect
(B) prevent
(C) treat
(D) assess

(A) 偵測
(B) 避免
(C) 對待
(D) 評估

正解 (B)

由❷得知，「開發者預計該系統將會減少 20% 的農場平均用水量」，空格前的 they 指的是前面的開發者，「他們也相信此系統能____農作物損害」，空格應填入選項 (B) prevent「避免」，上下文意通順，故為正解。

💡 應試者能透過段落中的前後句，判斷最符合句意的答案。

💡 應試者能理解書面文本中的詞彙，了解文章內容，並在四個不同動詞中，選出正確答案。

題目／中文翻譯

Questions 143-146 refer to the following article.

SHIRESBERRY (February 15)—❶ The second annual Shiresberry Film Festival begins on April 18 and

------ for five weeks. This year's offerings will not be limited to entries from North America and Europe. We
143.

will also be presenting ------ from Asia and South America. ❷ And everyone's favorite feature from last
144.

year's festival will be back: directors and screenwriters will hold question-and-answer sessions after their

films' initial screening. Make sure you do not miss this ------ event. Tickets always sell out quickly. ------
145. **146.**

Shiresberry Film Club members can now purchase priority tickets. Visit the Shiresberry Theater box office

or www.shiresberrytheater.com.

請參考以下報導，回答第 143 至 146 題。

SHIRESBERRY（2 月 15 日）—第二屆年度 Shiresberry 電影節於 4 月 18 日開幕，並且將會持續五個星期。
今年展出的電影將不限於北美洲和歐洲的參賽作品，我們也會放映來自亞洲和南美洲的電影。去年電影節大家最
喜歡的特點也將回歸——導演和編劇會在電影首映結束後進行問答環節，千萬不要錯過這個熱門的活動，門票
總是很快售完。*3 月 3 日會開放給一般民眾購買，Shiresberry 電影俱樂部的會員現在就可以優先購票，請洽
Shiresberry 電影院售票處或 www.shiresberrytheater.com。

*第 146 題插入句的翻譯

143. | Can understand grammar in written texts

(A) run   (A) 持續（現在式）
(B) has run   (B) 持續（現在完成式）
(C) will run   **(C) 持續（未來式）**
(D) ran   (D) 持續（過去式）

> **正解 (C)**
> 從開頭得知文章發布日期為 2 月 15 日，接著❶表示「第二屆年度 Shiresberry 電影節於 4 月 18 日開幕」，而空
> 格後提到「五週」，表示空格應填入未來式，故 (C) will run「持續」為正解。
> 其他選項皆不是未來式，故不符合文意。
>
> 💡 應試者能理解書面文本中的文法，並根據前後句判斷動詞的時態。

144. | Can connect information across multiple sentences in a single written text and across texts
       | Can understand vocabulary in written texts

(A) movies   **(A) 電影**
(B) clothing   (B) 服飾
(C) food   (C) 食物
(D) books   (D) 書籍

> **正解 (A)**
> 從❶可知為「電影節」以及❷提到「去年電影節大家最喜歡的特點也將回歸——導演和編劇會在電影首映結束後
> 進行問答環節」，得知文章與電影相關，故答案為選項 (A)，使上下文意通順。
>
> 💡 應試者能透過段落中的前後句子，連接文章訊息。
>
> 💡 應試者能理解書面文本中的詞彙，了解文章內容，並從四個不同名詞中，選出正確答案。

145.

Can connect information across multiple sentences in a single written text and across texts

Can understand vocabulary in written texts

(A) political
(B) popular
(C) practical
(D) preliminary

(A) 政治的
(B) 受歡迎的
(C) 實際的
(D) 初步的

重點解說

正解 (B)

根據❷提到「去年電影節大家最喜歡的特點也將回歸——導演和編劇會在電影首映結束後進行問答環節」，由此得知選項 (B) popular「受歡迎的」，最符合語意。

💡 應試者能透過段落中的前後句子，連接文章訊息。

💡 應試者能理解書面文本中的詞彙，了解文章內容，並在四個不同形容詞中，選出正確答案。

146.

Can connect information across multiple sentences in a single written text and across texts

(A) The awards will be presented by Hunter Johns.
(B) Renovations to the space are nearly complete.
(C) The later offerings were an even bigger success.
(D) Sales are open to the general public on March 3.

(A) 這個獎項將由 Hunter Johns 頒發。
(B) 這個空間的整修幾乎要完工。
(C) 後續推出的產品更加成功。
(D) 3 月 3 日會開放給一般民眾購買。

重點解說

正解 (D)

根據空格前一句和後一句，得知購票狀況和會員可以先購票的資訊，因此空格中應填入與售票相關的資訊，故選項 (D) 最為通順。
(A)、(B)、(C) 與前後的句子內容不連貫。(B) renovation「整修」；(C) offering「供給品、產品」。

💡 應試者能透過段落中的前後句子，判斷最符合句意的答案。

Questions 147-148 refer to the following advertisement.

Sedwick Electronics Hiring Event
March 2, 10 A.M.–5 P.M.
22 Myer Street, Hanover, PA 17331

❶ Sedwick Electronics is opening a new manufacturing facility in Hanover, Pennsylvania, and we need to fill many positions. We offer a wonderful work environment and great benefits to our employees.

❷ Come to the event and hear from employees from our Lancaster facility about their experience, learn about the open positions, and speak with our recruiters. No RSVP is necessary. Bring copies of your résumé.

請參考以下廣告，回答第 147 至 148 題。

Sedwick 電子 徵才活動
3 月 2 日上午 10 點到下午 5 點
Myer 街 22 號，漢諾威，PA 17331

Sedwick 電子公司在賓夕法尼亞州的漢諾威開設新的製造工廠，需要填補許多職位。我們提供員工一個舒適的工作環境以及優渥的福利。

歡迎參加徵才活動，聽聽看 Lancaster 廠區員工的經驗分享，了解職缺內容，還能和我們的招募人員談談。不需要回覆預約，只要攜帶你的履歷表即可。

147. | Can make inferences based on information in written texts

For whom is the advertisement intended?

(A) Recruiters
(B) Job seekers
(C) Local business owners
(D) Current Sedwick Electronics employees

這則廣告是為誰準備的？

(A) 招募人員
(B) 求職者
(C) 本地企業的老闆
(D) Sedwick 電子的在職員工

重點解說

正解 (B)

可以從大標題看到這是一個徵才活動，❶進一步說明這是一場為了求職者而辦的活動，例如：new facility……need to fill many positions。再從❷得知活動內容包括「員工的經驗分享」、「職缺內容」、「和招募人員談談」，故正解為選項 (B)。

💡 應試者能推測出廣告的目的，並能對文本細節做出判斷。

148. | Can locate and understand specific information in written texts

What is stated about Sedwick Electronics?

(A) It is moving its headquarters.
(B) It offers a training program for new employees.
(C) It requires employees to wear uniforms.
(D) It will have more than one location.

關於 Sedwick 電子的敘述何者正確？

(A) 總部正要搬遷。
(B) 提供新員工教育訓練。
(C) 要求員工穿著制服。
(D) 將會有不只一個據點。

重點解說

正解 (D)

❶第一行說明「Sedwick 電子公司在賓夕法尼亞州的漢諾威開設新的製造工廠」，而從❷可知，該公司在 Lancaster 也有一間工廠，由此可清楚知道，該公司原本就有一座工廠，並即將在第二個地點設立一座新工廠。故選項 (D) 為正解。

(A) headquarters「總部」。

💡 應試者能理解廣告中的訊息，即使選項換句話說，也能選出正確答案。

Questions 149-150 refer to the following notice.

Aguni Plumbing Supply Returns

Beginning March 1 at all Aguni Plumbing Supply locations, customers will be able to come to our stores to return purchases made online. For a complete refund, the return must be made within 30 days of purchase and must be accompanied by a receipt. In addition, the merchandise must be returned in the original packaging, and all components must be included. After 30 days, refunds will be limited to in-store credit only. Defective items may be exchanged for the same item only.

請參考以下通知，回答第 149 至 150 題。

Aguni 水電材料行退貨

從 3 月 1 日起，在所有的 Aguni 水電材料行地點，顧客都可以來我們的店裡退換網購商品。如需全額退款，必須在商品購買後 30 天內退貨並且附上收據。除此之外，商品必須以原包裝退回，且須包含所有零件。超過 30 天者，僅限以店內的消費點數作為退款。瑕疵品僅能以相同商品更換。

149.

Can locate and understand specific information in written texts

What will happen on March 1?

(A) A shipment will be returned.

(B) A new policy will go into effect.

(C) A promotional sale will take place.

(D) A customer survey will be published.

3 月 1 日將會發生什麼事？

(A) 貨物將被退回。

(B) 新政策將會開始生效。

(C) 將舉行促銷活動。

(D) 將發表顧客調查報告。

重點解說

正解 (B)

從第三行到第四行可知，退貨的期限和條件。第四行到第五行可知，退貨時的注意事項。由此可判斷，Aguni 水電材料行提出新的退貨政策，並從第一行得知此政策將於 3 月 1 日起生效，故選項 (B) 為正解。

(C) promotional sale「促銷活動」；(D) customer survey「顧客調查」。

💡 應試者能理解通知文件中的訊息，並推論文章的目的，選出正確答案，即使選項是以換句話說的方式表達。

150.

Can connect information across multiple sentences in a single written text and across texts

What is NOT a requirement for a complete refund?

(A) The return must be made at the original purchase location.

(B) The return must be made within a certain time frame.

(C) The item must be returned with all its components.

(D) The item must be returned in the original packaging.

為了得到全額退款下列哪一項不是必須的？

(A) 要在原購買地點退貨。

(B) 要在一定的期限內退貨。

(C) 商品須連同所有零件一起退回。

(D) 商品必須以原包裝退回。

重點解說

正解 (A)

從第二行可知，消費者可以進行網購商品的退貨，並沒有規定要退回原本購物的地方，故選項 (A) 為正解。

(B) 從第三行可知，退貨必須在購買後的 30 天內完成。

(C) 從第五行得知，所有的零件必須包含在原包裝裡；(D) 從第四行到第五行得知，商品必須要放在原本的包裝裡。選項中的 item「物品」指的是 merchandise「商品」。

(C) components「零件、成分」；(D) packaging「包裝」。

💡 應試者能理解此通知內的訊息，並將文章所提供關於退款的資訊連接起來。

題目/中文翻譯

Questions 151-152 refer to the following schedule

Peter,

❶ Here is my tentative schedule for Monday. Please check with these colleagues to confirm. Ani has arranged everything for my stay in sunny Samirabad—I certainly will not miss the weather here! My speech for the Samirabad Awards Banquet is nearly finalized. I will return to the office on Thursday, 15 February. If possible, please avoid making any appointments for the end of the week as I plan to focus on the Zoldanas Project when I return.

Sonya

❷ **Schedule for Sonya Barlow** **Monday, 12 February**	
8:30 A.M.	Breakfast with Evan Wong, Human Resources
9:45 A.M.	Phone conference financial update, Nasreen Akhtar
10:30 A.M.	Status of technology upgrades, Aaliyah Taffe
11:15 A.M.	New facilities proposal meeting, Mitch Carr
12:30 P.M.	Leave for airport
4:52 P.M.	Flight departs

請參考以下行程表,回答第 **151** 至 **152** 題。

Peter,

這是我星期一暫定的行程表,請和這些同事確認。Ani 已經幫我安排好在晴朗的 Samirabad 的所有事情,我當然不會錯過這裡的好天氣!我在 Samirabad 頒獎晚宴的演說即將定稿,我會在 2 月 15 日星期四返回辦公室。如果可能,請避免在週末有任何的安排,因為我打算回來時專注在 Zoldanas 專案上。

Sonya

Sonya Barlow 的行程表 **2 月 12 日 星期一**	
上午 8:30	和人力資源部門 Evan Wong 共進早餐
上午 9:45	電話會議確認財務更新,Nasreen Akhtar
上午 10:30	技術升級的狀況,Aaliyah Taffe
上午 11:15	新設施的提案會議,Mitch Carr
下午 12:30	離開前往機場
下午 4:52	飛機起飛

151. Can locate and understand specific information in written texts

What will Ms. Barlow do in Samirabad?

(A) Take a vacation
(B) Conduct a training session
(C) Attend a special dinner
(D) Meet an important client

Barlow 小姐將會在 Samirabad 做什麼事？

(A) 度假
(B) 進行教育訓練
(C) 參加特別的晚宴
(D) 和一位重要客戶見面

正解 (C)

重點解說

在❶第三行到第四行中，Barlow 小姐提到，「我在 Samirabad 頒獎晚宴的演說即將定稿」，banquet 意思是盛大且正式的晚餐，由此可判斷，Barlow 小姐要參加一個特別的晚宴，故選項 (C) 為正解。
(A) Barlow 小姐沒有提及任何有關度假的活動。
(B) Barlow 小姐沒有提及任何有關教育訓練的活動。conduct「舉辦、實行」。
(D) 從❶的第一行可得知是要和同事確認開會行程，並不是與客戶見面。

💡 應試者能理解時程表傳達的訊息，選出正確答案，即使選項是以換句話說的方式表達。

152. Can locate and understand specific information in written texts

Who will likely discuss a new idea?

(A) Mr. Wong
(B) Ms. Akhtar
(C) Ms. Taffe
(D) Mr. Carr

誰有可能討論新的想法？

(A) Wong 先生
(B) Akhtar 小姐
(C) Taffe 小姐
(D) Carr 先生

正解 (D)

重點解說

從❷行程表得知，上午 11:15 和 Carr 先生有一個新設施的提案會議，因此我們可以推斷這會是一個新的想法，故選項 (D) 為正解。
(A) Barlow 小姐將在早餐時與 Wong 先生會面，但內容沒有提及會討論新的想法。
(B) Akhtar 小姐負責提供財務更新，但內容沒有提及會討論新的想法。
(C) Taffe 小姐負責提供技術升級資訊，但內容沒有提及會討論新的想法。

💡 應試者能理解時程表的訊息，即使內容沒有直接表明，也可以推論出答案。

題目/中文翻譯

Questions 153-154 refer to the following text-message chain.

❶ **Javier Palomo [2:04 P.M.]**
Are you still at the farm? I haven't made a shelter for the new tractor yet, and rain has been forecast for today.

❷ **Conrad Genet [2:06 P.M.]**
I'm still here. It looks like it might rain any minute.

❸ **Javier Palomo [2:07 P.M.]**
Can you find a tarp to cover it?

❹ **Conrad Genet [2:12 P.M.]**
I couldn't find a spare one in the shed. There is a large black tarp covering the hay bales, though.

❺ **Javier Palomo [2:13 P.M.]**
That one needs to stay there. Could you search the barn?

❻ **Conrad Genet [2:17 P.M.]**
OK, I found a tarp, but it's quite dirty.

❼ **Javier Palomo [2:18 P.M.]**
<u>That's fine.</u> I'd rather clean the tractor than let it get drenched by the rain.

❽ **Conrad Genet [2:19 P.M.]**
Okay.

請參考以下簡訊對話，回答第 153 至 154 題。

Javier Palomo ［下午 2:04］
你還在農場嗎？我還沒為新的拖拉機蓋棚子，天氣預報說今天會下雨。

Conrad Genet ［下午 2:06］
我還在這裡，看起來隨時都會下雨。

Javier Palomo ［下午 2:07］
你可以找一條防水布蓋住它嗎？

Conrad Genet ［下午 2:12］
棚子裡找不到多餘的布，不過有一條大的黑色防水布蓋在牧草捲上。

Javier Palomo ［下午 2:13］
那一條必須留在那裡。你可以找一下穀倉嗎？

Conrad Genet ［下午 2:17］
好，我找到一條防水布了，但是它非常髒。

Javier Palomo ［下午 2:18］
沒關係。我寧願清理拖拉機，總比讓它被雨淋濕好。

Conrad Genet ［下午 2:19］
好的。

153. `Can make inferences based on information in written texts`

What does Mr. Palomo ask Mr. Genet to do?

(A) **Protect a piece of equipment**
(B) Check the weather forecast
(C) Put some tools in the shed
(D) Move some hay bales

Palomo 先生要 Genet 先生做什麼事？

(A) **保護一台設備**
(B) 查天氣預報
(C) 把一些工具放到棚子裡
(D) 移動一些牧草捲

正解 (A)

重點解說

Palomo 先生詢問 Genet 先生❶「你還在農場嗎？我還沒為新的拖拉機蓋棚子，天氣預報說今天會下雨。」接著又詢問❸「你可以找一條防水布蓋住它嗎？」句中的 it 指的是❶提到的拖拉機。由此可知，因為下雨天，Palomo 先生想要避免拖拉機進水。故選項 (A) 為正解。
(B) 由訊息可知對話的兩人都已知道天氣狀況。
(C) shed「棚子」，雖然在❹提到了棚子，但沒有提到棚子裡有任何工具。
(D) hay bales「牧草捲」，雖然在❹也有提及牧草捲，但沒有提到要移動它們。

💡 應試者能從簡訊內容與對話中的細節，推測出訊息的主要目的。

---

154. `Can make inferences based on information in written texts`

`Can connect information across multiple sentences in a single written text and across texts`

At 2:18 P.M., what does Mr. Palomo most likely mean when he writes, "That's fine"?

(A) He is pleased that the tractor is clean.
(B) He wants Mr. Genet to search the barn.
(C) **He is not concerned about the dirt.**
(D) He does not need Mr. Genet to work late.

Palomo 先生在下午 2 點 18 分寫到「That's fine」，最可能是什麼意思？

(A) 他很高興那台拖拉機是乾淨的。
(B) 他要 Genet 先生去穀倉找東西。
(C) **他並不擔心髒污。**
(D) 他不需要 Genet 先生加班。

正解 (C)

重點解說

Genet 先生提及❻「找到一條防水布了，但是它非常髒。」得知找到一條布之後，Palomo 先生說明❼「我寧願清理拖拉機，總比讓它被雨淋濕好。」由此可推測，Palomo 先生並不在意 Genet 先生找到的防水布是髒的，故選項 (C) 為正解。
(A) 訊息對話中沒有提到 Palomo 先生是否對拖拉機的狀態感到高興。
(B) 從❺可得知，Palomo 先生在下午 2 點 13 分已經要 Genet 先生去穀倉找東西。
(D) 從訊息對話中沒有跡象顯示 Genet 先生需要加班。

💡 應試者能從簡訊內容與對話中的細節，推測出訊息的主要目的。

💡 應試者能理解簡訊內容，並連結上下對話，選出正確答案。

Questions 155-157 refer to the following article.

Subway Sound to be Upgraded

❶ BOSTON (April 1)—The public address systems at selected subway stations are scheduled to be refurbished, the Transit Authority announced this week. The systems are used to make announcements to commuters both on the platforms and in the stations.

❷ Local commuters welcomed the news, although for some it was long overdue.

❸ "It can be pretty difficult to understand the announcements at some of the stations I use most frequently," said Ian Miller, who has taken the subway to work nearly every week for the past eighteen years. "I had heard the reports about it on TV, and all I can say is that it is about time!"

❹ Some of the systems currently in use are more than 30 years old. Worn-out speakers, wiring, microphones, and amplifiers will be replaced with new, more reliable devices. The work should be completed in October and cost more than $11 million.

❺ Boston's subway system came together in stages over the course of several years. The foundational component of the system's Green Line first opened on Tremont Street in the late 1890s. It was the first of its kind in the United States.

請參考以下報導,回答第 155 至 157 題

地鐵之音即將升級

波士頓(4月1日)—運輸管理局本週宣布,預計整修選定地鐵站的公共廣播系統。這些系統是用來廣播通知在月台上以及地鐵站裡的通勤者。

當地的通勤者對此消息表示歡迎,儘管對有些人來說早該如此。

「在幾個我最常使用的地鐵站當中,有些廣播都難以聽懂。」過去18年幾乎每週都搭乘地鐵上班的 Ian Miller 表示:「我之前在電視上得知這個消息,我只能說的確是時候了啊!」

部分運作中的系統已經使用超過30年,破舊的喇叭、線材、麥克風和擴大機都將被新的、更可靠的設備所取代。這項工程將於10月完工並耗資逾1100萬元。

波士頓地鐵系統經過數年的階段性發展後完成整合,該系統綠線的基礎部分於1890年代後期在 Tremont 街首次開通,是美國的首創先例。

155. Can make inferences based on information in written texts

What is the purpose of the article?

(A) To clarify where subway riders can locate information

(B) To describe improvements at some subway stations

(C) To announce the creation of a new subway line

(D) To explain why subway schedules will be revised

這篇文章的主旨為何？

(A) 釐清地鐵乘客在哪裡可以找到資訊

(B) 描述一些地鐵站的改進事宜

(C) 宣布開設新地鐵路線

(D) 解釋修改地鐵時刻表的原因

重點解說

正解 (B)

❶ 第一行到第三行說明廣播系統將會整修，❷、❸ 為當地通勤者對於升級的想法，從 ❹ 第二行到第四行得知，系統將替換成更可靠的設備。由此判斷，文章描述了地鐵站的改進事宜，故選項 (B) 為正解。improvement「改進」。

(D) 從 ❶ 第一行到第三行得知是在選定地鐵站內的廣播系統要整修，並不是地鐵時刻表會被修改。revise「修改」。

💡 應試者能理解文章內容所傳達的重點，並且可以從文本細節推測主旨。

156. Can make inferences based on information in written texts

Can connect information across multiple sentences in a single written text and across texts

How does Mr. Miller feel about the plans?

(A) He expects the project to fail.

(B) He is concerned about the cost.

(C) He believes the work is unnecessary.

(D) He has been waiting for the changes.

Miller 先生對於這些計畫的感覺如何？

(A) 他預期這個項目會失敗。

(B) 他擔心成本費用。

(C) 他認為這項工程是沒必要的。

(D) 他一直都在等待這些改變。

重點解說

正解 (D)

❷ 可得知「當地的通勤者對此消息表示歡迎，儘管對有些人來說早該如此。」❸ 第五行到第七行，Miller 先生提到他對這個消息的看法「的確是時候了啊！」由此可判斷，Miller 先生已經等這項改變許久，也欣然接受改變。故選項 (D) 為正解。

💡 應試者能從文本中的細節做出推測。

💡 應試者能將 Miller 先生說的話與前後文連接，理解文章中的訊息含意。

157. Can understand vocabulary in written texts

The word "stages" in paragraph 5, line 2, is closest in meaning to

(A) steps

(B) scenes

(C) train cars

(D) platforms

下列哪一個選項與第五段第二行的「stages」，意思最為接近？

(A) 階段

(B) 場景

(C) 列車車廂

(D) 月台

重點解說

正解 (A)

❺ 第一行到第二行提到「波士頓地鐵系統經過數年的階段性發展後完成整合」，接著第三行到第五行提到，「該系統綠線的基礎部分於 1890 年代後期在 Tremont 街首次開通」，由此判斷，文章中的 stages 意指這個工程是階段性的。故選項 (A) 為正解。

請注意，雖然 stages 有許多意思，但此篇上下文清楚表明正確答案是作為在過程或發展中的一個「階段」的意思。

💡 應試者能理解與生活情境相關的詞彙，並選出同義字。

題目 / 中 文 翻 譯

Questions 158-160 refer to the following Web page.

---

http://www.thesailboatfactory.fr/English/aboutus ▼

Enzo Moreau, Founder

❶ Enzo Moreau has always loved the sea, but he has not always been the shipbuilder he is known as today. — [1] —. A civil engineer in the early years, he took a consultant position in Marseille almost a decade ago in order to be closer to the ocean. — [2] —. Mr. Moreau soon found himself devoting nearly all of his free time to his passion—sailing. Taking a chance, he made yet another change: he used his life savings to start his own sailboat-restoration company, the Sailboat Factory. — [3] —. The company did so well in its first year that Mr. Moreau decided to share his success by giving back to the community. — [4] —. He has also written a number of articles about sailboat restoration for leading industry journals.

請參考以下網頁，回答第 **158** 至 **160** 題。

---

http://www.thesailboatfactory.fr/English/aboutus ▼

創辦人 Enzo Moreau

Enzo Moreau 一直以來都很熱愛海洋，但他並非一直是我們現在所熟知的造船者。早年他是一名土木工程師，為了更接近海洋，大約十年前他在馬賽擔任顧問一職。很快地，Moreau 先生發現他幾乎把所有的空閒時間投入在他熱愛的帆船。他冒險一試，做了另一項改變—他用畢生積蓄創辦屬於自己的帆船修復公司「The Sailboat Factory」。公司在第一年表現出色，因此 Moreau 先生決定透過回饋社會來分享他的成功，**＊舉例來說，他下班後開始在附近的湖泊提供帆船課程**，他也為產業期刊龍頭撰寫了多篇關於帆船修復的文章。

＊第 160 題插入句的翻譯

158.
`Can locate and understand specific information in written texts`

What was Mr. Moreau's first profession?

(A) Writer
(B) Engineer
(C) Shipbuilder
(D) Consultant

Moreau 先生最初的職業是什麼？

(A) 作家
(B) 工程師
(C) 造船者
(D) 顧問

正解 (B)

從❶第二行到第三行可得知，「早年他是一名土木工程師，為了更接近海洋，大約十年前他在馬賽擔任顧問。」由此可知，在擔任顧問之前，Moreau 先生的第一個職業是工程師，故選項 (B) 為正解。
(A) 雖然最後一句話提到 Moreau 先生寫過一些文章，但網頁內容表明這是發生在他職業生涯的後期。
(C) 由第一行我們可知造船者是 Moreau 先生目前的職業，並非最初的職業。
(D) 由第二行我們可知擔任顧問一職也是在工程師之後。

💡 應試者能理解網頁中的內容，並從關鍵訊息中選出正確答案。

159.
`Can locate and understand specific information in written texts`

What is indicated about Mr. Moreau?

(A) He is a business owner.
(B) He plans to retire soon.
(C) He won a community award.
(D) He grew up close to the ocean.

關於 Moreau 先生的敘述何者正確？

(A) 他是一位企業老闆。
(B) 他計畫即將退休。
(C) 他贏得一項社區獎項。
(D) 他在海邊長大。

正解 (A)

❶第五行寫著，「他用畢生積蓄創辦屬於自己的帆船修復公司。」由此可知，Moreau 先生自己有一間公司，故選項 (A) 為正解。
(B) retire「退休」，網頁內容沒有提及任何退休計畫。
(C) 雖然在第六到七行有提到 Moreau 先生將他的成功回饋給社會，但沒有提到他贏得獎項。
(D) 第二到三行僅提到 Moreau 先生為了更接近海洋而選擇擔任顧問，但並無任何線索可看出他是否在海邊長大。

💡 應試者能理解網頁中的事件與資訊，即使選項換句話說，也能選出正確答案。

160.
`Can make inferences based on information in written texts`

`Can connect information across multiple sentences in a single written text and across texts`

In which of the positions marked [1], [2], [3], and [4] does the following sentence best belong?
"He began offering sailing lessons at a nearby lake after hours, for example."

(A) [1]
(B) [2]
(C) [3]
(D) [4]

在標示 [1]、[2]、[3]、[4] 的地方中，哪一處最適合插入下列句子？
「舉例來說，他下班後開始在附近的湖泊提供帆船課程。」

(A) [1]
(B) [2]
(C) [3]
(D) [4]

正解 (D)

❶第六行到第七行寫著，「公司在第一年表現出色，因此 Moreau 先生決定透過回饋社會來分享他的成功」。在 [4] 插入句子後，提供帆船課程和前一句「將他的成功回饋給社會」來具體描述他怎麼回饋社會，上下文意通順流暢，故選項 (D) 為正解。

💡 應試者能從細節做出推測，選出句子最適切的位置。

💡 應試者能連結並理解網頁中的不同資訊。

Questions 161-163 refer to the following e-mail.

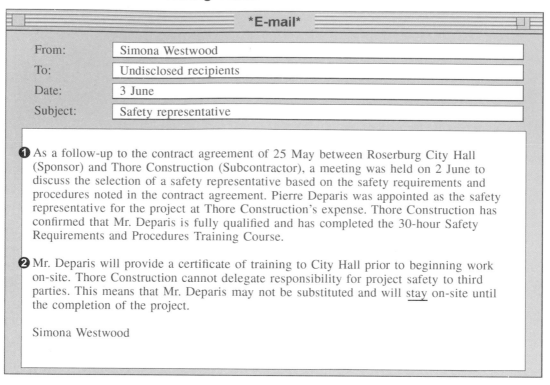

請參考以下電子郵件，回答第 161 至 163 題。

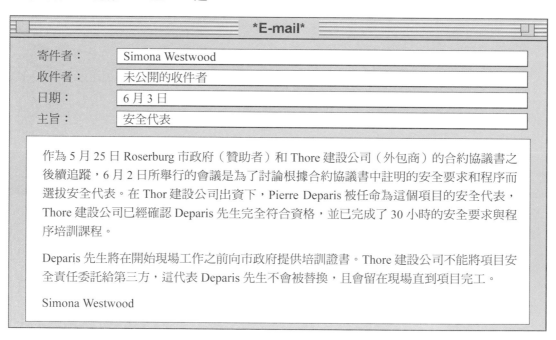

161.

> Can make inferences based on information in written texts

> Can connect information across multiple sentences in a single written text and across texts

What was the purpose of the meeting?

(A) To revise a list of safety requirements
(B) To discuss a proposed construction site
(C) To fill a position for a project
(D) To sign a final agreement

這個會議的目的是什麼？

(A) 修改安全需求表單
(B) 討論擬議的工地
(C) 填補一個項目的職位
(D) 簽署最終協議

重點解說

正解 (C)
❶第二行到第四行，提到會議是為了「討論根據合約協議書中註明的安全要求和程序而選拔安全代表」。選項 (C) 中 a position 表示 safety representative，故為正解。
(A) requirement「需求」，雖然❶第三行提到了 safety requirements，但內容沒有表明要修改表單。
(B) construction site「工地」，雖與建設公司有關，但信件內容沒有提到要討論工地。
(D) agreement「協議」，❶第一行提到此次會議是針對 5 月 25 日合約協議書的後續追蹤，由此可知最終協議已經簽署。

💡 應試者能從細節做出推測，並理解信件所傳達的目的。
💡 應試者能連結信件中的不同資訊，藉此判斷信件的目的。

162.

> Can locate and understand specific information in written texts

What will Mr. Deparis do before construction begins?

(A) Estimate expenses
(B) Contact his substitutes
(C) Advertise an open position
(D) Present proof of qualifications

在工程開始前，Deparis 先生將會做什麼事？

(A) 估計費用
(B) 聯絡他的代理人
(C) 刊登職缺廣告
(D) 出示資格證明

重點解說

正解 (D)
❷第一行到第二行提到「Deparis 先生將在開始現場工作之前向市政府提供培訓證書」。選項 (D) 以 proof of qualification 表示 certificate，故為正解。qualification「資格證明」。
(A) estimate「估計」，雖然❶第五行提到費用，但沒有提及費用需要估算。
(B) substitute「代替、代理人」，❷第三行提到「Deparis 先生不會被替換」，這表示他不能聯絡任何代理人。
(C) 由❶第四行到第五行，我們可知 Deparis 先生已被任命該職位。

💡 應試者能理解信件中的事件與資訊，即使選項換句話說，也能選出正確答案。

163.

> Can understand vocabulary in written texts

The word "stay" in paragraph 2, line 3, is closest in meaning to

(A) delay
(B) remain
(C) wait
(D) reside

下列哪一個選項與第二段第三行的「stay」，意思最為接近？

(A) 延遲
(B) 留下
(C) 等待
(D) 居住

重點解說

正解 (B)
從❷第二行到第三行得知，「Thore 建設公司不能將項目安全責任委託給第三方」，且❷第三行到第四行說明「Deparis 先生不會被替換，且會留在現場直到項目完工」，故選項 (B) remain 表示「留下」最恰當。

💡 應試者能理解文本中的詞彙，並選出可替換的單字。

Questions 164-167 refer to the following article.

E-Commerce Opening Doors for African Fashion Industry

❶ADDIS ABABA (6 May)—Africa's role as a consumer of fashion has been on the rise in recent years. This trend is largely due to the emergence of e-commerce, which provides Africans the opportunity to buy clothing from retailers with no physical presence on the continent.

❷ Perhaps more importantly, though, the growth of e-commerce is enabling small-scale African designers to also become *producers* of fashion, as they showcase their collections to consumers worldwide. African shopping Web sites like Jumjum and Longa are making the work of African designers available for purchase not just throughout the continent, but also as far away as London and New York. — [1] —.

❸ "African designers are finally gaining visibility," says Mazaa Absher, founder of Abbi Sportscore, Africa's fastest-growing athletic footwear company. "We have always had terrific design and production capacity here on the continent, but it was hard getting it out into the world. Now we are generating more sales online than we are in our stores." — [2] —.

❹ Even as Ms. Absher has transformed her company into an international powerhouse, she continues to highlight the advantages of manufacturing its products in her home city of Nazret. — [3] —. Africa's strong textile sector and innovative designs combine tradition and wearability, and this formula is allowing companies like hers to set their sights beyond the continent.

❺ "As more cities in Ethiopia—and all over Africa—improve their manufacturing capacity, it will become easier to reach the rest of the world," says Ms. Absher. — [4] —.

---

164. | Can make inferences based on information in written texts

What is the main topic of the article?

(A) New trends in marketing athletic footwear
(B) Increased competition in the African clothing market
(C) Recent growth in the African fashion industry
(D) The largest clothing companies in Africa

這篇報導的主旨是什麼？

(A) 運動鞋的行銷新趨勢
(B) 非洲服飾市場競爭加劇
(C) 非洲時尚產業近期的成長
(D) 非洲最大的服飾公司

> **重點解說**
>
> **正解 (C)**
> ❶第一行到第四行提及，「非洲作為時尚消費者的角色在近幾年不斷提升。這個趨勢最主要起因於電子商務的崛起」；❷第一行到第五行，說明電子商務讓非洲設計師得以向全世界展示他們的設計作品；❸第七行到第八行，「網路上創造的銷售額比實體店還多」。從以上敘述得知，這篇報導主旨為電子商務對非洲時裝產業帶來的成長與好處，故選項 (C) 為正解。
>
> 💡 應試者能從文中的細節推測此篇報導的核心概念和目的。

---

165. | Can connect information across multiple sentences in a single written text and across texts

What is indicated about Abbi Sportscore?

(A) It sells its products only online.
(B) It manufactures its shoes in Nazret.
(C) It will be moving its main offices soon.
(D) It was the first shoe company in Ethiopia.

以下關於 Abbi Sportscore 的敘述，何者正確？

(A) 它只在網路上販售產品。
(B) 它在 Nazret 生產鞋子。
(C) 它的主要辦公室即將搬遷。
(D) 它是衣索比亞第一間製鞋公司。

> **重點解說**
>
> **正解 (B)**
> ❹第三行提到 Absher 小姐「她仍持續強調在她家鄉 Nazret 製造產品的優勢。」由此可知，Abbi Sportscore 在 Nazret 生產鞋子，故選項 (B) 為正解。
> (A) 從❸最後二行得知，「現在，我們在網路上創造的銷售額比實體店還高」。由此可知，Abbi Sportscore 也有實體店。
>
> 💡 應試者能連結報導中的不同訊息，理解事件內容與資訊。

請參考以下報導,回答第 164 至 167 題。

電子商務為非洲時尚產業開啟大門

阿迪斯阿貝巴(5 月 6 日)—非洲作為時尚消費者的角色在近幾年不斷提升。這個趨勢最主要起因於電子商務的崛起,讓非洲人有機會從在非洲大陸沒有實體店面的零售商那裡購買衣服。

但或許更重要的是,電子商務的發展使得小規模的非洲設計師也能成為時尚生產者,因為他們向全球各地的消費者展示他們的服裝作品。非洲購物網站如 Jumjum 和 Longa,使非洲設計師的作品不僅可以在整個非洲大陸購買,遠在倫敦和紐約也能買到。

「非洲的設計師總算獲得關注了。」非洲發展最快速的運動鞋公司 Abbi Sportscore 創辦人 Mazaa Absher 表示:「我們在非洲大陸一直都有出色的設計和產能,但卻很難把它拓展到全世界。現在,我們在網路上創造的銷售額比實體店還高。」

即使 Absher 小姐已經把她的公司蛻變成國際大廠,她仍持續強調在她家鄉 Nazret 製造產品的優勢。***這座城市以有四間製衣廠而自豪,而第五間預計今年在附近的 Wonji 建成。**非洲強大的紡織業和創新設計融合了傳統和耐穿性,這個模式讓像她這樣的公司能夠將目光放在非洲大陸之外。

Absher 小姐說:「隨著衣索比亞和整個非洲的更多城市提高其製造能力,打入世界市場將變得更加容易。」

*第 167 題插入句的翻譯

---

166. Can locate and understand specific information in written texts

What is suggested about the Jumjum and Longa Web sites?

(A) They sell only handcrafted goods.
(B) They receive orders from around the world.
(C) They offer free shipping to London and New York.
(D) They are planning to open retail stores.

關於 Jumjum 和 Longa 網站,以下何者正確?

(A) 他們只販售手工製品。
(B) 他們收到來自世界各地的訂單。
(C) 他們提供到倫敦和紐約的免運服務。
(D) 他們正在計畫開零售店。

重點解說

正解 (B)
❷ 第七行提到,「非洲設計師的作品不僅可以在整個非洲大陸購買,遠在倫敦和紐約也能買到。」由此可知,Jumjum 和 Longa 的購物網站可以收到其他國家的訂單。故選項 (B) 為正解。

💡 應試者能理解報導中的事件與資訊,即使選項換句話說,也能選出正確答案。

---

167. Can make inferences based on information in written texts

Can connect information across multiple sentences in a single written text and across texts

In which of the positions marked [1], [2], [3], and [4] does the following sentence best belong?
"The city boasts four garment factories, with a fifth scheduled to be built this year in nearby Wonji."

(A) [1]
(B) [2]
(C) [3]
(D) [4]

在標示 [1]、[2]、[3]、[4] 的地方中,哪一處最適合插入下列句子?
「這座城市以有四間製衣廠而自豪,而第五間預計今年在附近的 Wonji 建成。」

(A) [1]
(B) [2]
(C) [3]
(D) [4]

重點解說

正解 (C)
❹ 第三行提到「她仍持續強調在她家鄉 Nazret 製造產品的優勢」。在 [3] 插入句子「這座城市以有四間製衣廠而自豪,而第五間預計今年在附近的 Wonji 建成。」用來說明前述所提到的優勢,故選項 (C) 為正解。

💡 應試者能理解報導的主要目的,並能從細節中做出推測。

💡 應試者能將報導中的資訊與獨立的句子連結,使語意通順。

Questions 168-171 refer to the following text-message chain.

❶ **Gary Park (10:23 A.M.)**
I e-mailed you the cover design for our September issue a few minutes ago. Did you receive it?

❷ **Jill Riley (10:26 A.M.)**
Yes, but is this the latest version? I thought we agreed that the background color should be lighter so the article titles are more visible.

❸ **Gary Park (10:28 A.M.)**
I forgot—sorry about that! I'm just now sending the file with the most recent version.

❹ **Jill Riley (10:30 A.M.)**
Opening it now… That's more like it. I'll forward it to Graphics and request a sample printout.

❺ **Jill Riley (10:35 A.M.)**
Good morning, Mr. Ojeda. Our new cover design is ready. When do you think you'll have a chance to work on it?

❻ **Frank Ojeda (10:38 A.M.)**
Send it to me now. I'll have a print copy ready for your approval after lunch.

168. Can make inferences based on information in written texts

Where do the people most likely work?

(A) At a bookstore
(B) At a public library
(C) At a television studio
(D) At a magazine publisher

這些人最有可能在哪裡工作？

(A) 書店
(B) 公共圖書館
(C) 電視攝影棚
(D) 雜誌出版社

重點解說

正解 (D)
❶Park 先生詢問 Riley 小姐是否收到九月號的封面設計，由此可推測他們是雜誌出版社，故選項 (D) 為正解。

💡 應試者能從長篇對話中，找出細節並做出推測。

請參考以下訊息對話，回答第 168 至 171 題。

Gary Park（上午 10：23）
幾分鐘前我把我們九月號的封面設計寄給你了。你有收到嗎？

Jill Riley（上午 10：26）
有，但這是最新的版本嗎？我以為我們同意背景顏色應該更淡一些，才能讓文章的標題比較明顯。

Gary Park（上午 10：28）
我忘記了，很抱歉！我現在正在傳送最新版本的檔案。

Jill Riley（上午 10：30）
正在開啟中⋯這樣好多了。我會把它轉給 Graphics 印刷並要求一份打樣。

Jill Riley（上午 10：35）
早安，Ojeda 先生。我們的新封面設計已經準備好了。你覺得你何時方便處理它？

Frank Ojeda（上午 10：38）
現在傳給我，午餐後我會準備好一份樣張供你審核。

169. Can connect information across multiple sentences in a single written text and across texts

Why does Mr. Park apologize?

(A) He sent the wrong file.
(B) He used an old e-mail address.
(C) He missed a project deadline.
(D) He lost an important document.

為什麼 Park 先生要道歉？

(A) 他寄錯檔案了。
(B) 他用了舊的電子郵件地址。
(C) 他錯過一項案子的截止日。
(D) 他遺失了一份重要文件。

重點解說

正解 (A)
❸Park 先生先向 Riley 小姐道歉，並說「我現在正在傳送最新版本的檔案。」由此可知，Park 先生之前寄的版本是未修正過的。故選項 (A) 為正解。
(B) e-mail address「電子郵件地址」；(D) document「文件」。

💡 應試者能理解訊息中的事件與資訊，即使內容並未提到「寄錯檔案」等字眼，也可以從訊息中推測而出。

170. Can make inferences based on information in written texts

Can connect information across multiple sentences in a single written text and across texts

At 10:30 A.M., what does Ms. Riley most likely mean when she writes, "That's more like it"?

(A) The budget is more reasonable.

(B) The color looks better.

(C) The story is more interesting.

(D) The schedule is more realistic.

Riley 小姐在上午 10：30 寫到，「That's more like it」，最有可能代表什麼意思？

(A) 預算比較合理。

(B) 顏色看起來比較好。

(C) 故事比較有趣。

(D) 行程比較實際。

正解 (B)

❷Riley 小姐提到，「我以為我們同意背景顏色應該更淡一些」，由此可知，Park 先生之後寄出的正確檔案，背景顏色是被修正過的。故選項 (B) 為正解。

(A) budget「預算」；(D) realistic「實際的」。

💡 應試者能理解訊息傳達的目的，並從細節中做出推測。

💡 應試者能連結訊息中的資訊，藉此判斷傳訊者的目的與含意。

171. Can connect information across multiple sentences in a single written text and across texts

What will Mr. Ojeda do by the afternoon?

(A) Approve a marketing plan

(B) Produce a sample

(C) Repair a printer

(D) Make copies of an agreement

Ojeda 先生下午會做什麼事？

(A) 核准一份行銷計畫

(B) 做出一個樣品

(C) 修理印表機

(D) 複印一份協議書

正解 (B)

❹Riley 小姐提到「我會把它轉給 Graphics 印刷並要求一份打樣」，隨後聯繫 Ojeda 先生。從❻得知，Ojeda 在午餐後會提供樣張。選項 (B) sample 表示 print copy，故為正解。

(A) approve「同意、核准」；(C) repair「修理」；(D) agreement「協議書」。

💡 應試者能理解訊息內容，即使內容中並未明確地表達，也能推測出正確答案。

Questions 172-175 refer to the following article.

Thredquest Outfitters

❶ WESTAN (March 6)—Thredquest Outfitters announced yesterday that it is the new sponsor of the Westan Panthers Basketball Team. The company officially replaced Marliner Sports on March 2. According to information from the Marliner Sports Web site, its longtime sponsorship agreement expired at the end of last season and was not renewed. Marliner Sports has since closed down its activewear division to focus on outdoor recreational equipment.

❷ Under the new sponsorship agreement, Thredquest Outfitters will pay for the official game balls and nets, according to an e-mail from the company's marketing director, Marta Hsu. The company will also provide the players' jerseys, shorts, and court shoes. "Transportation and lodging costs associated with out-of-town games will remain the team's responsibility and are largely covered by ticket sales," said the team's coach, Pedro Cardenas.

❸ Mr. Cardenas, along with the team's business manager and the facilities and equipment manager, helped negotiate the terms of the new sponsorship agreement. Mr. Cardenas studied athletic training at Halston University and worked for several competitive basketball teams in the region, advising on injury prevention and providing treatment. Then, he joined the Panthers as the coach. "We are looking forward to a long and fruitful relationship with Thredquest Outfitters," he said.

題目/中文翻譯

請參考以下報導，回答第 172 至 175 題。

Thredquest Outfitters

WESTAN（3 月 6 日）—Thredquest Outfitters 昨天宣布成為 Westan Panthers 籃球隊的新贊助商，該公司在 3 月 2 日正式取代 Marliner Sports。根據 Marliner Sports 網站的資訊，其長期贊助協議在上個賽季結束時到期且並未續約，Marliner Sports 自此已關閉其運動服裝部門，以專注在戶外休閒用品上。

根據新的贊助協議，Thredquest Outfitters 將會支付官方比賽的用球和籃網費用，該公司的行銷總監 Marta Hsu 在一封電子郵件中提到。該公司也將提供球員的球衣、短褲和球鞋。球隊教練 Pedro Cardenas 說：「到外地比賽相關的交通和住宿費用仍將由球隊負責，主要會以門票銷售來支付。」

Cardenas 先生與球隊的業務經理以及場地設備經理一起，幫助協商新贊助協議的條款。Cardenas 先生在 Halston 大學研讀運動訓練，並曾任職於該地區多支有競爭力的籃球隊，提供傷害預防建議及治療，接著他加入 Panthers 隊擔任教練。他說：「我們期待與 Thredquest Outfitters 共創長久而且成果豐碩的合作關係。」

172. Can make inferences based on information in written texts

What is the article about?

(A) A new basketball coach
(B) A change in a team's supporter
(C) A company's marketing plan
(D) An update to a team's schedule

這篇報導是關於什麼？

(A) 一位新的籃球教練
(B) 球隊贊助者的更換
(C) 公司的行銷計畫
(D) 球隊行程表的更新

重點解說

正解 (B)
從❶第二行到第四行得知，Thredquest Outfitters 取代 Marliner Sports 成為 Westan Panthers 籃球隊的新贊助商；❷第二行到第六行說明新贊助條約所包含的項目；❸第一行到第四行則說明 Cardenas 先生等人幫助協商新贊助協議的條款，因此選項 (B) 為正解。
(A) ❸第八行到第九行雖然提到 Cardenas 先生加入球隊當教練，但沒有提到是最近發生的。
(C) ❷第四到第五行雖然有提到 Marta Hsu 是 Thredquest Outfitters 的行銷總監，但文章沒有提及行銷計畫。
(D) 文章沒有討論球隊的行程表。

💡 應試者能理解報導的目的和主旨，並從細節中做出判斷。

173. Can locate and understand specific information in written texts

What is true about Marliner Sports?

(A) It no longer sells athletic clothing.
(B) It will close an outlet in Westan.
(C) It is now owned by Mr. Cardenas.
(D) It has merged with Thredquest Outfitters.

關於 Marliner Sports，以下何者正確？

(A) 它不再販售運動服飾。
(B) 它將會關閉一間在 Westan 的分店。
(C) 它現在是 Cardenas 先生所有。
(D) 它和 Thredquest Outfitters 合併了。

正解 (A)

重點解說

❶ 第九行提到，「Marliner Sports 自此已關閉其運動服裝部門，以專注在戶外休閒用品上。」由此可知，他們不再販售衣服類的產品，選項 (A) athletic clothing 與報導中的 activewear 皆代表運動服，故為正解。
(B) ❶ 第九行到第十行雖有提到 close down「關閉」，但指的是 Marliner Sports 的運動服裝部門，而非分店。
(C) 由整篇文章可得知，Cardenas 先生是球隊教練，文章內容沒有提到他擁有這兩間公司中的任一間。
(D) 整篇文章內容沒有提到兩間公司要合併。

💡 應試者能理解報導中的事件與資訊，並找出關鍵字，即使選項換句話說，也能選出正確答案。

174. Can locate and understand specific information in written texts

What part of the Westan Panthers' budget is funded by audience attendance at games?

(A) Basketball equipment
(B) Uniforms
(C) Footwear
(D) Team travel

Westan Panthers 哪一部分的預算是由觀眾出席率所提供？

(A) 籃球設備
(B) 制服
(C) 球鞋
(D) 球隊出行

正解 (D)

重點解說

❷ 第七行到第十行提到，「到外地比賽相關的交通和住宿費用仍將由球隊負責，主要會以門票銷售來支付。」選項 (D) team travel 包含了 transportation and lodging costs，而體育賽事的觀眾通常會購買門票進入，故此為正解。
(A)、(B)、(C) 由❷ 第二行到第六行可得知 Thredquest Outfitters 將會負責支付球隊比賽所需的籃球設備及服裝。

💡 應試者能理解報導中的事件與資訊，並找出關鍵字，即使選項換句話說，也能選出正確答案。

175. Can make inferences based on information in written texts

What most likely was Mr. Cardenas' previous job?

(A) Marketing director
(B) Business manager
(C) Facilities and equipment manager
(D) Sports trainer

以下何者最有可能是 Cardenas 先生的前一份工作？

(A) 行銷總監
(B) 業務經理
(C) 場地設備經理
(D) 運動訓練員

正解 (D)

重點解說

❸ 第四行到第八行提到，「Cardenas 先生在 Halston 大學研讀運動訓練，並曾任職於該地區多支有競爭力的籃球隊，提供傷害預防建議及治療。」由此可知，Cardenas 先生先前的工作與運動訓練最相關，故選項 (D) 為正解。
(A) 文章沒有提到 Cardenas 先生與行銷總監相關的資訊。
(B)、(C) 由❸ 第一行到第三行可知，Cardenas 先生與球隊的業務經理、場地設備經理是一同共事的關係，因此他不是擔任這兩個職務。

💡 應試者能根據報導內容推測主旨與目的，並從細節判斷出特定事實。

題目/中文翻譯

Questions 176-180 refer to the following e-mail and receipt.

1. 電子郵件

To:	riedewald@parasur.net.sr
From:	client_services@mhf.ca
Date:	April 2, 12:21 P.M.
Subject:	Your feedback

Dear Mr. Riedewald,

❶ Thank you for <u>filling out</u> the McMann Home Furnishings (MHF) survey. To show our appreciation, we have added reward points to your account. They can be applied to the purchase of products offered online as well as those offered in our retail stores. Clearance items and those priced $15.00 and above may not be purchased using credits.

❷ To use your reward points for an online purchase, select the items you would like to purchase and then check out. At the bottom of the page, select "Apply credits." The value of the applied credits will appear on your order receipt as a special discount.

❸ If you would prefer to use reward points at one of our retail locations, you can do so by logging in to your account on our Web site. Go to the My Rewards page, and then select "Print as a coupon." The coupon will have a bar code that can be scanned at the store's checkout counter.

Sincerely,

Client Services, McMann Home Furnishings

2. 收據

❶ Online Order #1157
McMann Home Furnishings Store
March 19, 11:31 A.M.

❷ Hand-Painted Picture Frame
Quantity: 1
Price: 10.00
Special Discount: -10.00

❸ Sailboat Ceramic Mug
Quantity: 4
Price: 40.00
Clearance Discount: -20.00

❹ Floral Blanket
Quantity: 1
Price: 25.00

❺ Photo Album
Quantity: 1
Price: 34.00
Seasonal Item Discount: -17.00

❻ Item total: 62.00
Shipping: Free
Total: 62.00

請參考以下電子郵件和收據，回答第 176 至 180 題。

收件者：	riedewald@parasur.net.sr
寄件者：	client_services@mhf.ca
日期：	4 月 2 日下午 12:21
主旨：	您的回饋

親愛的 Riedewald 先生，

感謝您填寫 McMann 家居用品店（MHF）的問卷。為了表達感謝，我們已將紅利點數加到您的帳戶裡。點數可用於網路購物以及購買我們零售店提供的商品，出清品和標價 15 美元以上的商品不能使用點數購買。

使用紅利點數線上購物，請選擇您要購買的商品並結帳。在頁面最下方，選擇「使用點數」，折抵的點數金額將會以特別折扣顯示在訂單收據上。

如果您想在其中一家零售店使用紅利點數，您可以透過在我們的網站登入帳號來使用。前往「我的獎勵」頁面，接著選擇「列印優惠券」，優惠券上的條碼可以在商店的結帳櫃檯掃描使用。

McMann 家居用品店 客戶服務 敬上

網路訂單 #1157
McMann 家居用品店
3 月 19 日 上午 11:31

手繪相框
數量：1
價格：10.00
特別折扣：-10.00

帆船陶瓷杯
數量：4
價格：40.00
出清折扣：-20.00

花卉毯子
數量：1
價格：25.00

相本
數量：1
價格：34.00
季節性商品折扣：-17.00

商品總金額：62.00
運費：免費
總金額：62.00

176. Can connect information across multiple sentences in a single written text and across texts

According to the e-mail, how did Mr. Riedewald receive reward points?

(A) He won an online contest.
(B) He participated in a customer survey.
(C) He spent a certain amount of money.
(D) He returned an item.

根據這封電子郵件，Riedewald 先生如何獲得紅利點數？

(A) 他贏得了線上比賽。
(B) 他參加了顧客問卷調查。
(C) 他花了一定程度的金額。
(D) 他退回商品。

重點解說

正解 (B)
❶電子郵件❶第一行到第二行提到，為了感謝完成顧客問卷調查，已將紅利點數加到 Riedewald 先生的帳戶中。故選項 (B) 為正解。
(A) contest「比賽」; (D) return「歸還、退回」。
💡 應試者能理解電子郵件中的訊息，並能連結信件和收據的內容，選出正確答案。

177. Can understand vocabulary in written texts

In the e-mail, the phrase "filling out" in paragraph 1, line 1, is closest in meaning to

(A) emptying
(B) supplying
(C) completing
(D) expanding

下列哪一個選項與電子郵件中第一段第一行的「filling out」，意思最為接近？

(A) 清空
(B) 提供
(C) 完成
(D) 拓展

重點解說

正解 (C)
❶電子郵件中❶第一行提到，感謝 Riedewald 先生填寫顧客調查，選項 (C) completing「完成」表示填完顧客調查，語意最為接近，故為正解。
💡 應試者能理解電子郵件中的詞彙，且能選出意義相近的單字。

178. Can connect information across multiple sentences in a single written text and across texts

How can customers apply their reward points in an MHF retail store?

(A) By entering their account number
(B) By entering their phone number
(C) By scanning a coupon's bar code
(D) By going to the Client Services Department

顧客如何在 MHF 的零售店使用紅利點數？

(A) 輸入他們的帳號
(B) 輸入他們的電話號碼
(C) 掃描優惠券上的條碼
(D) 前往客戶服務部門

重點解說

正解 (C)
❶電子郵件❸第一行到第二行說明，「您可以透過在我們的網站登入帳號」，接著第三行提及「優惠券上的條碼可以在商店的結帳櫃檯掃描使用」，故選項 (C) 為正解。
💡 應試者能理解電子郵件中提及的事實與資訊，即使選項換句話說，也能選出正確答案。

179.

> Can make inferences based on information in written texts

> Can connect information across multiple sentences in a single written text and across texts

According to the receipt, what is true about Mr. Riedewald?

(A) He paid for delivery of the items.
(B) He purchased the items in the evening.
(C) He paid over $70 for all items combined.
(D) He purchased only one item at regular price.

根據這張收據，以下關於 Riedewald 先生的敘述何者正確？

(A) 他有付商品運費。
(B) 他在傍晚購買商品。
(C) 他付超過 70 美元買所有的商品。
(D) 他只購買了一項原價商品。

> **重點解說**
>
> **正解 (D)**
> 從❷收據得知❷、❸、❺最後都有折扣金額，只有❹商品資訊中沒有註明折扣，由此可知，這四項產品中，只有一項沒有使用折扣，故選項 (D) 為正解。
> (A) 從收據中❻可知，shipping「運費」的欄位中是 free「免費的」，因此不需要付運費。delivery「運費」。
> (B) 收據中❶提及購買時間為 11:31A.M.，因此他是在上午購物，而不是在傍晚。
> (C) 從收據中❻可看到這次消費總額為 62 元，沒有超過 70 元。
>
> 💡 應試者能理解收據提供的資訊，並能從細節中判斷出正確答案。
> 💡 應試者能連結並理解電子郵件和收據中的資訊，以選出最適合的答案。

180.

> Can make inferences based on information in written texts

> Can connect information across multiple sentences in a single written text and across texts

What item did Mr. Riedewald most likely purchase using reward credits?

(A) The picture frame
(B) The ceramic mug
(C) The floral blanket
(D) The photo album

Riedewald 先生最有可能使用紅利點數購買下列哪一項商品？

(A) 相框
(B) 陶瓷杯
(C) 花卉毯子
(D) 相本

> **重點解說**
>
> **正解 (A)**
> ❶電子郵件中❷第三行提及「折抵的點數金額將會以特別折扣顯示在訂單收據上」。❷收據中❷的折扣名稱顯示為特別折扣，故選項 (A) 為正解。
>
> 💡 應試者能從電子郵件和收據中的資訊，推論出 Riedewald 先生買的東西。
> 💡 應試者能連結並理解電子郵件和收據中的資訊，以選出最適合的答案。

Questions 181-185 refer to the following e-mail and schedule.

1. 電子郵件

To:	All Staff
From:	Cassandra Clausen, Office Manager
Date:	February 17
Re:	Second quarter travel schedule

❶ The staff's travel schedule for the second quarter is now posted online. These months tend to be our busiest, so it is important that you keep the schedule updated. To avoid confusion, please include travel, whether domestic or international, only after it has been approved by a department supervisor. Do not forget that any travel exceeding ten consecutive business days is considered long-term and requires additional approval from the division head.

❷ Also, please note that there will likely be a few days of overlap in the travel dates of department supervisors during this quarter. For instance, Tessa Alexander has just been invited to lead several workshops in Seoul. Her dates are not yet confirmed, but her trip is expected to be at the same time as Natasha Danilchenko's trip to Denver. Bear in mind that any date-sensitive documents or approvals requiring the signature of a department supervisor should be acquired ahead of your departure.

❸ Let me know if you encounter difficulty viewing or editing the schedule. Have a fantastic second quarter.

Best,

Cassandra

2. 時程表

Garcia Architecture Group—Travel Schedule, April-June

Important Reminders

❶ — Requests for long-term travel should be directed to Laura Garcia.
❷ — This is a schedule of conferences and trade events requiring off-site travel. Please send information regarding sick leave and vacation time to Devon Taylor at Human Resources for entry into a separate calendar.

Dates	Name	Event, Location
❸ April 3–8	Natasha Danilchenko	Symposium on Modern City Structure, Denver
❹ April 22–27	Tania Schultz	Safety in Factory Design Workshop, Tokyo
❺ May 1–10	Gil Shaw	International Urban Architecture, Singapore
❻ May 1–10	Natasha Danilchenko	International Urban Architecture, Singapore
❼ June 7–12	Dionne O'Donnell	Reflections in Architecture Exposition, Ottawa

請參考以下電子郵件和時程表,回答第 181 至 185 題。

收件者:	全體員工
寄件者:	辦公室經理 Cassandra Clausen
日期:	2 月 17 日
回覆:	第二季出差時程表

員工的第二季出差時程表已經發布在網路。這幾個月往往是我們最忙的時間,所以隨時更新時程表是很重要的。為了避免造成混亂,無論是國內或國外出差,只有經過部門主管批准才能加入時程表。不要忘了,連續出差超過 10 個工作天視為長期出差,並且需要取得部門負責人的額外許可。

此外,請注意,這一季部門主管們的出差日期可能會有幾天是重疊的。例如 Tessa Alexander 剛獲邀在首爾主持多個研討會。雖然她的出差日期尚未確定,但行程預計會和 Natasha Danilchenko 前往丹佛的時間相同。請牢記在心,任何需要部門主管簽名的有時效性的文件或是批准,都應該在出發之前完成。

如果你在檢視或編輯這份時程表遇到問題,請讓我知道。祝各位有個很棒的第二季。

Cassandra 敬上

Garcia 建築集團— 4 月到 6 月出差時程表
重要事項提醒

— 長期出差的申請應直接向 Laura Garcia 提出。
— 這個時程表是關於有異地出差需求的會議以及貿易活動。請將病假和休假相關的資訊傳給人資部門的 Devon Taylor,以便輸入到另一個行事曆上。

日期	姓名	活動,地點
4 月 3 日到 8 日	Natasha Danilchenko	現代都市結構研討會,丹佛
4 月 22 日到 27 日	Tania Schultz	工廠設計安全工作坊,東京
5 月 1 日到 10 日	Gil Shaw	國際城市建築展覽,新加坡
5 月 1 日到 10 日	Natasha Danilchenko	國際城市建築展覽,新加坡
6 月 7 日到 12 日	Dionne O'Donnell	建築映象展覽,渥太華

題目／中文翻譯

181. Can make inferences based on information in written texts

What is the purpose of the e-mail?

(A) To invite employees to attend an event
(B) To request feedback on a recent meeting
(C) To encourage participation in conferences
(D) To announce the availability of an online document

這封電子郵件的目的是什麼？

(A) 邀請員工參加一個活動
(B) 對近期的會議要求回饋
(C) 鼓勵參與會議
(D) 公布一份可以使用的線上文件

正解 (D)

從 **1** 電子郵件 **❶** 的第一行提到「員工的第二季出差時程表已經發布在網路」，選項 (D) 中的 availability of an online document 與信件內容符合，故為正解。
(A) 電子郵件中沒有提及邀請員工參與活動。
(B) 電子郵件中沒有提及要提供對會議的回饋。
(C) 雖然電子郵件中有提及 workshop「研討會」，與 conference「會議」有相關，但信件內容沒有鼓勵員工參與會議。

💡 應試者能從細節推測出電子郵件的目的。

182. Can connect information across multiple sentences in a single written text and across texts

Why most likely are Ms. Alexander's travel plans not included on the schedule?

(A) Her travel dates fall within the third quarter.
(B) The schedule lists only confirmed travel.
(C) The schedule is limited to domestic travel.
(D) She missed the deadline for travel approval.

下列何者最有可能是 Alexander 小姐的出差計畫沒有包含在這份時程表的原因？

(A) 她的出差日期落在第三季。
(B) 時程表只列出已確認的出差。
(C) 時程表只限於國內出差。
(D) 她錯過了批准出差的期限。

正解 (B)

1 電子郵件 **❶** 的第三行到第四行提及「只有經過部門主管批准才能加入時程表」。接著在 **1** 電子郵件 **❷** 提到 Alexander 小姐的出差日期尚未確定，由此可知，她的出差計畫還不能加入時程表，故選項 (B) 為正解。
(A) 由 **1** 電子郵件 **❷** 的第二行到第四行可知 Alexander 小姐的出差日期預計與 Natasha Danilchenko 前往丹佛的時間相同，而 Natasha Danilchenko 的出差日已包含在 **2** 時程表。從 **1** 電子郵件 **❶** 的第一行可知時程表是第二季的，故她的出差日是在第二季。quarter「季度」。
(C) 由 **1** 電子郵件 **❶** 的第二行到第三行可知此時程表包含國內及國外的出差行程。domestic「國內的」。
(D) **1** 電子郵件及 **2** 時程表皆沒有提及期限。

💡 應試者能連接電子郵件與行程表提及的資訊，並從細節做出判斷。

183. Can locate and understand specific information in written texts

Why are employees asked to contact Ms. Taylor?

(A) To inform her of absences
(B) To request approval for long-term travel
(C) To report updates to their contact information
(D) To seek advice on presenting at trade shows

為什麼員工被要求要聯繫 Taylor 小姐？

(A) 通知她缺勤狀況
(B) 申請長期出差的許可
(C) 回報他們的聯絡資訊更新
(D) 尋求在貿易展上簡報的建議

正解 (A)

2 時程表中的 **❷** 提及，「請將病假和休假相關的資訊傳給人資部門的 Devon Taylor」，由此可知，請假或休假相關的缺勤事宜，要聯繫 Taylor 小姐。選項 (A) absences 表示 sick leave 和 vacation time，故為正解。
(B) 從 **2** 時程表中的 **❶** 可知長期出差的申請要找 Garcia 小姐。
(C) **1** 電子郵件及 **2** 時程表皆沒有要求員工回報聯絡資訊的更新。
(D) **1** 電子郵件及 **2** 時程表皆沒有要求員工提供簡報建議。

💡 應試者能理解時程表中注意事項提及的事件與資訊，即使選項換句話說，也能選出正確答案。

184. Can connect information across multiple sentences in a single written text and across texts

What is Ms. Garcia's job title?

(A) Office Manager
(B) Department Supervisor
(C) Division Head
(D) Head of Human Resources

Garcia 小姐的工作職稱是什麼？

(A) 辦公室經理
(B) 部門主管
(C) 部門負責人（層級高於 department）
(D) 人資主管

重點解說

正解 (C)
❷時程表中的❶提及長期出差應向 Laura Garcia 提出申請；❶電子郵件❶第四行到第六行提到「連續出差超過 10 個工作天視為長期出差，並且需要取得部門負責人的額外許可。」由此可知，Garcia 小姐是部門負責人，故選項 (C) 為正解。
(A) 由❶電子郵件的寄件者可得知辦公室經理為 Clausen 小姐。
(B) ❶電子郵件及❷時程表皆沒有提到部門主管是誰。
(D) ❷時程表中的❷提及 Devon Taylor 在人資部門，但沒有說明誰是該部門的主管。

💡 應試者能理解電子郵件中的內容，並且可以連接信件與行程表提及的資訊。

185. Can connect information across multiple sentences in a single written text and across texts

When will Ms. Alexander most likely be traveling?

(A) April 3–8
(B) April 22–27
(C) May 1–10
(D) June 7–12

Alexander 小姐最有可能在什麼時候出差？

(A) 4 月 3 日到 8 日
(B) 4 月 22 日到 27 日
(C) 5 月 1 日到 10 日
(D) 6 月 7 日到 12 日

重點解說

正解 (A)
❶電子郵件❷第三行到第四行提到，「雖然她的出差日期尚未確定，但行程預計會和 Natasha Danilchenko 前往丹佛的時間相同。」從❷時程表❸得知，Natasha Danilchenko 去丹佛的日期為 4 月 3 日到 8 日，故選項 (A) 為正解。

💡 應試者能理解電子郵件中的內容，並且可以連接信件與行程表中的資訊。

Questions 186-190 refer to the following press release and e-mails.

1. 新聞稿

FOR IMMEDIATE RELEASE

New Leader at Hilsun

❶ Vancouver (21 June)—Hilsun Media Company has selected Diana Silva as its new Chief Executive Officer. After graduating with a master's degree in business administration from Vardia University, Ms. Silva joined Cordha Networks, where she earned a reputation as a skilled negotiator. She presided over the merger of Cordha and Renar Universal five years ago. She has worked for Cordha for ten years, the last three as Vice President of Sales.

❷ Ms. Silva replaces Gregor Zuev, who announced his departure last year. After an extensive search, Ms. Silva was the board's unanimous choice for CEO. She will begin her new position in August.

2. 第一封電子郵件

To:	All staff
From:	Alex Briard
Subject:	CEO announcement
Date:	21 June

Dear Colleagues,

❶ As you know, we, the board of directors here at Hilsun Media have been searching for a new CEO. As of today, we can officially announce that Diana Silva has been selected for the position, and we are thrilled she will be joining us.

❷ At this time, we do not anticipate changes in departmental leadership, nor do we foresee new policies regarding promotions. Naturally, Ms. Silva may elect to revise both over time, but she has expressed her confidence in the assignments and policies as they currently stand.

❸ Ms. Silva will be welcomed with a luncheon in her honor on her first day. The tentative location for it is Tenley Hall. You can expect to see messages asking about menu preferences, scheduling, and special activities over the next few weeks.

All my best,

Alex Briard

3. 第二封電子郵件

To:	Diana Silva
From:	Alton Hague
Subject:	News
Date:	23 June

❶ I just heard the news about your new position, and I am so pleased for you. You have been wonderful to work with these past several years. The sales division in particular will miss your energy and leadership. I hope that we can continue to stay in touch and, with luck, work together in the future.

Best,

Alton

請參考以下新聞稿及兩封電子郵件，回答第 186 至 190 題。

即時發布

Hilsun 新領導人

溫哥華（6 月 21 日）— Hilsun Media 公司已任命 Diana Silva 作為新任執行長。Silva 小姐從 Vardia 大學獲得企業管理碩士學位後即加入 Cordha Networks，並在此獲得談判專家的盛名。五年前她主導了 Cordha 和 Renar Universal 的合併案。她在 Cordha 工作了十年，最後三年擔任銷售副總。

Silva 小姐取代去年宣布離職的 Gregor Zuev。在廣泛地調查後，Silva 小姐成為董事會一致認可的執行長，她將於八月上任新職位。

收件者：	全體員工
寄件者：	Alex Briard
主旨：	執行長公告
日期：	6 月 21 日

親愛的同事，

如各位所知，我們 Hilsun Media 的董事會一直在尋找新的執行長。從今天起，我們可以正式宣布 Diana Silva 被任命擔任此職務，我們非常高興她將加入我們。

此時此刻，我們預期部門負責人不會有所改變，也沒有預知和升遷相關的新政策。當然，Silva 小姐或許會選擇逐步修改兩者，但她已表示對於目前的任務和政策充滿信心。

Silva 小姐到職的第一天將舉行一個午餐會歡迎她，地點暫定為 Tenley Hall。接下來幾週，你們可能會收到詢問菜單喜好、行程，以及特別活動的訊息。

祝一切安好，

Alex Briard

題目/中文翻譯

收件者：	Diana Silva
寄件者：	Alton Hague
主旨：	最新消息
日期：	6 月 23 日

我剛聽到關於妳新職位的消息，我為妳感到非常高興。過去幾年與妳共事真的很開心，尤其是銷售部門，會想念妳的活力和領導力。希望我們可以持續保持聯絡，並且有幸未來能一起工作。

祝福妳，

Alton

186. | Can locate and understand specific information in written texts

What does the press release indicate about Ms. Silva?

(A) She used to work for Renar Universal.
(B) She was in charge of uniting two companies.
(C) She recently graduated from university.
(D) She hired Mr. Zuev at Cordha Networks.

這篇新聞稿中關於 Silva 小姐的敘述，以下何者正確？

(A) 她過去曾經在 Renar Universal 工作。
(B) 她負責兩間公司的合併。
(C) 她最近剛從大學畢業。
(D) 她在 Cordha Networks 雇用了 Zuev 先生。

重點解說

正解 (B)

1 新聞稿中的 **❶** 第四行到第五行提及，「五年前她主導了 Cordha 和 Renar Universal 的合併案」，選項 (B) unite 表示 merge「合併」，故為正解。in charge of「負責」。
(A) 從 **1** 新聞稿中 **❶** 第三行可知，Silva 小姐畢業後加入 Cordha Networks，並不是 Renar Universal。
(C) 從 **1** 新聞稿中 **❶** 第五行得知，Silva 小姐已經工作十年了，並不是近期畢業。
(D) 從 **1** 新聞稿中 **❷** 第一行得知，是 Silva 小姐取代了 Zuev 先生的職位，而非雇用 Zuev 先生。

💡 應試者能理解新聞稿提及的事件與資訊，即使選項以不同方式敘述，也能選出正確答案。

187. | Can make inferences based on information in written texts
| Can connect information across multiple sentences in a single written text and across texts

Who most likely is Mr. Briard?

(A) A department manager
(B) A member of Hilsun's board
(C) Ms. Silva's assistant
(D) Ms. Silva's former supervisor

Briard 先生最有可能是誰？

(A) 部門經理
(B) Hilsun 董事會的成員
(C) Silva 小姐的助理
(D) Silva 小姐的前主管

重點解說

正解 (B)

2 第一封電子郵件 **❶** 第一行指出，「我們 Hilsun Media 的董事會一直在尋找新的執行長」。由此判斷，Briard 先生是董事會的一員，故選項 (B) 為正解。
(C) assistant「助理」；(D) supervisor「監督者、管理者」。

💡 應試者能從書面文本的細節推測出主旨和目的。
💡 應試者能理解電子郵件內容，並連接整個信件中的資訊。

188. Can connect information across multiple sentences in a single written text and across texts

What is suggested about the luncheon for Ms. Silva?

(A) It will take place in August.
(B) It will be held at a local restaurant.
(C) The menu has been finalized.
(D) The company hosts it annually.

關於 Silva 小姐的午餐會何者正確？

(A) 將會在八月舉行。
(B) 將會在當地的餐廳舉辦。
(C) 菜單已經確定了。
(D) 公司每年舉辦一次。

> 重點解說
>
> **正解 (A)**
> ❶新聞稿❷第二行到第三行提到，「她將於八月上任新職位」。而在❷第一封電子郵件中❸第一行提及「Silva 小姐到職的第一天將有一個午餐歡迎會」，由此可判斷，她的午餐會將在八月舉行，故選項 (A) 為正解。
> (D) host「主辦」。
>
> 💡 應試者能理解新聞稿與電子郵件的內容，並連結兩者的訊息。

189. Can make inferences based on information in written texts

Why did Mr. Hague write the e-mail to Ms. Silva?

(A) To extend a job offer
(B) To schedule an appointment
(C) To offer his congratulations
(D) To discuss travel plans

為什麼 Hague 先生要寫這封電子郵件給 Silva 小姐？

(A) 提供一個工作機會
(B) 安排見面
(C) 表達他的祝賀之意
(D) 討論出差計畫

> 重點解說
>
> **正解 (C)**
> ❸第二封電子郵件❶第一行中，Hague 先生提到他很高興 Silva 小姐接到新職位，接著在第二行表示過去幾年很開心能和她一起共事，由此可判斷，這封信是為了感謝 Silva 小姐並傳達祝福，故選項 (C) 為正解。
> 💡 應試者能從細節推測出電子郵件的目的。

190. Can make inferences based on information in written texts

Can connect information across multiple sentences in a single written text and across texts

Where does Mr. Hague most likely work?

(A) At Hilsun Media
(B) At Vardia University
(C) At Renar Universal
(D) At Cordha Networks

Hague 先生最有可能在哪裡工作？

(A) Hilsun Media
(B) Vardia 大學
(C) Renar Universal
(D) Cordha Networks

> 重點解說
>
> **正解 (D)**
> ❸第二封電子郵件中❶第二行到第三行提到，「尤其是銷售部門，會想念妳的活力和領導力」，在❶新聞稿中的❶第五行到第六行提及，Silva 小姐在 Cordha 工作了十年，最後三年為銷售副總，由此可判斷，Hague 先生在 Cordha Networks 的銷售部門工作，故選項 (D) 為正解。
> 💡 應試者能從電子郵件的資訊做出推論。
> 💡 應試者能理解並連結書面文本中的所有事件與資訊。

題目/中文翻譯

Questions 191-195 refer to the following Web site, online form, and e-mail.

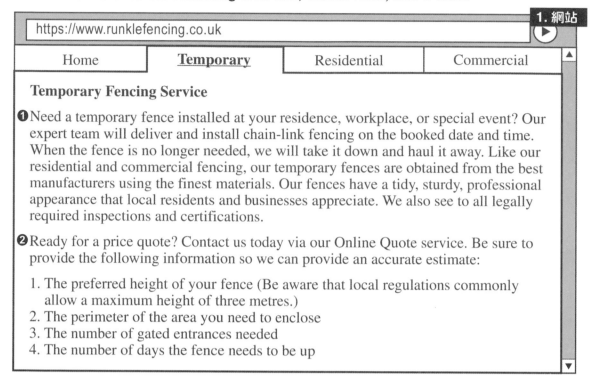

1. 網站

https://www.runklefencing.co.uk

| Home | **Temporary** | Residential | Commercial |

Temporary Fencing Service

❶ Need a temporary fence installed at your residence, workplace, or special event? Our expert team will deliver and install chain-link fencing on the booked date and time. When the fence is no longer needed, we will take it down and haul it away. Like our residential and commercial fencing, our temporary fences are obtained from the best manufacturers using the finest materials. Our fences have a tidy, sturdy, professional appearance that local residents and businesses appreciate. We also see to all legally required inspections and certifications.

❷ Ready for a price quote? Contact us today via our Online Quote service. Be sure to provide the following information so we can provide an accurate estimate:

1. The preferred height of your fence (Be aware that local regulations commonly allow a maximum height of three metres.)
2. The perimeter of the area you need to enclose
3. The number of gated entrances needed
4. The number of days the fence needs to be up

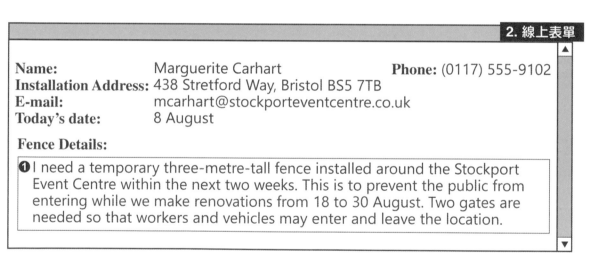

2. 線上表單

Name: Marguerite Carhart   **Phone:** (0117) 555-9102
Installation Address: 438 Stretford Way, Bristol BS5 7TB
E-mail: mcarhart@stockporteventcentre.co.uk
Today's date: 8 August

Fence Details:

❶ I need a temporary three-metre-tall fence installed around the Stockport Event Centre within the next two weeks. This is to prevent the public from entering while we make renovations from 18 to 30 August. Two gates are needed so that workers and vehicles may enter and leave the location.

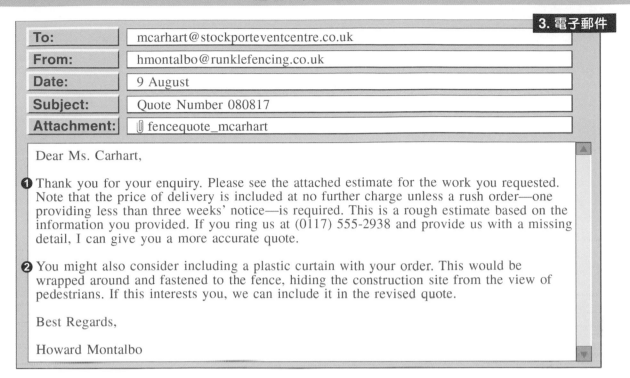

To:	mcarhart@stockporteventcentre.co.uk
From:	hmontalbo@runklefencing.co.uk
Date:	9 August
Subject:	Quote Number 080817
Attachment:	🔗 fencequote_mcarhart

Dear Ms. Carhart,

❶ Thank you for your enquiry. Please see the attached estimate for the work you requested. Note that the price of delivery is included at no further charge unless a rush order—one providing less than three weeks' notice—is required. This is a rough estimate based on the information you provided. If you ring us at (0117) 555-2938 and provide us with a missing detail, I can give you a more accurate quote.

❷ You might also consider including a plastic curtain with your order. This would be wrapped around and fastened to the fence, hiding the construction site from the view of pedestrians. If this interests you, we can include it in the revised quote.

Best Regards,

Howard Montalbo

請參考以下網頁、線上表單及電子郵件，回答第 191 至 195 題。

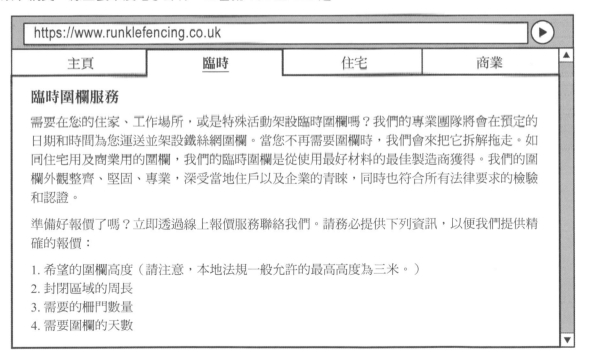

https://www.runklefencing.co.uk

| 主頁 | 臨時 | 住宅 | 商業 |

臨時圍欄服務

需要在您的住家、工作場所，或是特殊活動架設臨時圍欄嗎？我們的專業團隊將會在預定的日期和時間為您運送並架設鐵絲網圍欄。當您不再需要圍欄時，我們會來把它拆解拖走。如同住宅用及商業用的圍欄，我們的臨時圍欄是從使用最好材料的最佳製造商獲得。我們的圍欄外觀整齊、堅固、專業，深受當地住戶以及企業的青睞，同時也符合所有法律要求的檢驗和認證。

準備好報價了嗎？立即透過線上報價服務聯絡我們。請務必提供下列資訊，以便我們提供精確的報價：

1. 希望的圍欄高度（請注意，本地法規一般允許的最高高度為三米。）
2. 封閉區域的周長
3. 需要的柵門數量
4. 需要圍欄的天數

題目/中文翻譯

姓名：	Marguerite Carhart	電話：(0117) 555-9102

安裝地址：　　Stretford 路 438 號 , 布里斯托 BS5 7TB
電子郵件：　　mcarhart@stockporteventcentre.co.uk
今天的日期：　8 月 8 日

圍欄細節：

接下來兩週我需要一個三公尺高的臨時圍欄架設在 Stockport 活動中心附近，避免人群在 8 月 18 日到 30 日的整修期間通行。我們需要兩個柵門讓工人和車輛可以進出這個場所。

收件者：	mcarhart@stockporteventcentre.co.uk
寄件者：	hmontalbo@runklefencing.co.uk
日期：	8 月 9 日
主旨：	報價單號 080817
附件：	🔗 fencequote_mcarhart

親愛的 Carhart 小姐，

感謝您的詢價。請參閱附件針對您的需求做出的估價。請注意，除非是少於三週的急件訂單，否則運費已包含在內，無須額外費用。

這是根據您提供的資料做出的粗略估算。如果您來電 (0117) 555-2938，提供我們遺漏的細節，我可以給您更準確的報價。

您也可以考慮加訂一個塑膠遮簾，可以圍繞並固定在圍欄上，讓施工現場隱藏於行人的視線。如果您對此感興趣，我們可以把它加到修改後的報價單裡。

Howard Montalbo 敬上

191.　Can locate and understand specific information in written texts

What does the Web site indicate about fences taller than three meters?

(A) They are made of plastic.
(B) They are usually prohibited by law.
(C) They require special transportation.
(D) They must be ordered directly from the manufacturer.

關於網站上提到高於三公尺的圍欄，以下何者正確？

(A) 它們是塑膠做的。
(B) 它們通常是被法律禁止的。
(C) 它們需要特殊運輸。
(D) 它們必須直接從製造商下訂單。

重點解說

正解 (B)

1️⃣ 網站中的 2️⃣ 第一點提到圍欄的高度，並補充「請注意，本地法規一般允許的最高高度為三米。」由此可知，圍欄的高度是有法律上的限制，故選項 (B) 為正解。

💡 應試者能理解網頁上提及的資訊，即使選項換句話說，也能選出正確答案。

192. Can locate and understand specific information in written texts

According to the form, why does Ms. Carhart need a temporary fence installed?

(A) To mark a property line
(B) To draw attention to an exhibit
(C) To control a crowd at a special event
(D) To limit public access to a work site

根據這張表單，為什麼 Carhart 小姐需要架設臨時圍欄？

(A) 標記地界線
(B) 引起人們對展覽的注意
(C) 在特殊活動中控制人潮
(D) 限制民眾進入工地

正解 (D)
❷ 線上表單中的 ❶ 第二行到第三行提到，這次架設圍欄的原因是為了「避免人群在 8 月 18 日到 30 日的整修期間通行」，故選項 (D) 為正解。
(A) property line「地界線」；(B) exhibit「展覽」；(C) crowd「人潮」
💡 應試者能理解線上表單中的事實訊息，即使選項換句話說，也能選出正確答案。

193. Can connect information across multiple sentences in a single written text and across texts

What information does Ms. Carhart fail to give about the fence she needs?

(A) The height of the fence to be erected
(B) The dates when the fence is needed
(C) The perimeter of the area to be enclosed
(D) The number of entrances needed

關於 Carhart 小姐所需的圍欄，她沒有提供什麼資訊？

(A) 要架設的圍欄高度
(B) 需要圍欄的日期
(C) 封閉區域的周長
(D) 需要的入口數量

正解 (C)
❷ 線上表單中 ❶ 第一行到第二行提到，「需要一個三公尺高的臨時圍欄」。接著第二行到第四行提到，「避免人群在 8 月 18 日到 30 日的整修期間通行」、「我們需要兩個柵門讓工人和車輛可以進出這個場所。」由此可知，她並沒有提到 ❶ 網站中的 ❷ 的第二點「封閉區域的周長」，故選項 (C) 為正解。
💡 應試者能理解網站和線上表單的內容，並能連結兩者的資訊和事件。

194. Can connect information across multiple sentences in a single written text and across texts

What is implied about Ms. Carhart's fence project?

(A) There will be a charge for delivery.
(B) The project involves work at several job sites.
(C) Extra workers must be hired to install the fence.
(D) Inspectors must first approve the project.

Carhart 小姐的圍欄工程暗示著什麼？

(A) 將會收取運費。
(B) 這個工程涉及在多個工作地點工作。
(C) 必須雇用額外的工人來架設圍欄。
(D) 檢驗人員必須先核准這項工程。

正解 (A)
❸ 電子郵件中 ❶ 第二行提到，運費已包含在內，無須額外費用，除非是少於三週的急件訂單。由此可知，Carhart 小姐的訂單是需要運費的，故選項 (A) 為正解。
(B) involve「涉及」；(C) install「安裝、架設」；(D) inspector「檢驗人員」。
💡 應試者能理解電子郵件中的訊息，即使選項以不同方式敘述，也能選出正確答案。

195. Can locate and understand specific information in written texts

Why does Mr. Montalbo recommend adding a curtain?

(A) It would act as a noise barrier.
(B) It would help keep in dust.
(C) It would serve as a visual screen.
(D) It would improve safety conditions.

為什麼 Montalbo 先生建議增加一個遮簾？

(A) 它可充當隔音牆。
(B) 它有助於防塵。
(C) 它用來當作視覺屏障。
(D) 它可以加強安全條件。

重點解說

正解 (C)
❸電子郵件中的❷第二行提到，「讓施工現場隱藏於行人的視線。」由此可知，新增塑膠遮簾是為了作為視覺屏障，故選項 (C) 為正解。

💡應試者能理解電子郵件的訊息，即使選項換句話說，也能選出正確答案。

Questions 196-200 refer to the following Web page and e-mails.

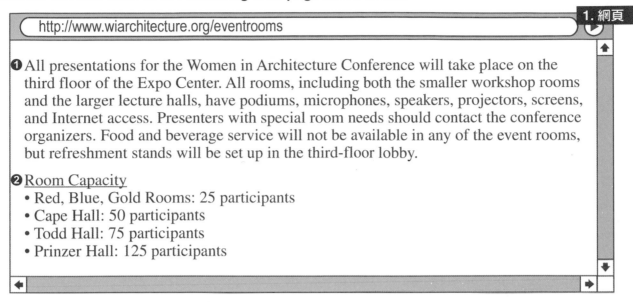

http://www.wiarchitecture.org/eventrooms

1. 網頁

❶ All presentations for the Women in Architecture Conference will take place on the third floor of the Expo Center. All rooms, including both the smaller workshop rooms and the larger lecture halls, have podiums, microphones, speakers, projectors, screens, and Internet access. Presenters with special room needs should contact the conference organizers. Food and beverage service will not be available in any of the event rooms, but refreshment stands will be set up in the third-floor lobby.

❷ Room Capacity
• Red, Blue, Gold Rooms: 25 participants
• Cape Hall: 50 participants
• Todd Hall: 75 participants
• Prinzer Hall: 125 participants

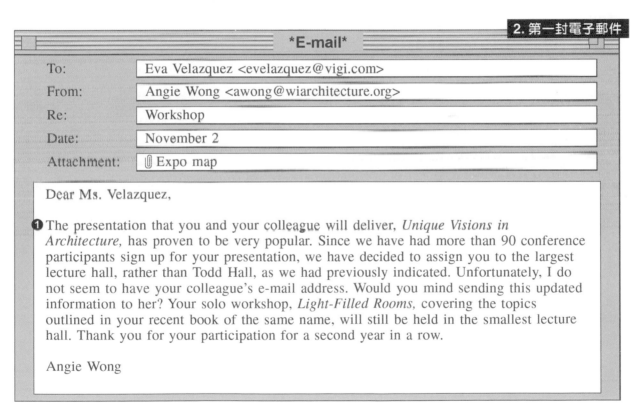

2. 第一封電子郵件

E-mail

To:	Eva Velazquez <evelazquez@vigi.com>
From:	Angie Wong <awong@wiarchitecture.org>
Re:	Workshop
Date:	November 2
Attachment:	📎 Expo map

Dear Ms. Velazquez,

❶ The presentation that you and your colleague will deliver, *Unique Visions in Architecture,* has proven to be very popular. Since we have had more than 90 conference participants sign up for your presentation, we have decided to assign you to the largest lecture hall, rather than Todd Hall, as we had previously indicated. Unfortunately, I do not seem to have your colleague's e-mail address. Would you mind sending this updated information to her? Your solo workshop, *Light-Filled Rooms,* covering the topics outlined in your recent book of the same name, will still be held in the smallest lecture hall. Thank you for your participation for a second year in a row.

Angie Wong

題目／中文翻譯

E-mail

To:	Amalia Harris <aharris@vigi.com>
From:	Eva Velazquez <evelazquez@vigi.com>
Re:	Workshop
Date:	November 2
Attachment:	📎 Expo map

Hello Amalia,

❶ Please see the forwarded message and the attached map Ms. Wong sent to me this morning. It looks like we have been upgraded to a larger room due to the popularity of our presentation—great news! It might be a good idea if we get together next week to go through our presentation and finalize the agenda and the handouts we have chosen to distribute. Let me know what time might work for you.

Thanks,

Eva

請參考以下網頁和兩封電子郵件，回答第 **196** 至 **200** 題。

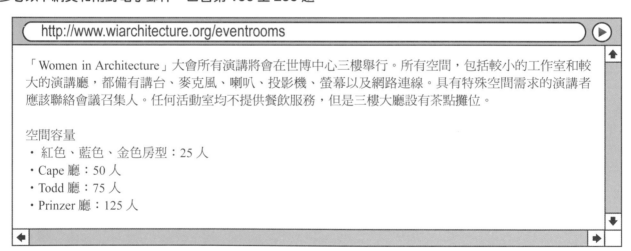

http://www.wiarchitecture.org/eventrooms

「Women in Architecture」大會所有演講將會在世博中心三樓舉行。所有空間，包括較小的工作室和較大的演講廳，都備有講台、麥克風、喇叭、投影機、螢幕以及網路連線。具有特殊空間需求的演講者應該聯絡會議召集人。任何活動室均不提供餐飲服務，但是三樓大廳設有茶點攤位。

空間容量
・紅色、藍色、金色房型：25 人
・Cape 廳：50 人
・Todd 廳：75 人
・Prinzer 廳：125 人

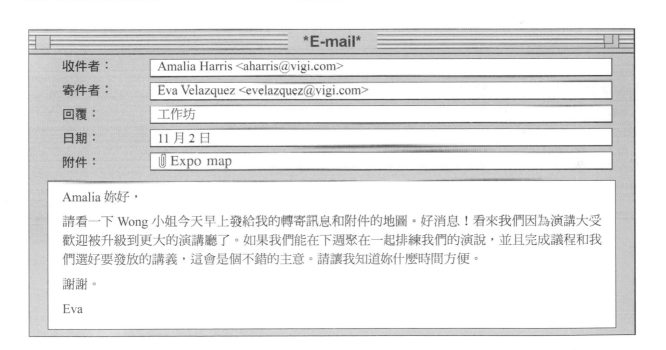

E-mail

收件者：	Eva Velazquez <evelazquez@vigi.com>
寄件者：	Angie Wong <awong@wiarchitecture.org>
回覆：	工作坊
日期：	11 月 2 日
附件：	📎 Expo map

親愛的 Velazquez 小姐，

您和您同事將發表的演講「Unique Visions in Architecture」非常受歡迎。由於我們已經有超過 90 位與會者報名參加您們的演講，我們決定將您們分配到最大的展演廳，而不是之前指定的 Todd 廳。不幸的是，我似乎沒有您同事的電子郵件地址，您方便把這個更新資訊傳給她嗎？概述了您近期同名書主題的個人工作坊「Light-Filled Rooms」，依然會在最小的演講廳舉行。感謝您連續兩年的參與。

Angie Wong

E-mail

收件者：	Amalia Harris <aharris@vigi.com>
寄件者：	Eva Velazquez <evelazquez@vigi.com>
回覆：	工作坊
日期：	11 月 2 日
附件：	📎 Expo map

Amalia 妳好，

請看一下 Wong 小姐今天早上發給我的轉寄訊息和附件的地圖。好消息！看來我們因為演講大受歡迎被升級到更大的演講廳了。如果我們能在下週聚在一起排練我們的演說，並且完成議程和我們選好要發放的講義，這會是個不錯的主意。請讓我知道妳什麼時間方便。

謝謝。

Eva

196. Can locate and understand specific information in written texts

According to the Web page, what is unavailable in the event rooms?

(A) Podiums
(B) Projectors
(C) Internet
(D) Catering

根據網頁，活動室內沒有提供什麼？

(A) 講台
(B) 投影機
(C) 網路
(D) 餐飲

重點解說	**正解 (D)**

1 網頁中的 **❶** 第五行提到，「任何活動室均不提供餐飲服務。」故選項 (D) catering「餐飲」表示 food and beverage 為正解。選項 (A)、(B)、(C) 在 **1** 網頁中 **❶** 的第三行到第四行皆有提到。

💡 應試者能理解網頁中的資訊，以及和內文意義相近的詞彙。

197. Can locate and understand specific information in written texts

What is suggested in the first e-mail about Ms. Velazquez?

(A) She prefers to present in smaller rooms.
(B) She has published a book.
(C) She is a conference organizer.
(D) She has not presented at this conference before.

第一封電子郵件中，關於 Velazquez 小姐的敘述何者正確？

(A) 她偏好在比較小的空間演說。
(B) 她出版了一本書。
(C) 她是會議召集人。
(D) 她之前沒有在這個會議上演說過。

重點解說	**正解 (B)**

2 第一封電子郵件中 **❶** 第六行到第七行提及，「概述了您近期同名書主題的個人工作坊『Light-Filled Rooms』」，由此可知，Velazquez 小姐曾出版過書籍。故選項 (B) 為正解。

💡 應試者能理解電子郵件中的事件與資訊，即使文本中並未明顯指出，也能選出正確答案。

198. Can make inferences based on information in written texts

Can connect information across multiple sentences in a single written text and across texts

Where will the presentation *Unique Visions in Architecture* be given?

(A) In the Blue Room
(B) In Cape Hall
(C) In Todd Hall
(D) In Prinzer Hall

「Unique Visions in Architecture」的演講將會在哪裡舉行？

(A) 藍色房型
(B) Cape 廳
(C) Todd 廳
(D) Prinzer 廳

重點解說	**正解 (D)**

2 第一封電子郵件中 **❶** 第二行到第四行提到，「由於我們已經有超過 90 位與會者報名參加您們的演講。」而根據 **1** 網頁中的 **❷** 第四點得知，Prinzer 廳可容納 125 個人，因此選項 (D) 為正解。

💡 應試者能從電子郵件及網頁的資訊做出推論。

💡 應試者能理解文章內容，並能連結網頁和電子郵件中的資訊。

199. Can locate and understand specific information in written texts

What does Ms. Wong ask Ms. Velazquez to do?

(A) Forward an e-mail
(B) Register for an event
(C) Confirm her payment details
(D) Provide biographical details

Wong 小姐請 Velazquez 小姐做什麼事？

(A) 轉寄一封電子郵件
(B) 報名一個活動
(C) 確認她的付款細節
(D) 提供個人簡介的細節

重點解說

正解 (A)
② 第一封電子郵件中❶第四行到第五行提及，Wong 小姐沒有 Velazquez 小姐同事的電子郵件，並在第五行詢問，「您方便把這個更新資訊傳給她嗎？」由此可知，Wong 小姐希望 Velazquez 小姐幫忙轉傳消息，故選項 (A) 為正解。
(B) register「登記、報名」；(C) payment「支付、付款」；(D) biographical「生平簡介、傳記」。

💡 應試者能理解電子郵件中的事件與訊息，即使文本中並未明確地表達，也能選出正確答案。

200. Can make inferences based on information in written texts

Can connect information across multiple sentences in a single written text and across texts

Who most likely is Ms. Harris?

(A) Ms. Velazquez's classmate
(B) Ms. Wong's editor
(C) Ms. Velazquez's work colleague
(D) Ms. Wong's assistant

Harris 小姐最有可能是誰？

(A) Velazquez 小姐的同學
(B) Wong 小姐的編輯
(C) Velazquez 小姐的工作同事
(D) Wong 小姐的助理

重點解說

正解 (C)
③ 第二封電子郵件中❶第一行，Velazquez 小姐要 Harris 小姐確認 Wong 小姐轉發的消息和地圖，呼應②第一封電子郵件中❶第五行到第六行，Wong 小姐請 Velazquez 小姐轉寄信件給她的同事。再者，③第二封電子郵件中❶第二行提到，「看來我們因為演講大受歡迎被升級到更大的演講廳了」，由此可知 Harris 小姐是 Velazquez 小姐的同事，故選項 (C) 為正解。

💡 應試者能從電子郵件的資訊做出推論。

💡 應試者能連結並理解兩則電子郵件的資訊與目的。

151

題目／中文翻譯

101.
`Can understand grammar in written texts`

The coaches are ------- that the Gremon Soccer Club will win tomorrow night.

(A) hope
(B) hopes
(C) hopeful
(D) hopefully

教練們希望 Gremon 足球俱樂部明天晚上能獲勝。

(A) 希望（原形動詞）
(B) 希望（第三人稱單數動詞）
(C) 抱有希望的（形容詞）
(D) 滿懷希望地（副詞）

重點解說

正解 (C)
空格前為 be 動詞，因此空格應為形容詞表示人（coaches）的狀態，選項 (C) 是唯一的形容詞，故為正解。
(A) 為原形動詞；(B) 為第三人稱單數動詞；(D) 為副詞，這些選項都沒有正確符合句子的語法。

💡 應試者能理解書面文本中的文法，選出 hope「希望」的適當形態。

102.
`Can understand grammar in written texts`

Mr. Hodges ------- that volunteers sign up to assist with the Hannock River cleanup by Friday.

(A) requesting
(B) to be requested
(C) requests
(D) to request

Hodges 先生要求志願者們在週五前報名協助 Hannock 河的清理工作。

(A) 要求（現在分詞）
(B) 被要求（被動式不定詞）
(C) 要求（第三人稱單數現在式動詞）
(D) 要求（不定詞）

重點解說

正解 (C)
空格後為 that 子句，空格應填入一般動詞，因為 Hodges 先生為第三人稱，唯選項 (C) 為第三人稱單數動詞最合適，故為正解。volunteer「志願者」，sign up「報名、註冊」，assist「協助」。
(A)、(B)、(D) 都沒有正確符合句子的語法。

💡 應試者能理解書面文本中的文法，並了解句子結構，選出動詞 request「要求」的適當形態。

103.
`Can understand vocabulary in written texts`

The office's copy machine will be out of service until ------- notice.

(A) extra
(B) temporary
(C) further
(D) ongoing

辦公室的影印機將暫停服務直到另行通知為止。

(A) 額外的
(B) 暫時的
(C) 進一步的
(D) 持續的

重點解說

正解 (C)
全部選項皆為形容詞。空格後為名詞 notice「通知」，因此空格應填入選項 (C) further「進一步的、另外的」最符合語意，故為正解。copy machine「影印機」，out of service「暫停服務、故障」。
(A)、(B)、(D) 在此沒有以有意義的方式修飾 notice，也沒有正確地完成句子。

💡 應試者能理解書面文本中的詞彙，並從不同形容詞中選出適切的答案。

104. Can understand grammar in written texts

If ------- are not satisfied with an item, return it for a full refund within 30 days of purchase.

(A) you
(B) your
(C) yours
(D) yourself

如果你對某項商品感到不滿意，在購買後 30 天內退貨可全額退款。

(A) 你（主格）
(B) 你的（所有格形容詞）
(C) 你的（所有格代名詞）
(D) 你自己（反身代名詞）

重點解說

正解 (A)

以「If...」為首的條件句，空格後為 be 動詞，因此空格應填入一個名詞（主詞），選項 (A) you 是主詞代名詞最為合適。satisfied「滿意的」，return「歸還」，refund「退款」。
(B) 所有格形容詞，(D) 反身代名詞，此兩個選項皆不能作為主詞；(C) 所有格代名詞，雖然有些所有格代名詞可以作為主詞，但它們前面必須有先行詞才可以。

💡 應試者能理解書面文本中的文法，依照句子結構選出正確的主詞形式。

105. Can understand vocabulary in written texts

Our most recent survey was sent to clients just last week, ------- it is too soon to send another one.

(A) when
(B) since
(C) so
(D) finally

我們上週才剛把最新的問卷寄給客戶，所以現在發送另一份還太早。

(A) 當
(B) 自從
(C) 所以
(D) 終於

重點解說

正解 (C)

空格前後為兩個完整句子，故應填入連接詞連接兩句，選項 (C) so「所以」語意最為合適，故為正解。
(A) when「當」及 (B) since「既然、自從」皆為連接詞，語意不合適；(D) finally「終於」為副詞，文法不正確。

💡 應試者能理解書面文本中的詞彙，並從不同單字中選出適切的答案。

106. Can understand grammar in written texts

Guests were ------- with the table decorations for the company banquet.

(A) impressive
(B) impressed
(C) impressing
(D) impressively

來賓們對公司晚宴的餐桌布置感到印象深刻。

(A) 令人印象深刻的（形容詞）
(B) 感到印象深刻的（過去分詞、形容詞）
(C) 印象深刻（現在分詞）
(D) 令人印象深刻地（副詞）

重點解說

正解 (B)

空格前為 be 動詞，主詞為 guests「來賓、客人」，因此空格應填入形容詞，描述來賓因餐桌布置而產生的狀態，填入選項 (B) impressed，動詞＋ ed 為過去分詞，可當形容詞使用，與前面的 be 動詞結合成為被動式，表示「對…感到印象深刻的」，故為正解。decoration「裝飾」，banquet「晚宴」。
(A) 雖然是形容詞，但指的是主詞令人印象深刻；(C) 現在分詞，指的是主詞正在做使人印象深刻的行為；(D) 副詞，此選項不符合語法。

💡 應試者能理解書面文本中的文法，辨別動詞 impress「印象深刻」過去分詞與現在分詞的使用時機。

107. Can understand vocabulary in written texts

After a 10 percent increase in delivery costs last year, management decided to look for a new paper -------.

(A) officer
(B) supplier
(C) finder
(D) starter

去年運送成本增加 10% 後，管理階層決定尋找新的紙張供應商。

(A) 官員
(B) 供應商
(C) 發現者
(D) 參賽者

正解 (B)

選項皆為名詞。逗號之前的語意為「去年運送成本增加 10% 後」，逗號之後的語意為「管理階層決定尋找新的紙張 ____」，選項 (B) supplier「供應商」最符合語意，因四個選項中，只有供應商是唯一能提供購買紙張的選項，故為正解。delivery「運送」。

💡 應試者能理解書面文本中的詞彙，並從不同名詞中選出適切的答案。

108. Can understand grammar in written texts

Inclement weather was ------- responsible for the low turnout at Saturday's Exton Music Festival.

(A) largely
(B) large
(C) largest
(D) larger

惡劣天氣是週六 Exton 音樂節到場人數低的主要原因。

(A) 主要地（副詞）
(B) 大的（形容詞）
(C) 最大的（最高級）
(D) 比較大的（比較級）

正解 (A)

空格中就算不填入任何字，句子也符合文法及語意，因此空格應填入可修飾後面形容詞 responsible 的副詞，故選項 (A) largely「主要地」為正解。inclement「（天氣）惡劣的」，turnout「到場人數、出席者」。

💡 應試者能理解書面文本中的文法，辨別一個完整句子的結構，並選出正確的單字詞性。

109. Can understand vocabulary in written texts

The location of next month's online gaming forum is yet to be -------.

(A) concluded
(B) prevented
(C) invited
(D) decided

下個月線上遊戲座談會的地點尚未決定。

(A) 結束
(B) 防止
(C) 邀請
(D) 決定

正解 (D)

選項皆為動詞過去分詞形態，與空格前的 be 動詞組合為被動式（be 動詞＋過去分詞），空格應填入選項 (D) decided「被決定」，語意最為合適，故為正解。其他選項則無法有意義的完成句子。forum「座談會、論壇」。

💡 應試者能理解書面文本中的詞彙，並從不同動詞中選出適切的答案。

110. Can understand grammar in written texts

The annual report has been posted online, ------- the director's office has not yet received a printed copy.

(A) but
(B) why
(C) with
(D) once

年度報告已經在網上發布了，但是主任辦公室還沒有收到紙本。

(A) 但是
(B) 為什麼
(C) 和
(D) 一旦

正解 (A)

此題是兩個完整的子句，中間以空格隔開。包含空格的句子語意為「年度報告已經在網上發布了，____ 主任辦公室還沒有收到紙本。」空格應填入連接詞，連接兩個完整子句，選項 (A) but「但是」語意最為合適，故為正解。annual「年度的」，receive「接收」。
(B) why「為什麼」當連接詞時，通常會和 the reasons 做搭配，語意不合適；(C) with「和、用」為介系詞，要接名詞；(D) once「一旦…」，語意不符。

💡 應試者能理解書面文本中的文法，並選出合適的連接詞。

111. Can understand grammar in written texts

Tomorrow at ------- 12:15 P.M., the mayor will break ground at the site of the new courthouse.

(A) precise
(B) precision
(C) precisely
(D) preciseness

明天中午 12:15 整，市長將會在新的法院大樓預定地破土動工。

(A) 精確的（形容詞）
(B) 精確（性）（名詞）
(C) 精確地（副詞）
(D) 精確性（名詞）

正解 (C)

通常英文把時間放在句尾，故這句也能以「The mayor will break ground at the site of the new courthouse tomorrow at 12:15 P.M.」呈現，當時間放句首時，是為了強調動作發生的時間點。空格中就算不填入任何字，這個句子也符合文法及語意，因此空格應填入副詞，修飾後面的 12:15 P.M.，選項 (C) 在此表示「正好、整」，故為最合適的答案。break ground「破土、挖掘」，courthouse「法院大樓」。

💡 應試者能理解書面文本中的文法，並辨別 precise「精確的」適當的形態。此外，也能理解不常見的句子結構。

112. Can understand vocabulary in written texts

Compri Tech, Inc., was able to increase its profits ------- making its processes more efficient.

(A) around
(B) by
(C) to
(D) for

Compri 科技公司能夠藉由讓流程更有效率來增加利潤。

(A) 在…周圍
(B) 藉由…
(C) 到…
(D) 為了…

正解 (B)

選項皆可作為介系詞。空格之前的句子語意為「Compri 科技公司能夠增加利潤」，空格後提供了原因，以選項 (B) by「藉由」連接句子，解釋此科技公司是如何增加利潤，語意最為通順，故為正解。increase「增加」，profit「收益、利潤」。
(C) to 後面應接原形動詞。

💡 應試者能理解書面文本中的詞彙，並選出合適的介系詞。

113. Can understand grammar in written texts

An online module will be provided for those ------- cannot attend the training session.

(A) who
(B) what
(C) when
(D) where

線上模組將會提供給那些無法參加培訓課程的人。

(A) 人（關係代名詞）
(B) 物（複合關係代名詞）
(C) 時間（關係副詞）
(D) 地點（關係副詞）

重點解說

正解 (A)

根據空格後的句子判斷，空格為後面句子的主詞，主詞為人，因此空格應填入選項 (A) who 關係代名詞，引導形容詞子句修飾先行詞 those。those who = people who，故選項 (A) 為正解。module「模組、組件」，attend「參加、出席」。

💡 應試者能理解書面文本中的文法，並能辨別關係代名詞的使用時機。

114. Can understand grammar in written texts

Before the updated design can go into -------, it must be approved by management.

(A) product
(B) producer
(C) productive
(D) production

在更新的設計可以投入生產前，必須得到管理階層的許可。

(A) 產品（名詞）
(B) 製作人（名詞）
(C) 具生產力（形容詞）
(D) 生產（名詞）

重點解說

正解 (D)

空格前面為動詞片語 go into「開始（投入）…」，介系詞 into 後面應接名詞，選項 (D) 語意最為合適，故為正解。updated「更新的」，management「管理階層」。
(A) product「產品」雖然是名詞，但產品是生產的結果，不符合語意；(B) producer「製作人、生產者」雖然也是名詞，但是指進行製作的人，並不符合語意。

💡 應試者能理解書面文本中的文法，並選出 produce「生產」的適當形態。

115. Can understand vocabulary in written texts

Ms. Valdez' sales numbers are good ------- for her to be considered for the employee-of-the-month award.

(A) forward
(B) even
(C) ahead
(D) enough

Valdez 小姐的銷售數字好到足以讓她列入當月最佳員工獎的考量。

(A) 前進
(B) 甚至
(C) 前面
(D) 足夠地

重點解說

正解 (D)

全部選項皆可作為副詞。空格應為副詞，修飾空格之前的形容詞 good，選項 (D) enough「足夠地」最為合適。
(A)、(B)、(C) 在此沒有以有意義的方式修飾 good，也沒有正確地完成句子。

💡 應試者能理解書面文本中的詞彙，並選出合適的副詞。

116. `Can understand vocabulary in written texts`

Mr. Nigam was ------- retirement when his boss asked him to be the head of security at the new facility.

(A) under
(B) ahead of
(C) nearby
(D) close to

Nigam 先生即將退休時，他的老闆要求他擔任新設施的安全負責人。

(A) 在…之下
(B) 在…前面
(C) 附近
(D) 接近

重點解說

正解 (D)

when 之前的語意為「Nigam 先生 ____ 退休」，包括 when 之後的句子語意為「當他的老闆要求他擔任新設施的安全負責人時」，選項 (D) close to「接近」，最符合語意，故為正解。其他選項無法正確地完成句子。retirement「退休」。

💡 應試者能理解書面文本中的詞彙，並從四個單字中選出合適的答案。

117. `Can understand grammar in written texts`

Milante Shoes ------- altered the firm's marketing strategy after a recent economic shift.

(A) quick
(B) quickest
(C) quickly
(D) quicken

在近期的經濟變動後，Milante 製鞋快速地改變公司的行銷策略。

(A) 快速的（形容詞）
(B) 最快的（最高級）
(C) 快速地（副詞）
(D) 加快（動詞）

重點解說

正解 (C)

空格中就算不填入任何字，這個句子也符合文法及語意。由整個句子可推知，空格應為副詞，修飾後面的動詞 alter「改變、更改」。空格應填選項 (C) quickly「快速地」，最為合適，故為正解。其他選項無法正確地完成句子。strategy「策略」，shlft「轉變」。

💡 應試者能理解書面文本中的文法，並辨別 quick「快速的」適當的形態。

118. `Can understand vocabulary in written texts`

The Auto Tools Manufacturing Convention will begin with an informal ------- on Friday evening.

(A) destination
(B) section
(C) reception
(D) invention

汽車工具製造大會將於週五晚上以一場非正式的接待會揭開序幕。

(A) 終點
(B) 部分
(C) 接待會
(D) 發明

重點解說

正解 (C)

全部選項皆為名詞，空格前以 informal「非正式的」來修飾，唯選項 (C) reception「接待會」符合語意，故為正解。convention「大會、會議」。

💡 應試者能理解書面文本中的詞彙，並從四個名詞中選出合適的答案。

題目/中文翻譯

---

119. Can understand grammar in written texts

The Rockton Restaurant chain employs standardized practices to ensure a ------- customer experience.

(A) consist
(B) consistent
(C) consisting
(D) consistently

Rockton 連鎖餐廳採用標準化做法以確保一致的客戶體驗。

(A) 組成（動詞）
(B) 一致的（形容詞）
(C) 組成（現在分詞）
(D) 始終如一地（副詞）

重點解說

正解 (B)

空格之前有冠詞 a，後有名詞片語 customer experience「客戶體驗」，因此空格應為修飾名詞的形容詞，故選項 (B) consistent「一致的」為正解。其他選項皆不正確。chain「連鎖店」，standardized「標準化的」，ensure「確保」。

💡 應試者能理解書面文本中的文法，並選出 consist「組成」的適當形態。

---

120. Can understand grammar in written texts

The third-shift lead position ------- available and can be applied for in person at the warehouse.

(A) to become
(B) had to become
(C) has become
(D) becoming

大夜班領班的職位已經釋出，可以親自去倉庫申請。

(A) 成為（to 不定詞）
(B) 成為（have to 的過去式加原形動詞）
(C) 已經成為（現在完成式）
(D) 成為（現在分詞）

重點解說

正解 (C)

空格之前有名詞 position「位置」，後有形容詞 available「可得到的、可用的」作為 become 的表語。選項 (C) has become「已經成為」最為合適，因為現在完成式最能表達該句狀況。

💡 應試者能理解書面文本中的文法，並選出動詞 become「變成、成為」的適當形態。

---

121. Can understand vocabulary in written texts

As our regular provider did not have the desks we needed in stock, we ordered from a local store -------.

(A) namely
(B) instead
(C) otherwise
(D) though

由於我們固定的供應商沒有我們所需的桌子庫存，所以我們改從當地商店訂購。

(A) 那就是
(B) 作為替代
(C) 否則
(D) 雖然

重點解說

正解 (B)

全部選項皆為副詞，逗號前的語意為「由於我們固定的供應商沒有我們所需的桌子庫存」，逗號後的語意為「我們從當地商店訂購 ____」，選項 (B) instead「作為替代」最符合語意，故為正解。regular「固定的、常規的」，in stock「有存貨」。
(A) namely「那就是」不能放句尾。

💡 應試者能理解書面文本中的詞彙，並從四個副詞中選出最合適的答案。

122. Can understand grammar in written texts

Aaron Park's new book features photographs of homes designed and built by the homeowners -------.

(A) itself
(B) himself
(C) themselves
(D) ourselves

Aaron Park 的新書是以屋主自己設計和建造的房屋照片為特色。

(A) 它自己
(B) 他自己
(C) 他們自己
(D) 我們自己

重點解說

正解 (C)
當反身代名詞放句尾時為強調語氣，空格之前為名詞 homeowners「屋主」，因此選項 (C) themselves「他們自己」最符合語意，故為正解。

 應試者能理解書面文本中的文法，並選出正確的反身代名詞。

123. Can understand vocabulary in written texts

Kieu Tech Services ------- to build three more data centers in southern Vietnam in the next two years.

(A) refers
(B) delivers
(C) intends
(D) indicates

Kieu 科技服務公司打算在未來兩年內於越南南部再多建造三座數據中心。

(A) 把…歸類於
(B) 運送
(C) 打算
(D) 指示

重點解說

正解 (C)
全部選項皆為動詞，動詞後接不定詞，代表主詞的目的。句中提及的時間是在「未來兩年內」，選項 (C) intends「打算、計畫」語意最為合適，因為它指的是對未來行動的計畫，故為正解。

 應試者能理解書面文本中的詞彙，並從四個動詞中選出最合適的答案。

124. Can understand vocabulary in written texts

------- our public relations manager, Ms. Ghazarian has just been appointed vice president of media relations.

(A) Sincerely
(B) Immediately
(C) Solely
(D) Formerly

我們先前的公共關係經理，Ghazarian 小姐剛被任命為媒體關係部副總裁。

(A) 真誠地
(B) 即刻地
(C) 單獨地
(D) 先前

重點解說

正解 (D)
全部選項皆為副詞。空格應填選項 (D) formerly「先前」，語意最為合適，故為正解。appoint「指派」。

 應試者能理解書面文本中的詞彙，並從四個副詞中選出最合適的答案。

159

125. Can understand grammar in written texts

The Dubai Physicians Group believes that ongoing ------- between researchers and practitioners is essential.

(A) collaborate
(B) collaborated
(C) collaboration
(D) collaborates

杜拜醫生團隊認為研究學者和從業人員間的持續合作是很重要的。

(A) 合作（動詞）
(B) 合作（過去式動詞）
(C) 合作（名詞）
(D) 合作（第三人稱單數動詞）

重點解說	正解 (C) 空格之前為形容詞 ongoing「持續的、不間斷的」，因此空格應填入名詞，唯選項 (C) 最為合適，故為正解。physician「醫生」。 💡 應試者能理解書面文本中的文法，並辨別 collaborate「合作」的適當形態。

126. Can understand grammar in written texts

All Hershel Industries employees must have a valid ID card ------- enter the building.

(A) in order to
(B) as long as
(C) regarding
(D) always

所有 Hershel 工業的員工必須持有有效身分證件才能進入大樓。

(A) 為了
(B) 只要
(C) 關於
(D) 總是

重點解說	正解 (A) 空格之前的語意為「所有 Hershel 工業的員工必須持有有效身分證件」，空格之後的語意為「進入大樓」，選項 (A) in order to「為了」最符合語意，故為正解。valid「有效的」。 (B) as long as「只要」為片語，後需接完整句子；(C) regarding「關於」為介系詞，後面要接名詞。 💡 應試者能理解書面文本中的文法，並理解語意，選出合適的答案。

127. Can understand vocabulary in written texts

Hotels and universities are ------- to recycle their used mattresses through the city's recycling program.

(A) systematic
(B) eligible
(C) familiar
(D) successful

旅館業者和大學有資格透過這座城市的回收計畫來回收他們的二手床墊。

(A) 有系統的
(B) 有資格的
(C) 熟悉的
(D) 成功的

重點解說	正解 (B) 全部選項皆為形容詞。空格之前為 be 動詞，空格應填入選項 (B) eligible「有資格的」，語意最合適，故為正解。be eligible to「有資格去做某事」。mattress「床墊」。 💡 應試者能理解書面文本中的詞彙，並從四個形容詞中選出最合適的答案。

128. Can understand vocabulary in written texts

Kovox Ltd. aims to optimize quality ------- reducing the impact on the environment.

(A) which
(B) while
(C) because
(D) unless

Kovox 有限公司目標在於優化品質的同時也減少對環境的影響。

(A) 事物（關係代名詞）
(B) 當…的時候
(C) 因為
(D) 除非

正解 (B)

空格之前的語意為「Kovox 有限公司目標在於優化品質」，空格之後的語意為「減少對環境的影響」。其中，選項 (B) while「當…的時候」，語意最為合適，故為正解。
(A) which 為關係代名詞，用於代替前面的先行詞，語意不合適；(C) because 及 (D) unless 皆為連接詞，須連接兩個完整句子。

💡 應試者能理解書面文本中的詞彙，並從四個單字中選出最適合的答案。

129. Can understand grammar in written texts

------- the potential success of a product is often done through market research.

(A) Calculate
(B) Calculation
(C) Calculating
(D) Calculated

計算一個產品的潛在成功通常是透過市場調查來完成。

(A) 計算（原形動詞）
(B) 計算（名詞）
(C) 計算（現在分詞）
(D) 計算（過去式動詞）

正解 (C)

此句的動詞為單數 is，空格為此句的主詞，動名詞可當主詞表示動作這件事本身，唯選項 (C) 最為合適，故為正解。potential「潛在的」。
(B) 雖然也是名詞，但因缺少介系詞 of（Calculation of the...），故此選項不能正確完成句子。

💡 應試者能理解書面文本中的文法，並辨別 calculate「計算」的適當形態。

130. Can understand grammar in written texts

Despite initial ------- over the size of the venue, the Westover Fashion Show was a great success.

(A) critical
(B) criticize
(C) critically
(D) criticism

儘管最初對場地規模有受到批評，但 Westover 時裝秀仍然獲得巨大的成功。

(A) 批判的（形容詞）
(B) 批評（動詞）
(C) 批判性地（副詞）
(D) 批評（名詞）

正解 (D)

句首 despite「儘管」後面要接名詞片語，空格之前是形容詞 initial「最初的」，因此空格應填入名詞，故選項 (D) criticism「批評」為正解。venue「場地」。

💡 應試者能理解書面文本中的文法，並辨別 criticize「批評」適當的形態。

Questions 131-134 refer to the following letter.

Dear PGD Account Holder,

PGD Bank strives ------- the highest levels of client security and service. This applies not only to online-
131.
and telephone-based services, but also to our brick-and-mortar locations. Our three branch offices have

proudly been a part of the community ------- a combined total of 40 years.
132.

To assist you even better in the future, ❶ **our Smithville branch will be temporarily closed for renovations**

July 8–22. ------- . In the meantime, our other two regional branches in Pine Grove and Bradford will
133.

maintain normal business ------- . We value your feedback and will respond to any concerns that you may
134.

have as soon as possible.

Sincerely,

Edwin Chen, Operations Manager
PGD Bank

請參考以下信件，回答第 131 至 134 題。

親愛的 PGD 帳戶持有人，

PGD 銀行致力於提供最高等級的客戶安全與服務，這不只適用於網路和電話服務，也包含我們的實體服務處。
我們三間分行很榮幸成為這個社區的一份子，前後共有 40 年的時間。

為了提供更好的服務，Smithville 分行將從 7 月 8 日到 22 日暫時關閉進行整修。＊若造成您的不便我們深表歉意。
於此同時，我們另外兩間位在 Pine Grove 和 Bradford 的地區分行將會維持正常營業時間。我們重視您的回饋並
且會盡快回覆任何您可能會遇到的問題。

Edwin Chen 營運經理 敬上
PGD 銀行

＊第 133 題插入句的翻譯

131. | Can understand grammar in written texts

(A) to provide
(B) provided
(C) providing
(D) to be provided

(A) 提供（不定詞）
(B) 提供（過去分詞）
(C) 提供（現在分詞）
(D) 提供（被動式不定詞）

重點解說

正解 (A)

空格前有動詞 strives「努力、奮鬥」，通常當 strive 以現在式狀態在句子中作動詞時，後面可接 to ＋原形動詞（不
定詞），表示「努力去做某事」。唯有選項 (A) 最為符合，故為正解。

💡 應試者能理解書面文本中的文法，選出動詞 provide「提供」在此封信件中的適當時態。

132.

Can understand vocabulary in written texts

(A) except
(B) amid
(C) near
(D) for

(A) 除了…之外
(B) 在…之間
(C) 接近
(D) 達

正解 (D)

空格之後為 a combined total of 40 years「總共 40 年」，因此空格應填入時間介系詞。其中選項 (D) for ＋一段時間，最為合適，故為正解。

💡 應試者能理解此封信件內容及與時間長度相關的單字。

133.

Can connect information across multiple sentences in a single written text and across texts

(A) Unfortunately, services will be limited.
(B) We thank you for trusting in PGD Bank over these years.
(C) We apologize for any inconvenience this may cause.
(D) Traffic on the boulevard has increased lately.

(A) 很抱歉，服務將會受到限制。
(B) 感謝您多年來對 PGD 銀行的信任。
(C) 若造成您的不便我們深表歉意。
(D) 最近林蔭大道上的車流量增加了。

正解 (C)

空格前的句子語意為「Smithville 分行將從 7 月 8 日到 22 日暫時關閉進行整修」，表示客戶在此時間內無法享有銀行各項服務，因此空格應填入選項 (C)「若造成您的不便我們深表歉意。」語意最為合適，故為正解。
(D) boulevard「大街、林蔭大道」。

💡 應試者能理解此封信件的內容，並從前後句子判斷最符合句意的答案。

134.

Can connect information across multiple sentences in a single written text and across texts

Can understand vocabulary in written texts

(A) investments
(B) hiring
(C) hours
(D) interests

(A) 投資
(B) 雇用
(C) 時間
(D) 興趣

正解 (C)

選項皆為名詞，包括空格的句子意思是「我們另外兩間位在 Pine Grove 和 Bradford 的地區分行將會維持正常營業 ＿＿＿」。❶ 提到有一間分行暫時關閉，空格填入選項 (C) hours，在此 business hours 表示「營業時間」，表示另外兩間分行不會關閉，故為正解。

💡 應試者能理解此封信件的內容，並從前後句子判斷最符合語意的答案。

💡 應試者能理解此封信件中產業領域的常見單字／慣用語。

Questions 135-138 refer to the following letter.

August 29
Greene & Lauer Logistics
2334 Hoyt Street
Boston, MA 02121

Dear Hiring Manager:

I am pleased to be writing this letter of recommendation for Mr. Nobuo Omoto. He __135.__ as an intern for our Finance Department. During this time, Mr. Omoto worked on a variety of tasks, from __136.__ data for budget reports to reviewing files ahead of our annual audit. Mr. Omoto quickly mastered our regular procedures, and he routinely made suggestions for making our workflow processes more efficient. In fact, some of these __137.__ have since been incorporated into the department's everyday operations.

I strongly recommend Mr. Omoto for any entry-level position in the financial services industry. __138.__ . If I can be of any further assistance, please do not hesitate to contact me at the above address or by e-mail at ojimenez@greenelauer.com.

Sincerely,

Oscar Jimenez
Financial Officer

請參考以下信件，回答第 135 至 138 題。

8 月 29 日
Greene & Lauer 物流
2334 號 Hoyt 街
波士頓，麻薩諸塞州 02121

親愛的招募經理，

我很高興能為 Nobuo Omoto 先生寫這封推薦信。他曾在我們的財務部門擔任實習生，在此期間，Omoto 先生做了非常多種類的工作項目，從蒐集預算報告的數據，到在年度審計前檢查文件。Omoto 先生很快地掌握我們的常規程序，他經常提出建議讓工作流程更有效率。事實上，其中一些改變已被納入部門的日常運作。

我強烈推薦 Omoto 先生擔任金融服務行業的任何初階職位。＊他將會成為貴公司的寶貴人才。如果需要進一步的協助，請隨時透過上述地址或是寄電子郵件至 ojimenez@greenelauer.com 與我聯繫。

順頌商祺
Oscar Jimenez
財務總監

＊第138 題插入句的翻譯

135.

Can connect information across multiple sentences in a single written text and across texts

Can understand vocabulary in written texts

(A) networked
(B) applied
(C) served
(D) followed

(A) 使（電腦）連網
(B) 應用
(C) 擔任
(D) 追隨

重點解說

正解 (C)
包含空格的句子意思是「他曾在我們的財務部門 ＿＿＿ 實習生」。空格後有一個介系詞 as，因此空格應填入選項 (C) serve 搭配 as 使用，serve as... 為「擔任…」，正好符合 Omoto 先生作為實習生角色的文意，故為正解。

💡 **應試者能理解較長的信件，並能將訊息連結起來得知信件主題。**

💡 **應試者能理解書面文本中的詞彙，和常見的動詞搭配。**

136.

(A) gathers
(B) gathering
(C) having gathered
(D) gathered

(A) 蒐集（第三人稱單數現在式動詞）
(B) 蒐集（動名詞或現在分詞）
(C) 蒐集（現在完成式）
(D) 蒐集（過去分詞）

正解 (B)

包含空格的句子意思是「Omoto 先生做了非常多種類的工作項目，從 ＿＿＿ 預算報告的數據，到在年度審計前檢查文件」。這邊的介系詞片語為「from...to...」表示範圍變化「從…到…」，介系詞後須接動名詞，選項 (B) gathering 最合適，故為正解。

💡 應試者能理解書面文本中的文法，以及不常見的文法結構。

137.

(A) instruments
(B) changes
(C) events
(D) resources

(A) 樂器
(B) 改變
(C) 活動
(D) 資源

正解 (B)

包括空格的句子意思是「其中一些 ＿＿＿ 已被納入部門的日常運作」。前一句提到，Omoto 先生經常提出能使工作流程更有效率的建議，因此空格應填入選項 (B) changes「改變」，表示前面所提到的建議，最符合語意，故為正解。

💡 應試者能理解較長的信件，並連結整個文本中的訊息。

💡 應試者能理解這篇信件中與職場相關的單字／慣用語。

138.

(A) He will be a great asset to your organization.
(B) He will be completing his internship very soon.
(C) I hope to work with Mr. Omoto one day.
(D) Please send your application to me directly.

(A) 他將會成為貴公司的寶貴人才。
(B) 他很快就會完成他的實習。
(C) 我希望有天能和 Omoto 先生一起工作。
(D) 請直接把你的申請書寄給我。

正解 (A)

空格前的句子是「我強烈推薦 Omoto 先生擔任金融服務行業的任何初階職位」。空格填入選項 (A) 後，表明 Omoto 先生能為公司帶來幫助，上下文意通順流暢，故為正解。asset「人才、資產」。
(B) internship「實習」；(D) application「申請」。

💡 應試者能透過前後句子判斷最符合句意的答案。

Questions 139-142 refer to the following e-mail.

To: Mason Wu <mwu@wustudios.co.nz>
From: Trent Tuiloma <ttuiloma@canterburyairport.co.nz>
Subject: Canterbury Airport project
Date: Monday, 2 July

Dear Mr. Wu,

Thank you for agreeing to consult on the Canterbury Airport redesign project. _____ **139.** . As a result, I am particularly eager to hear your ideas about upgrading our main terminal.

Can we meet this week? There are a number of _____ **140.** restaurants near my office. If you are available this Friday, we could meet at Celia's Café on Cumberland Street. I would also like a few of my colleagues to _____ **141.** us. They would appreciate _____ **142.** ways to enhance the airport user's experience.

I look forward to hearing from you soon.

Sincerely,

Trent Tuiloma
Chairman, Canterbury Airport Redesign Team

請參考以下電子郵件，回答第 139 至 142 題。

收件者：Mason Wu <mwu@wustudios.co.nz>
寄件者：Trent Tuiloma <ttuiloma@canterburyairport.co.nz>
主旨：Canterbury 機場計畫
日期：7 月 2 日，週一

親愛的 Wu 先生，

感謝您同意對 Canterbury 機場重新設計計畫提供諮詢。* **我一直很欽佩您為地區機場所做的努力。**因此，我特別渴望聽聽您對升級我們主要航廈的想法。

這週我們可以見個面嗎？我的辦公室附近有許多很棒的餐廳，如果您這週五有空，我們可以在 Cumberland 街的 Celia's 咖啡廳見面。我也想請幾位同事加入我們，他們會很高興討論提升機場使用者體驗的方法。

期待能早日收到您的回覆。

致上誠摯敬意

Trent Tuiloma
Canterbury 機場重新設計團隊主席

*第 139 題插入句的翻譯

139. | Can connect information across multiple sentences in a single written text and across texts

(A) I can meet you when you arrive.
(B) Scheduling flights can be quite tricky.
(C) I have long admired your work on regional airports.
(D) There are several dining options at the airport.

(A) 當您抵達時我可以跟您見面。
(B) 安排航班可能非常棘手。
(C) 我一直很欽佩您為地區機場所做的努力。
(D) 機場有許多餐飲的選擇。

正解 (C)

重點解說

空格前的句子是「感謝您同意對 Canterbury 機場重新設計計畫提供諮詢」，空格後的句子是「因此，我特別渴望聽聽您對升級我們主要航廈的想法」，因此空格應填入選項 (C)，表明對於 Wu 先生工作的敬佩，上下文意通順流暢，故為正解。regional「地區的、區域的」。
(A) arrive「抵達」；(B) tricky「棘手的」。

💡 應試者能理解電子郵件的內容，並能透過前後句子判斷最符合句意的答案。

140. Can understand grammar in written texts

(A) excel　　　　　　　　　　　　　　　(A) 勝過（現在式動詞）
(B) excellent　　　　　　　　　　　　**(B) 出色的（形容詞）**
(C) excellently　　　　　　　　　　　　(C) 出色地（副詞）
(D) excelled　　　　　　　　　　　　　(D) 勝過（過去分詞）

重點解說

正解 (B)
空格之後為名詞 restaurant「餐廳」，因此空格應填入形容詞來修飾名詞，唯有選項 (B) 最為合適，故為正解。

💡 應試者能理解書面文本中的文法，選出 excel「勝過」在文章中的適當時態與詞性。

141. Can connect information across multiple sentences in a single written text and across texts

Can understand vocabulary in written texts

(A) join　　　　　　　　　　　　　　**(A) 參加**
(B) pay　　　　　　　　　　　　　　　(B) 付錢
(C) remind　　　　　　　　　　　　　(C) 提醒
(D) defend　　　　　　　　　　　　　(D) 保衛

重點解說

正解 (A)
包含空格的句子意思是「我也想請幾位同事 ＿＿＿ 我們」，上一句指出「我們可以在 Cumberland 街的 Celia's 咖啡廳見面」，此部分的電子郵件是關於共事的人計畫碰面的內容，因此空格應填入 (A) join「加入、參加」，語意最為合適，故為正解。

💡 應試者能透過段落中的前後句子，判斷最符合句意的答案。

💡 應試者能理解書面文本中的詞彙、了解文章內容，並從四個不同動詞中選出正確答案。

142. Can understand grammar in written texts

(A) to discuss　　　　　　　　　　　(A) 討論（不定詞）
(B) discussing　　　　　　　　　　**(B) 討論（動名詞）**
(C) discuss　　　　　　　　　　　　(C) 討論（原形動詞）
(D) discussed　　　　　　　　　　　(D) 討論（過去分詞）

重點解說

正解 (B)
空格之前有動詞 appreciate「感激」，appreciate 後面須接名詞或動名詞，唯有選項 (B) 最符合文法規則，故為正解。

💡 應試者能理解書面文本中的文法，選出動詞 discuss「討論」在文章中的適當時態。

Questions 143-146 refer to the following e-mail.

To: anna.goldstein@mail.com
From: jhlee@lindstromuniversity.co.uk
Subject: Executive Management Certificate
Date: 10 February

Dear Anna,

On behalf of Lindstrom University, I am writing to welcome you to the Executive Management Certificate program.

As a member of the incoming class, you ‾‾‾143.‾‾‾ in an intensive yearlong online curriculum. While the majority of the training takes place via online classes, the program begins with a three-day ‾‾‾144.‾‾‾ workshop to be held on the campus of Lindstrom University from 25 to 27 May.

Prior to the session, you will have access to course materials as well as some preliminary assignments. These assignments must be completed ‾‾‾145.‾‾‾ the training in May. We will use this work as a starting point for the workshop. ‾‾‾146.‾‾‾ .

Many congratulations, Anna. We look forward to seeing you in May.

Ju Hae Lee
Dean of Admission, Lindstrom University

請參考以下電子郵件，回答第 143 至 146 題。

收件者：anna.goldstein@mail.com
寄件者：jhlee@lindstromuniversity.co.uk
主旨：行政管理證書
日期：2 月 10 日

親愛的 Anna，

謹代表 Lindstrom 大學寫信歡迎你參加行政管理證書學程。

身為新生班的一員，你將會參加為期一年的密集線上課程。雖然大多數的培訓課程都是線上進行，但這個課程將從 5 月 25 日到 27 日在 Lindstrom 大學校園舉行為期三天的入門工作坊作為開端。

課程開始之前，你會得到課程教材以及一些預習作業，這些作業必須在五月的培訓前完成，我們將以這份作業作為工作坊的起點。* 我們期望學生們認真看待每一項作業。

非常恭喜你 Anna，我們期待在五月與你相見。

Ju Hae Lee
Lindstrom 大學招生主任

*第 146 題插入句的翻譯

143. | Can connect information across multiple sentences in a single written text and across texts

(A) participated
(B) will be participating
(C) have participated
(D) have been participating

(A) 參加（過去式）
(B) 參加（未來進行式）
(C) 參加（現在完成式）
(D) 參加（現在完成進行式）

重點解說

正解 (B)

空格前的句子是「身為新生班的一員」，可以得知目前課程尚未開始，因此空格應填入未來式，故選項 (B) 為正解。

💡 應試者能透過段落中的前後句子，連結文章訊息並選出正確的動詞形態。

144. Can understand grammar in written texts

(A) introduce
(B) introducing
(C) introductory
(D) introductorily

(A) 介紹（現在式）
(B) 介紹（現在分詞）
(C) 首次的（形容詞）
(D) 首次地（副詞）

重點解說

正解 (C)
空格之後有名詞 workshop「工作坊」，因此空格應填入形容詞，修飾後面的名詞，故選項 (C) introductory「首次的」語意最通順，故為正解。

💡 應試者能理解書面文本中的文法，並根據前後句子判斷 introduce「介紹」在文章中的適當時態與詞性。

---

145. Can connect information across multiple sentences in a single written text and across texts

Can understand vocabulary in written texts

(A) before
(B) behind
(C) despite
(D) throughout

(A) 在…之前
(B) 在…後面
(C) 儘管
(D) 遍及

重點解說

正解 (A)
包含空格的句子意思是「這些作業必須完成 ＿＿＿ 五月的培訓」，後一句子表示，「我們將以這份作業作為工作坊的起點」，由此可知，這些作業必須在上課前完成，選項 (A) before「之前」最為合適，故為正解。

💡 應試者能透過段落中的前後句子，連結文章訊息。

💡 應試者能理解書面文本中的詞彙、了解文章內容，並從四個不同介系詞中選出正確答案。

---

146. Can connect information across multiple sentences in a single written text and across texts

(A) You performed very well in your interview.
(B) Your application stood out to the faculty.
(C) Thank you for attending all of the preliminary sessions.
(D) We expect students to give each assignment careful attention.

(A) 你在面試時表現得很好。
(B) 你的申請書在教職員中脫穎而出。
(C) 感謝你參加所有的先修課程。
(D) 我們期望學生們認真看待每一項作業。

重點解說

正解 (D)
空格前的句子是「我們將以這份作業作為工作坊的起點」，空格應填入選項 (D)，表示這些作業的重要性，再接續說明希望學生能認真完成作業，上下文意通順流暢，故為正解。

💡 應試者能理解信件的內容，並能透過段落中的前後句子判斷最符合句意的答案。

題目／中文翻譯

Questions 147-148 refer to the following coupon.

AMS
Encounters with Science and Technology
$3 OFF

$3 off the price of one admission

❶ Present this coupon at AMS and receive $3 off one general admission ticket. Limit one per household. Coupon cannot be combined with any other offers, including group rates and senior discount tickets. Valid for all permanent exhibits and galleries (not valid for featured exhibits or planetarium).

❷ Regular hours: Tue–Sun, 9 a.m.–5 p.m.
❸ Summer hours (June 12–September 5):
Open every day 9 a.m.–7 p.m.

1 011000110 011110100 0

請參考以下折價券，回答第 147 至 148 題。

AMS
科學和科技的邂逅
$3 折價券

一張門票優惠 3 美元

在 AMS 出示此折價券，一張全票可折扣 3 美元，每戶家庭限使用一張。折價券不得和其他優惠合併使用，包含團體票價以及敬老優待票。適用所有常設展以及畫廊（不適用於特展或天文館）。

正常開放時間：週二到週日上午 9 點到下午 5 點
夏季時間（6 月 12 日至 9 月 5 日）：
每日上午 9 點到晚上 7 點開放

1 011000110 011110100 0

147.  Can make inferences based on information in written texts

What most likely is AMS?

(A) A museum
(B) A repair facility
(C) An electronics store
(D) An energy provider

AMS 最有可能是什麼？

(A) 博物館
(B) 維修中心
(C) 電子產品商店
(D) 能源供應者

重點解說

正解 (A)

從❶第三行到第四行可知，這張折價券「適用所有常設展以及畫廊（不適用於特展或天文館）。」由此可推斷，AMS 是一間擁有展覽和畫廊的博物館，故選項 (A) 為正解。

💡 應試者能理解文本內容，並從折價券的細節推斷出主題和目的。

148.

Can make inferences based on information in written texts

Can connect information across multiple sentences in a single written text and across texts

What happens at AMS during the summer?

(A) It closes earlier.
(B) It opens at a later time.
(C) It is open an extra day.
(D) It is closed for special events.

夏季期間 AMS 會發生什麼事？

(A) 提早關門。
(B) 比較晚開門。
(C) 多開放一天。
(D) 為了特殊活動而關閉。

重點解說

正解 (C)

從❷可得知，平常開放時間為週二到週日，然而❸指出，夏季營業時間為每天早上 9 點到晚上 7 點，由此可知，夏季時博物館也會在週一營業，比平常多一天，故選項 (C) 為正解。

💡 應試者能理解折價券所傳達的內容，並從文本中的細節做出推斷。

💡 應試者能理解折價券的內容，並連結上下訊息選出正確答案。

Questions 149-150 refer to the following e-mail.

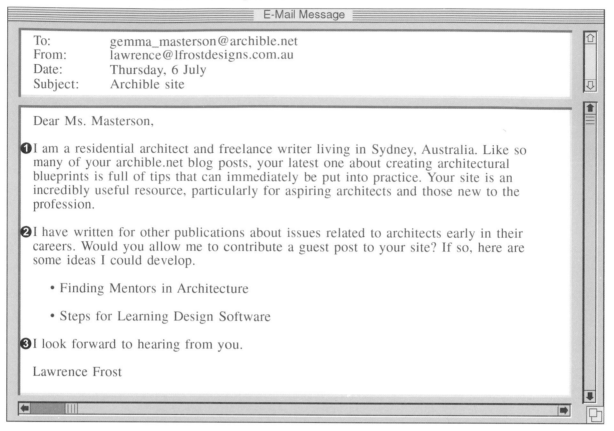

請參考以下電子郵件，回答第 **149** 至 **150** 題。

149. `Can make inferences based on information in written texts`

What does Mr. Frost suggest he likes about archible.net?

(A) **Its informative content**
(B) Its interactive features
(C) Its directory of architects
(D) Its collection of drawing tools

Frost 先生表示他喜歡 archible.net 的什麼？

(A) **具資訊性的內容**
(B) 具互動功能
(C) 建築師名錄
(D) 繪圖工具的收藏

重點解說

正解 (A)

❶第二行 Frost 先生提到，最新一篇文章充滿了可以立即運用在實務的技巧。選項 (A) informative content 指的是❶第三行所提到的 tips「技巧」，故為正解。
(B) interactive「互動的」；(C) directory「指南、名錄」；(D) collection「收藏」。

💡 應試者能理解電子郵件的內容，並從細節做出推斷。

150. `Can connect information across multiple sentences in a single written text and across texts`

What does Mr. Frost list in the e-mail?

(A) Articles he published on his own site
(B) Posts by Ms. Masterson that he enjoyed
(C) Problems he noticed on the Web site
(D) **Topics that he would like to write about**

Frost 先生在電子郵件中列出什麼？

(A) 他在自己的網站發布的文章
(B) 他喜歡的 Masterson 小姐的文章
(C) 他在網站上注意到的問題
(D) **關於他想寫的主題**

重點解說

正解 (D)

❷第二行 Frost 先生詢問，「請問能讓我在妳的網站投稿一篇客座文章嗎？」並補充說明「如果可以，以下是一些我可以發揮的想法」。由電子郵件的開頭我們可知 Frost 先生是自由作家，而他列的兩點是他為自己潛在的客座文章所提出的寫作主題，故選項 (D) 為正解。

💡 應試者能理解此電子郵件的資訊，並判別信件中列點的目的。

Questions 151-152 refer to the following information.

Springfield Community School
Computer Courses

Internet Safety
❶ This course teaches students everything they need to navigate the Web safely.

	Course ID	Class Time	Instructor	Room
❷	249800: 01	Tuesday 5:30–7:30 P.M.	Patrick McCann	211
❸	249800: 02	Saturday 1:00–3:00 P.M.	Nora Farid	166

Spreadsheet Basics
❹ This course teaches the basics of online spreadsheets. Students will learn how to create effective charts for calculating and analyzing data clearly and easily.

	Course ID	Class Time	Instructor	Room
❺	225810: 01	Thursday 5:30–8:30 P.M.	Remi Sanders	118
❻	225810: 02	Sunday 1:00–4:00 P.M.	Nora Farid	315

請參考以下資訊，回答第 151 至 152 題。

Springfield 社區學校
電腦課程

網路安全
本課程教導學生安全瀏覽網頁所需的一切。

課程代號	上課時間	講師	教室
249800: 01	週二下午 5:30 到 7:30	Patrick McCann	211
249800: 02	週六下午 1:00 到 3:00	Nora Farid	166

電子試算表基礎
本課程教導線上試算表的基礎知識。學生們將學習如何建立有效的圖表，以便清晰易懂且不費力地計算並分析數據。

課程代號	上課時間	講師	教室
225810: 01	週四下午 5:30 到 8:30	Remi Sanders	118
225810: 02	週日下午 1:00 到 4:00	Nora Farid	315

151. Can connect information across multiple sentences in a single written text and across texts

Why would people enroll in the course taught by Ms. Sanders?

(A) To practice designing Web sites
(B) To improve their Internet searches
(C) To get tips on creating spreadsheets
(D) To learn how to advertise on the Internet

為什麼大家要報名參加由 Sanders 小姐教學的課程？

(A) 為了練習網站設計
(B) 為了改善他們的網路搜尋能力
(C) 為了獲得建立試算表的技巧
(D) 為了學習如何在網路上做廣告

重點解說

正解 (C)
❺標示了 Sanders 小姐的上課資訊，由此可知，她是教試算表相關的知識。❹第一行到第三行說明這堂課會教線上試算表的基礎知識，以及「如何建立有效的圖表，以便清晰易懂且不費力地計算並分析數據。」故選項 (C) 為正解。spreadsheet「電子試算表」。

💡 應試者能理解此文本中的內容，並能連結課程的介紹與資訊，選出正確答案。

152. Can connect information across multiple sentences in a single written text and across texts

What is indicated about Ms. Farid?

(A) She also teaches children.
(B) She is Ms. Sanders' supervisor.
(C) She teaches twice a week.
(D) She used to work as a data analyst.

關於 Farid 小姐，以下敘述何者正確？

(A) 她也教小孩。
(B) 她是 Sanders 小姐的主管。
(C) 她一週授課兩次。
(D) 她曾經當過數據分析師。

重點解說

正解 (C)
從❸得知，Farid 小姐在週六有一堂關於網路安全的課程，此外，❻Farid 小姐在週日還有一堂電子試算表基礎課程。由此可知，Farid 小姐一週教兩堂課，故選項 (C) 為正解。
(B) supervisor「主管、指導者」。

💡 應試者能理解此文本中的內容，並能連結課程的介紹與資訊，選出正確答案。

Questions 153-154 refer to the following text-message chain.

Sally Witham (4:47 P.M.)
❶ Hi Wakiko. I just finished up here at the Kyoto store. I'll be on the train that arrives in Tokyo at 11:35 tomorrow morning. How should I get to your location?

Wakiko Ohara (4:48 P.M.)
❷ I'll have an associate pick you up at the station. How do things look in Kyoto?

Sally Witham (4:49 P.M.)
❸ The Kyoto store is doing a great job. It has everything that we at the home office are looking for. Athletic shoes and sandals are displayed according to specifications, and sales associates are friendly and knowledgeable.

Wakiko Ohara (4:51 P.M.)
❹ You should like things here, too. Do you want to begin your visit after lunch, say at 2:00?

Sally Witham (4:52 P.M.)
❺ Sounds good. See you tomorrow.

153. Can make inferences based on information in written texts

Why did Ms. Witham contact Ms. Ohara?

(A) To review sales figures
(B) To arrange a store visit
(C) To discuss employee performance reviews
(D) To determine the most convenient train to take

為什麼 Witham 小姐要聯絡 Ohara 小姐？

(A) 為了檢視銷售額
(B) 為了安排巡店
(C) 為了討論員工績效評估
(D) 為了決定最便利的火車

重點解說

正解 (B)
❸ Witham 小姐提到京都店的優點，❹ Ohara 小姐詢問 Witham 小姐「妳想在午餐後開始巡店嗎，2 點如何？」由此可知，此次聯繫主要是要安排巡店，故選項 (B) 為正解。
(A) sales figures「銷售額」；(C) performance reviews「績效評估」。

💡 應試者能理解簡訊內容，並從對話細節推斷出目的。

請參考以下簡訊內容，回答第 153 至 154 題。

> **Sally Witham**（下午 4:47）
> Wakiko 妳好，我剛完成在京都店的工作。明天早上我將會搭乘 11:35 抵達東京的火車。我該怎麼前往妳的位置呢？

> **Wakiko Ohara**（下午 4:48）
> 我會請一位同事去車站接妳。京都的情況如何？

> **Sally Witham**（下午 4:49）
> 京都店表現得很好，它有我們總店期待的一切。運動鞋和涼鞋都按照規範擺設，而且銷售人員很親切博學。

> **Wakiko Ohara**（下午 4:51）
> 妳應該也會喜歡這裡的。妳想在午餐後開始巡店嗎，2 點如何？

> **Sally Witham**（下午4:52）
> 聽起來不錯，明天見。

154.
> Can make inferences based on information in written texts

> Can connect information across multiple sentences in a single written text and across texts

At 4:51 P.M., what does Ms. Ohara most likely mean when she writes, "You should like things here, too"?

(A) The Tokyo store is being run according to corporate policy.
(B) Ms. Witham will find the athletic shoes she needs.
(C) Ms. Ohara's associate is always punctual.
(D) The Tokyo store is located next to a popular restaurant.

下午 4:51，Ohara 小姐說「You should like things here, too」最有可能代表什麼？

(A) 東京店正按照公司政策經營。
(B) Witham 小姐將會找到她需要的運動鞋。
(C) Ohara 小姐的同事總是很準時。
(D) 東京店位在一間熱門的餐廳隔壁。

重點解說

正解 (A)

❸Witham 小姐提到京都店的優點，包含第三行到第四行「運動鞋和涼鞋都按照規範擺設」，以及第五行到第六行「銷售人員很親切博學」。❹Ohara 小姐回覆「妳應該也會喜歡這裡的」，表示東京店也是按照公司政策經營，故選項 (A) 為正解。run「經營」，corporate「公司的」。
(C) associate「同事、夥伴」，punctual「準時的」。

💡 應試者能理解簡訊內容，並從對話細節推斷出目的。

💡 應試者能理解此訊息的內容，並將上下訊息的對話連接起來，選出正確的答案。

Questions 155-157 refer to the following report.

❶ **Structure:** Blaine River Drawbridge	❹ **Location:** Ridgeline Highway, KM 147
❷ **Main span material:** Steel girder	❺ **Owner:** State Highway Agency
❸ **Age of structure:** 30 years	❻ **Report completed by:** Vivian Tulio
	❼ **Date:** October 17

❽ **Notes:**
The bridge is overall structurally sound. Inform Department of Transportation about small cracks in asphalt.

❾ Bridge component	Rating	❿ Key to ratings
Support elements	4	**1** Failed; immediate closure required
Towers	4	**2** Deteriorated; may fail soon
Road surface	3	**3** Shows deterioration but still functions within acceptable parameters
Drainage features	4	**4** Shows minor wear
Safety barriers	5	**5** New condition
Sidewalk or walkway	6	**6** Not applicable

請參考以下報告，回答第 155 至 157 題。

建造物：Blaine River 吊橋	地點：Ridgeline 公路 147 公里
主跨材料：鋼梁	隸屬：州公路局
建物年齡：30 年	製作報告者：Vivian Tulio
	日期：10 月 17 日

備註：
橋梁整體結構完好。通知交通部關於柏油上的小裂縫。

橋梁構件	評分	評分指標
支撐構件	4	1 坍塌；需要即刻關閉
橋塔	4	2 損壞；可能很快會坍塌
橋面	3	3 呈現劣化狀態但仍在可接受範圍內運作
排水系統	4	4 呈現輕微磨損
安全護欄	5	5 全新狀態
人行道或走道	6	6 不適用

155. Can make inferences based on information in written texts

What did Ms. Tulio most likely do? | Tulio 小姐最有可能做了什麼？

(A) Make repairs
(B) Hire a contractor
(C) Perform an inspection
(D) Authorize a construction plan

(A) 維修
(B) 雇用承包商
(C) 執行檢驗
(D) 核准施工計畫

正解 (C)

重點解說

❶指出這次評估的建物為 Blaine River 吊橋，❽備註寫到「橋梁整體結構完好。通知交通部關於柏油上的小裂縫」，❾為各項吊橋組成部分評分。由此可推知，Tulio 小姐填寫的是檢查報告，故選項 (C) 為正解。
(B) contractor「承包商」；(D) authorize「核准、授權」，construction「建造、施工」。

💡 應試者能理解報告所傳達的目的，並從文本細節推斷出正確答案。

156. Can connect information across multiple sentences in a single written text and across texts

What part of the structure is in most need of maintenance? | 這項建造物的哪一部份最需要維修？

(A) The support elements
(B) The road surface
(C) The drainage features
(D) The safety barriers

(A) 支撐構件
(B) 橋面
(C) 排水系統
(D) 安全護欄

正解 (B)

重點解說

❿「評分指標」可得知每一個分數代表的狀況。選項 (B) the road surface「橋面」為 3 分，代表「呈現劣化狀態但仍在可接受範圍內運作」，由此可知，橋面是最需要加強維護的，故為正解。
(A) the support elements「支撐構件」和 (C) the drainage features「排水系統」為 4 分，代表「呈現輕微磨損」；
(D) the safety barriers「安全護欄」為 5 分，代表「全新狀態」。故選項 (A)、(C)、(D) 皆不符合題意。

💡 應試者能連結報告評分以及評分指標的含意，理解橋梁構件的狀況。

157. Can make inferences based on information in written texts

Can connect information across multiple sentences in a single written text and across texts

What is probably true about the Blaine River Drawbridge? | 關於 Blaine River 吊橋，下列敘述何者可能為真？

(A) It was not designed for pedestrian use.
(B) It will be closed for the month of October.
(C) It does not have the required signage.
(D) It is the oldest bridge on the Ridgeline Highway.

(A) 它不是設計給行人使用。
(B) 它將在 10 月關閉。
(C) 它沒有所需要的標示牌。
(D) 它是 Ridgeline 公路上最老的橋。

正解 (A)

重點解說

從❹得知這個吊橋位於 Ridgeline 公路上，由此可推斷，吊橋是給汽車行駛的，並非設計給行人通行。此外，❾橋梁構件中的 Sidewalk or walkway「人行道或走道」項目，其評分為 6，根據❿評分指標，6 表示「不適用」，這表示吊橋無法讓行人走動通行。故選項 (A) 為正解。pedestrian「行人」。
(B)❼所指的日期是檢查報告的日期，而不是吊橋關閉的日期。
(C) signage「標示牌、廣告牌」。

💡 應試者能理解報告所傳達的目的，並從文本細節推斷出正確答案。

💡 應試者能將報告提及的資訊連接起來，理解文章的訊息含意。

TEST 2

Questions 158-160 refer to the following article.

Alma Poised for Growth

❶This month has seen a huge jump in sales of Condor PX brand wheat seed in Argentina. Last year, across much of this nation, there were above-average temperatures and below-average rainfall, causing fields to <u>yield</u> sharply less wheat overall. But despite the adverse weather conditions, Condor PX wheat did comparatively well.

❷Condor PX was bred by Alma Seed Company in Brazil. Although Alma has been selling Condor PX through its Argentinian distributors for several years, it was slow to catch on until now. Investors also have taken notice of Alma's rapidly improving fortunes.

請參考以下文章，回答第 **158** 至 **160** 題。

Alma 蓄勢待發

本月，Condor PX 牌小麥種子在阿根廷的銷售量大幅增長。去年全國大部分地區，高於平均的氣溫及低於平均的降雨量，造成麥田整體<u>生產量</u>大幅降低。但儘管天氣條件不利，Condor PX 小麥的表現相對較好。

Condor PX 是由巴西的 Alma 種子公司所培育出來的。雖然多年來 Alma 一直透過阿根廷的經銷商銷售 Condor PX，但直到現在才流行起來。投資者也注意到 Alma 的迅速增長。

158. Can locate and understand specific information in written texts

According to the article, what is one condition that affected wheat harvests?

(A) Excessive rain
(B) Unusually warm weather
(C) A shortage of wheat seeds
(D) A loss of wheat fields

根據這篇文章，影響小麥收成的條件之一是什麼？

(A) 過多的雨量
(B) 異常溫暖的天氣
(C) 小麥種子短缺
(D) 麥田的損失

重點解說

正解 (B)

從❶第三行到第五行得知，「高於平均的氣溫及低於平均的降雨量，造成麥田整體生產量大幅降低。」故選項 (B) 為正解。

(A) excessive「過多的」；(C) shortage「缺少」。

💡 應試者能理解文章中的事件與資訊，並能透過關鍵訊息，選出正確的答案。

159. Can understand vocabulary in written texts

The word "yield" in paragraph 1, line 5, is closest in meaning to

(A) allow
(B) fail
(C) follow
(D) produce

下列哪一個選項與第一段第五行的「yield」，意思最為接近？

(A) 允許
(B) 失敗
(C) 跟隨
(D) 生產

重點解說

正解 (D)

❶第三行到第五行提到，「高於平均的氣溫及低於平均的降雨量，造成麥田整體生產量大幅降低。」選項 (D) 動詞形式的 produce「生產」，意思最接近 yield 在此句的前後文，使語意最為通順，故為正解。

💡 應試者能理解書面文本中的詞彙，並能選出可替換的單字。

160. Can make inferences based on information in written texts

According to the article, what did Alma Seed Company do?

(A) Relocate to Argentina
(B) Purchase Condor PX
(C) Develop a type of wheat
(D) Invest in a new company

根據這篇文章，Alma 種子公司做了什麼？

(A) 搬遷至阿根廷
(B) 購買 Condor PX
(C) 研發出一種小麥
(D) 投資一間新公司

重點解說

正解 (C)

❶第六行到第八行得知，「儘管天氣條件不利，Condor PX 小麥的表現相對較好。」由此可知，Condor PX 是一種小麥的品種。而從❷第一行得知，Condor PX 是 Alma 種子公司所培育，故選項 (C) 為正解。

(A) relocate「搬遷」；(D) invest「投資」。

💡 應試者能推斷文章內容的主要目的，並能針對細節做出推論。

Questions 161-163 refer to the following e-mail.

To:	All Staff
From:	Selene Hong
Date:	March 25
Subject:	Reminder

Dear Staff,

❶I would like to draw your attention to several new procedures regarding business trip expense reports. — [1] —. Beginning next month, business-related dining receipts must be accompanied by a listing of each dinner attendee. Also, please make sure that you do not include receipts for any non-work-related items or activities with your report. — [2] —. Finally, note that our accounting software will now automatically calculate for you the total to be reimbursed. You need only to upload images of your receipts for the software to do this.

❷I will be happy to respond to your questions. — [3] —. However, I will be flying to Tokyo this Friday to meet clients, so I will not be checking e-mail that day. — [4] —.

Sincerely,

Selene Hong
Assistant Director, Human Resources Department
Datoric Systems

請參考以下電子郵件，回答第 161 至 163 題。

收件者：	全體員工
寄件者：	Selene Hong
日期：	3 月 25 日
主旨：	提醒事項

親愛的同仁，

我想請你們注意一些關於出差費用報告的新程序。*跟著這些步驟將讓我們加快發放你的核銷費用。從下個月開始，業務相關的餐飲收據必須附上每位用餐出席者的名單。除此之外，請確保你的報告中不包含任何非工作相關之物品或活動收據。最後，請知悉我們的會計軟體現在可以幫你自動計算核銷的總金額，你只需要上傳收據的影像讓軟體來處理。

我很樂意回覆各位的問題。不過，本週五我將會飛往東京與客戶會面，所以那天不會查看電子郵件。

誠摯地祝福

Selene Hong
人力資源部門副總監
Datoric 系統公司

*第 163 題插入句的翻譯

161. Can locate and understand specific information in written texts

What is indicated about Datoric Systems?

(A) It has increased the spending amount allowed for business dinners.

(B) It will adopt new procedures for filing travel expense reports.

(C) It has office locations in several countries.

(D) It plans to hold a company celebration.

關於 Datoric 系統公司，下列敘述何者正確？

(A) 它提高了商務晚餐的消費金額。

(B) 它將採用新的程序來填報差旅費用報告。

(C) 它在許多國家有辦公室駐點。

(D) 它計畫舉行公司慶祝活動。

重點解說

正解 (B)

❶ 第一行「我想請你們注意一些關於出差費用報告的新程序。」由此可知，這封電子郵件的目的是為了告訴員工新的差旅費核銷程序，故選項 (B) 為正解。expense「花費、費用」。

💡 應試者能理解電子郵件中的訊息，即使選項改寫，也能選出正確答案。

---

162. Can locate and understand specific information in written texts

Why is the accounting software mentioned?

(A) To highlight a special capability it has

(B) To encourage staff to install it

(C) To help employees log on to it

(D) To point out that it will be replaced

為什麼提到會計軟體？

(A) 強調它具備的特殊功能

(B) 鼓勵員工安裝

(C) 幫助職員登入

(D) 指出它將會被取代

重點解說

正解 (A)

❶ 第五行到第七行提到，「我們的會計軟體現在可以幫你自動計算核銷的總金額，你只需要上傳收據的影像讓軟體來處理。」由此可知，提到會計軟體是為了告知員工可以用它來計算費用，故選項 (A) 為正解。(B) install「安裝」；(C) log on「登入」。

💡 應試者能理解電子郵件中的實際資訊，即使內文沒有直接說明，也能選出正確答案。

---

163. Can make inferences based on information in written texts

Can connect information across multiple sentences in a single written text and across texts

In which of the positions marked [1], [2], [3], and [4] does the following sentence best belong?

"Following these steps will enable us to quickly issue your reimbursement payment."

(A) [1]

(B) [2]

(C) [3]

(D) [4]

在標示 [1]、[2]、[3]、[4] 的地方中，哪一處最適合插入下列句子？

「跟著這些步驟將讓我們加快發放你的核銷費用。」

(A) [1]

(B) [2]

(C) [3]

(D) [4]

重點解說

正解 (A)

❶ 第二行到第三行提到，「業務相關的餐飲收據必須附上每位用餐出席者的名單。」❶ 第三行到第四行提到，「請確保你的報告中不包含任何非工作相關之物品或活動收據」，在 [1] 插入句子，these steps「這些步驟」承接❶ 第二行到第四行所提到報銷時要留意的事項，上下文意通順，故選項 (A) 為正解。

💡 應試者能推斷電子郵件的目的，並能針對細節做出推論。

💡 應試者能連結電子郵件中提及的資訊，以此判斷信件目的。

題目／中文翻譯

Questions 164-167 refer to the following text-message chain.

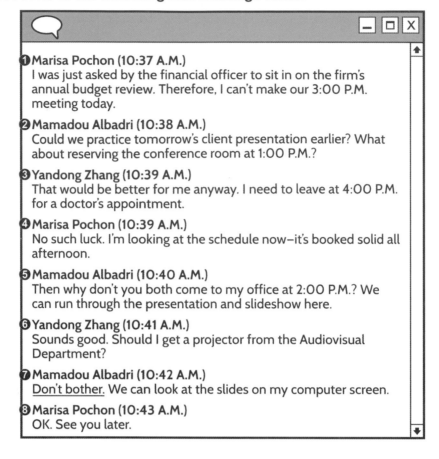

請參考以下簡訊對話，回答第 164 到 167 題。

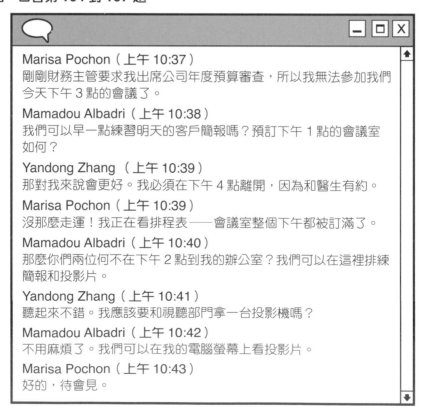

164.

`Can locate and understand specific information in written texts`

Why is Ms. Pochon unavailable at 3:00 P.M.?

(A) She has a phone call with important clients.

(B) She has to give a presentation.

(C) She has been asked to attend a meeting.

(D) She has a medical appointment.

為什麼 Pochon 小姐下午 3 點沒空？

(A) 她要和重要客戶通電話。

(B) 她要發表簡報。

(C) 她被要求參加一個會議。

(D) 她有預約看診。

重點解說

正解 (C)

❶Pochon 小姐被財務主管要求出席公司年度預算審查，所以沒辦法參加下午 3 點的會議，由此可知，Pochon 小姐下午 3 點有別的會議要出席，故選項 (C) 為正解。

(D) appointment「預約」。

💡 應試者能理解簡訊對話的實際資訊，即使問題換句話詢問，也能選出正確答案。

165.

`Can make inferences based on information in written texts`

Why does Mr. Albadri suggest using his office?

(A) Because it can accommodate a lot of people

(B) Because it is located near the finance office

(C) Because his audiovisual equipment has been upgraded

(D) Because the conference room is unavailable

為什麼 Albadri 先生提議使用他的辦公室？

(A) 因為它可以容納很多人

(B) 因為它位於財務辦公附近

(C) 因為他的視聽設備升級了

(D) 因為會議室不能使用

重點解說

正解 (D)

❹當 Pochon 小姐在看會議室的排程時提到，「會議室整個下午都被訂滿了。」由此可知，他們沒辦法預約會議室，故選項 (D) 為正解。unavailable「不能使用的」。

(A) accommodate「容納」；(C) audiovisual「視聽的」，equipment「設備、器材」。

💡 應試者能理解簡訊對話所提及的資訊，並能針對文本中的細節做出推論。

166.

`Can make inferences based on information in written texts`

`Can connect information across multiple sentences in a single written text and across texts`

At 10:42 A.M., what does Mr. Albadri most likely mean when he writes, "Don't bother"?

(A) He should not be disturbed this afternoon.

(B) Ms. Pochon should not reserve a room.

(C) Mr. Zhang does not have to come to a meeting.

(D) Mr. Zhang does not need to bring a projector.

Albadri 先生在上午 10:42 寫到「Don't bother」，最有可能代表什麼意思？

(A) 今天下午他不應該被打擾。

(B) Pochon 小姐不應該預訂會議室。

(C) Zhang 先生不用去參加會議。

(D) Zhang 先生不用帶一台投影機。

重點解說

正解 (D)

❻Zhang 先生詢問「我應該要和視聽部門拿一台投影機嗎？」Albadri 先生回答❼底線句子「不用麻煩了。」後面接著回覆，「我們可以在我的電腦螢幕上看投影片」。由此可知，Zhang 先生不需要帶一台投影機到辦公室，故選項 (D) 為正解。projector「投影機」。

(B) reserve「預定、預約」。

💡 應試者能理解簡訊對話內容，並能針對細節做出推論。

💡 應試者能連結文本中提及的資訊，並判斷 Albadri 先生說話的目的。

167. | Can locate and understand specific information in written texts

When will the three people meet? 這三人將在幾點見面？

(A) At 1:00 P.M.

(B) At 2:00 P.M.

(C) At 3:00 P.M.

(D) At 4:00 P.M.

(A) 下午 1 點

(B) 下午 2 點

(C) 下午 3 點

(D) 下午 4 點

重點解說

正解 (B)

❺Albadri 先生詢問「那麼你們兩位何不在下午 2 點到我的辦公室？」❻Zhang 先生認為這個點子不錯，❽Pochon 小姐也提到「好的，待會見」。由此可知，他們三人下午 2 點會在 Albadri 先生的辦公室見面，故選項 (B) 為正解。

💡 應試者能理解簡訊對話中提到的實際資訊，並能從三人對話中，找出正確答案。

Questions 168-171 refer to the following article.

Nairobi Daily Journal

2 April

❶ Two supermarket chains are currently competing to be number one in Kenya. Both retailers, AT Mart and Duggan's, have announced that they are determined to place first with consumers. — [1] —.

❷ In March, AT Mart, which is based in the United Kingdom, announced it was planning to launch its first store in Nairobi. — [2] —. It is one of the largest supermarket chains in the world. Duggan's, on the other hand, is not well-known outside of Africa, but it is South Africa's most dominant supermarket chain and has established a presence here. Now there are eight Duggan's stores in Kenya with a loyal customer base.

❸ — [3] —. Some supermarket chains, such as Wentworth's, which is based in the United States, have not been willing to pay what they consider to be exorbitant leasing fees when their stores simply were not attracting a significant number of shoppers. As a result, Wentworth's closed all three of its stores after only two years in Kenya.

❹ Duggan's, however, has an advantage. — [4] —. The company created its own real estate division, D Properties Ltd. This company has built four shopping complexes with Duggan's as the main tenant in each. Moreover, Duggan's has paid special attention to tailoring its product inventory to the local culture. It also has developed an effective supply-and-delivery system to service its famous on-site bakeries, butcher shops, and produce sections. AT Mart may have much wider name recognition, but it will need to be more innovative to compete against the popular Duggan's.

--**Susan Kotter, Staff Reporter**

請參考以下報導，回答第 168 至 171 題。

奈洛比每日新聞

4 月 2 日

肯亞兩間連鎖超級市場目前正在爭奪第一。AT Mart 和 Duggan's 這兩間零售商，都宣告他們決心成為消費者的首選。

今年三月，總部位在英國的 AT Mart 宣布計畫在奈洛比開設第一間店。它是世界上最大的連鎖超市之一。另一方面，Duggan's 在非洲以外並不有名，但它是南非最主要的連鎖超市，並且早已進駐此地。現在肯亞有八間 Duggan's 的店面，並擁有忠實的客群。

* 理想的超市地點，租金通常特別貴。 有一些連鎖超市，例如總部位在美國的 Wentworth's，在店面無法吸引大量消費者的情況下，一直不願意支付他們認為過高的租賃費。因此，Wentworth's 在肯亞僅兩年就關閉了全部三間店。

然而，Duggan's 有一個優勢。該公司建立了自己的房地產事業處—— D 地產有限公司。這間公司已建造出四間購物中心，並由 Duggan's 做為每一間購物中心的主要承租者。此外，Duggan's 特別專注於針對當地文化調整產品庫存。它也開發出一套有效的供給和運送系統來服務知名的現場烘焙麵包店、肉舖和生鮮區。AT Mart 或許有更廣的品牌知名度，但它需要更具創新才能與廣受歡迎的 Duggan's 競爭。

——**本報記者 Susan Kotter**

*第 171 題插入句的翻譯

題目／中文翻譯

168. Can make inferences based on information in written texts

What is the article mainly about?

(A) Business strategies that work well
(B) The competition within an industry
(C) Places to find bargains in Kenya
(D) The growth of new shopping malls

這篇報導主要是關於什麼？

(A) 執行良好的商業策略
(B) 業內競爭
(C) 在肯亞能找到便宜貨的地方
(D) 新購物中心的成長

重點解說

正解 (B)

❶第一行提到「肯亞兩間連鎖超級市場目前正在爭奪第一。」兩間連鎖超市分別是 AT Mart 和 Duggan's。❷分別介紹 AT Mart 和 Duggan's 超市，❸提到其他連鎖超市 Wentworth's 的經營狀況，❹提及 Duggan's 的優勢。由此可知，這篇文章主要比較各連鎖超市產業，故選項 (B) 為正解。
(A) strategy「策略」；(C) bargain「便宜貨、議價」。

💡 應試者能從長篇報導中，找出細節並推斷出文章主旨。

169. Can locate and understand specific information in written texts

What is indicated about Wentworth's?

(A) It has a loyal customer base.
(B) Its branch stores were mostly in South Africa.
(C) Its business in Kenya was relatively short-lived.
(D) It is a family-owned enterprise.

關於 Wentworth's 的敘述何者正確？

(A) 它擁有忠實的客群。
(B) 它的分店大多位在南非。
(C) 它在肯亞的生意相對短暫。
(D) 它是一間家族企業。

重點解說

正解 (C)

❸第三行到第七行提到，當 Wentworth's 超市沒有吸引大量消費者時，不願意支付過高的租賃費用。接著補充，「因此，Wentworth's 在肯亞僅兩年就關閉了全部三間店。」由此可知，Wentworth's 超市的分店都沒有經營太久，故選項 (C) 為正解。short-lived「短暫的」。
(A) loyal「忠誠的」；(B) branch「分店」；(D) enterprise「企業」。

💡 應試者能理解報導中的實際資訊，並能透過關鍵訊息，選出正確答案。

170. Can connect information across multiple sentences in a single written text and across texts

What is NOT mentioned as an accomplishment of Duggan's?

(A) Establishing a real estate division
(B) Creating an efficient delivery system
(C) Setting up on-site bakeries
(D) Developing a global reputation

關於 Duggan's 的成就，下列哪一項沒有提到？

(A) 建立一個房地產事業處
(B) 開發一個有效的運送系統
(C) 設立現場烘焙的麵包店
(D) 發展全球的聲譽

重點解說

正解 (D)

選項 (A) 出現在❹第二行到第三行「該公司建立了自己的房地產事業處——D 地產股份有限公司。」(B)、(C) 則出現在❹第八行到第十一行「它也開發出一套有效的供給和運送系統來服務知名的現場烘焙麵包店」。唯有 (D) developing a global reputation「發展全球的名譽」在報導中並未提及，故為正解。reputation「名譽、聲望」。
(A) real estate「房地產」，division「處、分部」；(B) delivery「運送」；(C) on-site「現場的」。

💡 應試者能連結報導所提到的資訊，並能找到關鍵字，選出正確的答案。

171.

Can make inferences based on information in written texts

Can connect information across multiple sentences in a single written text and across texts

In which of the positions marked [1], [2], [3], and [4] does the following sentence best belong?

"Rents in desirable locations for supermarkets are often extremely high."

(A) [1]
(B) [2]
(C) [3]
(D) [4]

在標示 [1]、[2]、[3]、[4] 的地方中，哪一處最適合插入以下句子？

「理想的超市地點，租金通常特別貴。」

(A) [1]
(B) [2]
(C) [3]
(D) [4]

正解 (C)

重點解說

❸ 以 Wentworth's 超市為例，在第三行到第七行提到，「在店面無法吸引大量消費者的情況下，一直不願意支付他們認為過高的租賃費」，在 [3] 插入句子時，與後面 Wentworth's 超市不願支付過高的租賃費用的部分前後呼應，上下文意通順。desirable「渴望獲得的」。

💡 應試者能理解報導傳達的目的，並能針對細節做出推論。

💡 應試者能理解報導內容，並連結上下句子的訊息，選出正確答案。

Questions 172-175 refer to the following letter.

8 February

Ms. Mala Chelvi
60 Jalan Tun Razak
54200 Kuala Lumpur

Dear Ms. Chelvi,

❶ We are delighted to inform you that you have been nominated as a finalist for the Small Business Challenge competition this year. Now in its fifth year, this competition is designed to highlight innovative products and services launched by young entrepreneurs. The Web application that you developed, which provides a means of matching charitable organizations with volunteers, earned one of the top scores from our panel of judges.

❷ In the next round of the challenge, you will participate in a live presentation about your product before a panel of expert judges. The three people with the best presentations will receive one-time grants of MYR 10,000 each to invest in their businesses.

❸ Please go to sbc.org/competition and submit an outline of your presentation, a brief video that clearly <u>illustrates</u> the use of your application, and a passport-sized photograph of yourself. You will also need to sign a consent form allowing us to use your name and photo, if needed, in promotional materials on our Web site. The deadline for submission of these materials is 10 March.

Best regards,

Felix Pang

Felix Pang
Chairperson, Small Business Challenge Committee

請參考以下信件，回答第 172 至 175 題。

2 月 8 日

Mala Chelvi 小姐
Tun Razak 街 60 號
54200 吉隆坡

親愛的 Chelvi 小姐，

我們很高興通知您，您已經被提名為今年小型企業挑戰賽的決賽選手。這個競賽已邁入第五個年頭，旨在突顯由年輕企業家發展出的創新產品和服務。您所開發的網路應用程式，提供方法媒合慈善團體和志願者，在我們評審團中獲得最高分之一。

下一輪挑戰中，您將會參加一場現場簡報，在專業評審團面前介紹您的產品。獲得最佳簡報的三人，每位將獲得 10,000 元馬幣的一次性補助金來投資他們的事業。

請前往 sbc.org/competition 並提交您的簡報大綱、一個能清楚說明您的應用程式用途的短片，以及一張護照規格尺寸的個人照片。您也需要簽署一份同意書，允許我們在有需要的情況下，使用您的名字和照片作為網站宣傳素材。繳交這些資料的期限是 3 月 10 日。

獻上誠摯的祝福

Felix Pang

Felix Pang
小型企業挑戰委員會主席

172. Can locate and understand specific information in written texts

What is the purpose of the letter?

(A) To seek volunteers for an event
(B) To notify a contest finalist
(C) To sell business consultation services .
(D) To offer a small-business loan

這封信件的目的是什麼？

(A) 尋找活動的志願者
(B) 通知競賽的決賽選手
(C) 銷售企業顧問服務
(D) 提供小型企業貸款

重點解說

正解 (B)

❶第一行到第二行提到，「我們很高興通知您，您已經被提名為今年小型企業挑戰賽的決賽選手。」❷提及比賽模式，❸提及比賽需要繳交的文件和檔案。由此可知，這封信的目的是通知決賽選手比賽的相關訊息，故選項 (B) 為正解。

(A) volunteer「志願者」; (C) consultation「顧問、諮詢」; (D) loan「貸款」。

💡應試者能理解信件中實際資訊，並透過關鍵訊息，選出正確答案。

173. Can make inferences based on information in written texts

What does Ms. Chelvi most likely specialize in?

(A) Law
(B) Technology
(C) Finance
(D) Marketing

Chelvi 小姐最有可能專攻什麼？

(A) 法律
(B) 科技
(C) 財務
(D) 行銷

重點解說

正解 (B)

❶第四行到第五行提到，Chelvi 小姐開發的網路應用程式，提供方法媒合慈善團體和志願者。由此可知，Chelvi 小姐專攻科技，故選項 (B) 為正解。

💡應試者能理解信件內容所傳達的目的，並能從文本中的細節做出推論。

174. Can understand vocabulary in written texts

The word "illustrates" in paragraph 3, line 2, is closest in meaning to

(A) represents
(B) translates
(C) lightens
(D) decorates

下列哪一個選項與第三段第二行的「illustrates」意思最為接近？

(A) 說明
(B) 翻譯
(C) 減輕
(D) 裝飾

重點解說

正解 (A)

由❸第一行到第二行可知，必須繳交短片來說明應用程式的用途。其中選項 (A) represents「說明、表達」意思最接近，語意也最為合適，故為正解。

請注意，雖然 illustrate 有許多意思，但由此處的上下文，清楚表明在此的意思接近正確答案 represent，表示利用範例或比較來解釋某事。

💡應試者能理解書面文本中的詞彙，並選出可替換的單字。

175. Can connect information across multiple sentences in a single written text and across texts

What is Ms. Chelvi asked to do by March 10 ?

(A) Update a Web page design
(B) Give a presentation
(C) Sign a consent form
(D) Pay a fee

Chelvi 小姐在 3 月 10 日前要做什麼？

(A) 更新網頁設計
(B) 發表簡報
(C) 簽署同意書
(D) 付費

重點解說

正解 (C)

❸ 第三行提到，「您也需要簽署一份同意書」，接著第五行提到，繳交這些資料的期限為 3 月 10 日。這邊的資料也包含上述所提的 consent form「同意書」，故選項 (C) 為正解。consent「同意」。

(A) update「更新」；(D) fee「費用」。

💡 應試者能理解信件的內容，並連結文本中的訊息，選出正確的答案。

Questions 176-180 refer to the following letter and order.

1. 信件

Two Swan Press
72 Holywell Road, Edinburgh EH8 8PJ

4 December

Mr. Albert Morello
17 Peyton Avenue
Kingston 5
Jamaica, W.I.

Dear Mr. Morello:

❶ Enclosed please find your royalty payment for *Understanding Our Oceans*. You should have recently received an e-mail that listed the sales figures and the royalties due to you for the print and electronic versions of your book.

❷ We are proud to announce that Two Swan Press was given the Publisher of the Year Award by the UK Book Industry in October. We thank the authors who have worked with us since our founding five years ago.

❸ All Two Swan Press authors are entitled to an author discount of 40 percent off any title on our Web site. Simply use the code AUX1417 for your discount.

❹ If you have any questions at all, please do not hesitate to contact me.

Kind regards,

Sarah Wicklin

Sarah Wicklin

Encl.

2. 訂單

https://www.twoswanpress.co.uk/orderconfirmation

THANK YOU FOR YOUR ORDER!

❶ Special December Offer—free shipping on all orders over £35

❷ **Name:** Duncan Booth

❸ **E-mail:** mbooth@silvertech.co.uk

❹ **Date of purchase:** 12 December

❺ **Ship to:** Duncan Booth
321 Maslin St.
Coatbridge ML5 1LZ, Scotland, UK

❻ _1_ *Business in Our Lives* by Elaine Schuyler   £75.00
❼ Discount Applied (AUX1417)   −30.00
❽ Balance Due   £45.00
❾ Paid by Credit Card ****5732

❿ Items from multiple orders may be combined in the same package. We will notify you when your order has shipped.

請參考以下信件和訂單，回答第 176 至 180 題。

Two Swan 出版社
Holywell 路 72 號，愛丁堡 EH8 8PJ

12 月 4 日

Albert Morello 先生
Peyton 大道 17 號
Kingston 5
牙買加，西印度群島

親愛的 Morello 先生，

隨信附上《Understanding Our Oceans》的版稅款項。您最近應該已經收到一封電子郵件，上面列出您的書籍印刷版和電子書的銷售數字和版稅。

我們很自豪地宣布，Two Swan 出版社在 10 月獲得由英國圖書產業頒發的年度出版社獎。感謝自五年前成立以來與我們合作的作者們。

所有 Two Swan 出版社的作者在我們網站上購買任何書都能享有六折的作者優惠，只要輸入折扣碼 AUX1417 即可使用優惠。

如果您有任何問題，請隨時與我聯繫。

致上親切的問候
Sarah Wicklin

附件

https://www.twoswanpress.co.uk/orderconfirmation

感謝您的訂購！

12 月特別優惠——訂單金額超過 35 英鎊免運費

姓名：	Duncan Booth
電子郵件：	mbooth@silvertech.co.uk
購買日期：	12 月 12 日
配送資訊：	Duncan Booth Maslin 街 321 號 Coatbridge ML5 1LZ，蘇格蘭，英國

___1___ 《Business in Our Lives》，作者 Elaine Schuyler　　75.00 英鎊
使用優惠（AUX1417）　　　　　　　　　　　　　　　-30.00
應付金額　　　　　　　　　　　　　　　　　　　　45.00 英鎊

信用卡付款 ****5732
不同訂單的品項可以合併在同一個包裹，當您的訂單出貨時我們將會通知您。

176. Can make inferences based on information in written texts

What is a purpose of the letter?

(A) To ask Mr. Morello to write a book
(B) To explain an enclosed contract
(C) To notify Mr. Morello of a payment
(D) To describe an updated personnel policy

這封信件的目的是什麼？

(A) 要求 Morello 先生寫一本書
(B) 解釋隨信附上的合約
(C) 通知 Morello 先生一筆付款
(D) 敘述更新的人事政策

重點解說

正解 (C)

❶ 信件中 ❶ 第一行提及，「隨信附上《Understanding Our Oceans》的版稅款項」。由此可知，這封信件的目的是為了通知 Morello 先生應得的版稅，故選項 (C) 為正解。
(B) enclosed「隨信附上的」，contract「合約」。

💡 應試者能理解信件內容的主要目的，並能根據文本細節做出推論。

---

177. Can locate and understand specific information in written texts

What was sent in a previous message to Mr. Morello?

(A) Incorrect contact information
(B) Detailed sales numbers
(C) A list of suggested changes
(D) A link to an electronic book

先前發給 Morello 先生的訊息是什麼？

(A) 不正確的聯繫方式
(B) 詳細的銷售數字
(C) 建議更改的清單
(D) 電子書的連結

重點解說

正解 (B)

❶ 信件中 ❶ 第一行到第三行提到，Morello 先生最近應該收到一封電子郵件，其中列出了他出版書籍的銷售數字和版稅。由此可知，Morello 先生先前收到的信件已告知銷售數字和版稅金額，故選項 (B) 為正解。

💡 應試者能理解信件中的實際資訊，並選出正確答案。

---

178. Can locate and understand specific information in written texts

What does Ms. Wicklin mention about Two Swan Press?

(A) It moved to a new location in October.
(B) It has launched a new program for its fifth anniversary.
(C) It has won an industry award.
(D) It has decided to focus on scientific publications.

關於Two Swan出版社，Wicklin小姐提到了什麼？

(A) 它在 10 月搬到新的地點。
(B) 它推出一個五週年新計畫。
(C) 它獲得一個產業獎項。
(D) 它決定要專注在科學出版物。

重點解說

正解 (C)

❶ 信件中 ❷ 第一行到第二行提到「Two Swan 出版社在 10 月獲得由英國圖書產業頒發的年度出版社獎」，故選項 (C) 為正解。

💡 應試者能理解信件中的實際資訊，並選出正確答案。

179.

Can make inferences based on information in written texts

Can connect information across multiple sentences in a single written text and across texts

What is suggested about Mr. Booth?

(A) He is a Two Swan Press author.
(B) He wrote *Business in Our Lives*.
(C) He is an acquaintance of Mr. Morello.
(D) He has purchased items from Two Swan Press before.

關於 Booth 先生的敘述，何者正確？

(A) 他是 Two Swan 出版社的一位作者。
(B) 他撰寫《Business in Our Lives》。
(C) 他是 Morello 先生的熟人。
(D) 他之前在 Two Swan 出版社買過東西。

重點解說

正解 (A)
1 信件中的 ❸ 第一行到第二行提到，所有 Two Swan 出版社的作者都能享有六折的作者優惠。根據 **2** 訂單中的 ❼ 得知，Booth 先生有使用作者專屬折扣，由此可知，Booth 先生也是 Two Swan 出版社的作者之一，故選項 (A) 為正解。
(C) acquaintance「熟人」。

💡 應試者能理解信件中的事實訊息，即使文章並未明確說明，也能做出推論。

💡 應試者能連結信件和訂單中的訊息，在兩個文本之間找出關聯。

180.

Can connect information across multiple sentences in a single written text and across texts

What is indicated about the order?

(A) It has been delayed.
(B) It has not yet been paid.
(C) It contains multiple books.
(D) It includes free shipping.

關於這張訂單何者正確？

(A) 它延遲了。
(B) 它尚未付款。
(C) 它包含多本書。
(D) 它有免運費。

重點解說

正解 (D)
2 訂單中 ❶ 12 月特別優惠得知，「訂單金額超過 35 英鎊免運費」。在 ❽ 應付金額中，得知訂購者還須付 45 英鎊，因此這次的訂單不用運費，故選項 (D) 為正解。

💡 應試者能理解訂單的內容，並連結多個訊息，選出正確答案。

Questions 181-185 refer to the following e-mails.

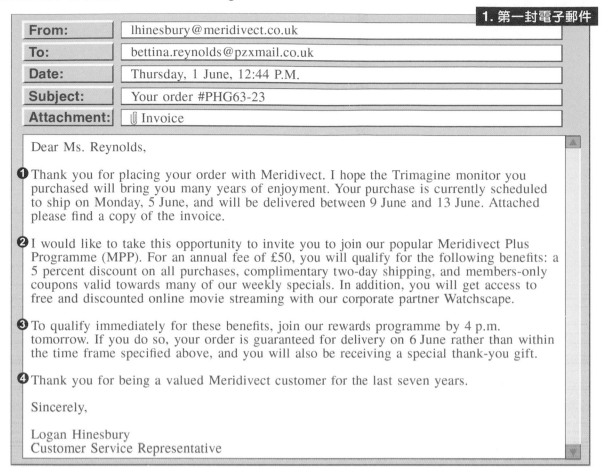

From:	lhinesbury@meridivect.co.uk
To:	bettina.reynolds@pzxmail.co.uk
Date:	Thursday, 1 June, 12:44 P.M.
Subject:	Your order #PHG63-23
Attachment:	Invoice

Dear Ms. Reynolds,

❶ Thank you for placing your order with Meridivect. I hope the Trimagine monitor you purchased will bring you many years of enjoyment. Your purchase is currently scheduled to ship on Monday, 5 June, and will be delivered between 9 June and 13 June. Attached please find a copy of the invoice.

❷ I would like to take this opportunity to invite you to join our popular Meridivect Plus Programme (MPP). For an annual fee of £50, you will qualify for the following benefits: a 5 percent discount on all purchases, complimentary two-day shipping, and members-only coupons valid towards many of our weekly specials. In addition, you will get access to free and discounted online movie streaming with our corporate partner Watchscape.

❸ To qualify immediately for these benefits, join our rewards programme by 4 p.m. tomorrow. If you do so, your order is guaranteed for delivery on 6 June rather than within the time frame specified above, and you will also be receiving a special thank-you gift.

❹ Thank you for being a valued Meridivect customer for the last seven years.

Sincerely,

Logan Hinesbury
Customer Service Representative

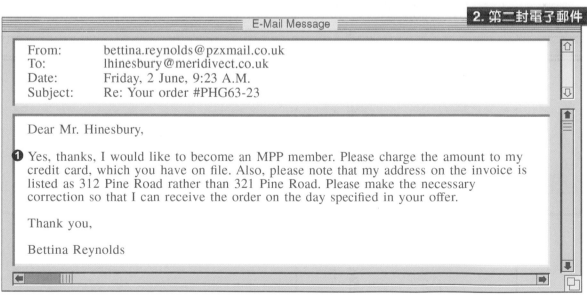

E-Mail Message

From:	bettina.reynolds@pzxmail.co.uk
To:	lhinesbury@meridivect.co.uk
Date:	Friday, 2 June, 9:23 A.M.
Subject:	Re: Your order #PHG63-23

Dear Mr. Hinesbury,

❶ Yes, thanks, I would like to become an MPP member. Please charge the amount to my credit card, which you have on file. Also, please note that my address on the invoice is listed as 312 Pine Road rather than 321 Pine Road. Please make the necessary correction so that I can receive the order on the day specified in your offer.

Thank you,

Bettina Reynolds

請參考以下兩封電子郵件，回答第 181 至 185 題。

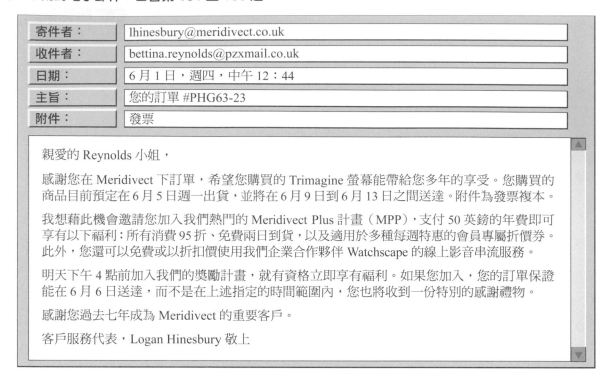

寄件者：	lhinesbury@meridivect.co.uk
收件者：	bettina.reynolds@pzxmail.co.uk
日期：	6 月 1 日，週四，中午 12：44
主旨：	您的訂單 #PHG63-23
附件：	發票

親愛的 Reynolds 小姐，

感謝您在 Meridivect 下訂單，希望您購買的 Trimagine 螢幕能帶給您多年的享受。您購買的商品目前預定在 6 月 5 日週一出貨，並將在 6 月 9 日到 6 月 13 日之間送達。附件為發票複本。

我想藉此機會邀請您加入我們熱門的 Meridivect Plus 計畫（MPP），支付 50 英鎊的年費即可享有以下福利：所有消費 95 折、免費兩日到貨，以及適用於多種每週特惠的會員專屬折價券。此外，您還可以免費或以折扣價使用我們企業合作夥伴 Watchscape 的線上影音串流服務。

明天下午 4 點前加入我們的獎勵計畫，就有資格立即享有福利。如果您加入，您的訂單保證能在 6 月 6 日送達，而不是在上述指定的時間範圍內，您也將收到一份特別的感謝禮物。

感謝您過去七年成為 Meridivect 的重要客戶。

客戶服務代表，Logan Hinesbury 敬上

E-Mail Message

寄件者：bettina.reynolds@pzxmail.co.uk
收件者：lhinesbury@meridivect.co.uk
日期：6 月 2 日，週五，上午 9：23
主旨：回覆：您的訂單 #PHG63-23

親愛的 Hinesbury 先生，

好的，謝謝，我想成為 MPP 會員，請用我儲存的那張信用卡扣款。另外，請注意，我在發票上的地址被列為 Pine 路 312 號，而不是 Pine 路 321 號，請務必修正，以便我可以在您優惠所指定的日期收到我的訂單。

謝謝。

Bettina Reynolds

181. Can make inferences based on information in written texts

What is one reason why the first e-mail was sent?

(A) To announce a delay in delivery
(B) To advertise a new product
(C) To introduce a new service
(D) **To promote a special customer benefit**

發送第一封電子郵件的原因為何？

(A) 通知延遲到貨
(B) 宣傳新產品
(C) 推出新服務
(D) **推廣特別顧客福利**

重點解說

正解 (D)
1 第一封電子郵件中 **②** 第一行到第二行提到，「我想藉此機會邀請您加入我們熱門的 Meridivect Plus 計畫（MPP）」，並在 **②** 第二行到第五行說明加入計畫能享有的福利。由此可知，推廣 MPP 計畫給顧客是其中一個寄信原因，故選項 (D) 為正解。
(B) advertise「宣傳、登廣告」。

💡 應試者能理解電子郵件的目的，並能針對細節做出推論。

182. Can connect information across multiple sentences in a single written text and across texts

What is NOT mentioned as a feature of the Meridivect Plus Programme?

(A) Membership with an online movie service
(B) Free shipping on purchases
(C) **Access to an online music library**
(D) Discounts on merchandise

關於 Meridivect Plus 計畫的特色，何者沒有提到？

(A) 線上影音服務的會員資格
(B) 購物免運費
(C) **使用線上音樂庫**
(D) 商品的折扣

重點解說

正解 (C)
從 **1** 第一封電子郵件中 **②** 第四行到第五行得知，加入的會員可以免費或以折扣價使用 Watchscape 的線上影音串流服務。**②** 第三行也提到，「所有消費 95 折、免費兩日到貨」。唯有選項 (C) 在文章中並未提及，故為正解。
(D) merchandise「商品」。

💡 應試者能理解電子郵件的事實資訊，並能連結整個文本中所提到的訊息。

183. Can locate and understand specific information in written texts

What is indicated about Ms. Reynolds?

(A) She recently moved to a new address.
(B) **She has been a Meridivect customer for several years.**
(C) She is already a Watchscape customer.
(D) She makes most of her purchases online.

關於 Reynolds 小姐的敘述，何者正確？

(A) 她最近搬到新的地址。
(B) **她是 Meridivect 多年的客戶。**
(C) 她已經是 Watchscape 的顧客。
(D) 她大多數在網路購物。

重點解說

正解 (B)
1 第一封電子郵件中 **④** 提到，「感謝您過去七年成為 Meridivect 的重要客戶」。由此可知，Reynolds 小姐已成為 Meridivect 客戶很多年了，故選項 (B) 為正解。

💡 應試者能理解電子郵件的內容，即使選項改寫，也能選出正確答案。

184. Can connect information across multiple sentences in a single written text and across texts

When will Ms. Reynolds' order arrive?

(A) On June 2
(B) On June 6
(C) On June 9
(D) On June 13

Reynolds 小姐的訂單什麼時候會送達？

(A) 6 月 2 日
(B) 6 月 6 日
(C) 6 月 9 日
(D) 6 月 13 日

重點解說

正解 (B)
❶第一封電子郵件中❸第二行到第三行提到，如果 Reynolds 小姐加入獎勵計畫，她的訂單即可在 6 月 6 日送達。隨後從❷第二封電子郵件中❶第一行可知，Reynolds 小姐想要加入這個計畫，因此她的訂單會在 6 月 6 日送達。透過連接此兩個資訊，我們可知選項 (B) 為正解。

💡 應試者能理解電子郵件的內容，並能連結兩封電子郵件各別提及的資訊。

185. Can locate and understand specific information in written texts

What problem does Ms. Reynolds report?

(A) She could not open the attached invoice.
(B) She did not receive any coupons.
(C) Her credit card has been canceled.
(D) Her house number was listed incorrectly.

Reynolds 小姐回報了什麼問題？

(A) 她無法開啟附件的發票。
(B) 她沒有收到任何折價券。
(C) 她的信用卡被取消了。
(D) 她的門牌號碼被寫錯了。

重點解說

正解 (D)
在❷第二封電子郵件❶第二行到第三行中，Reynolds 小姐提及「請注意，我在發票上的地址被列為 Pine 路 312 號，而不是 Pine 路 321 號」。由此可知，她的門牌號碼被寫錯了，故選項 (D) 為正解。
(A) invoice「發票」；(B) coupons「折價券」。

💡 應試者能理解電子郵件中的內容，並選出正確答案。

Questions 186-190 refer to the following e-mail, form, and article.

To:	All Staff
From:	Personnel Department
Date:	June 20
Subject:	Mentoring Program
Attachment:	📎 Application

❶ Employees who have been with Broadside Electronics for less than eighteen months are invited to apply to participate in a new mentoring program that will match a maximum of ten junior employees with long-term company veterans. The goal is that junior employees will sharpen corporate skills, better understand company culture, and develop a more focused career path. Mentees will be assigned to a mentor based strictly on their work assignment and professional interests. The pairs will meet at mutually convenient times throughout the year, from three to five hours per month.

❷ To be considered for participation in this initiative, complete the attached application and return to Mentoring Program Director Tim Wrigley at t.wrigley@broadsideelec.com by July 1. Mr. Wrigley will send notification of his selections by July 15.

MENTORING PROGRAM APPLICATION

❶ **Name:** <u>Cara Drummond</u>   ❷ **Extension:** <u>144</u>

❸ **Division:** <u>Sales</u>

❹ **Professional areas of interest:**
<u>I am most interested in learning about our markets abroad and developing my sales-presentation abilities for these international markets. I am also interested in general career guidance.</u>

❺ **Best workdays and times for meeting:**
<u>Any weekday morning except Monday.</u>

題目/中文翻譯

3. 文章

The Broadside Company Newsletter

Mentoring Program Sees Results

❶ Long-time employee and Vice President of Sales Alena Russo was intrigued when a Personnel Department director approached her about mentoring a less experienced employee under a program that began last year. She is glad to have accepted the assignment. "After working with Ms. Drummond, I am more satisfied with my own duties, because I know I have helped a professional who is just getting started. I only wish that I had had someone looking out for me in my early years," remarked Ms. Russo.

❷ Ms. Drummond explains that she "needed pointers on how to make better sales pitches." She reports that her sales are up by 20 percent now. She better understands the opportunities Broadside Electronics has to offer and what is required to become a manager. "Thanks to Ms. Russo, I have been able to define my career goals, and I am a happier person when I arrive to work every day."

❸ New mentorship pairs are now being formed. Interested parties should contact Tim Wrigley in the Personnel Department.

請參考以下電子郵件、表單和文章，回答第 186 至 190 題。

收件者：	全體員工
寄件者：	人事部門
日期：	6 月 20 日
主旨：	指導計畫
附件：	申請表

在 Broadside 電子公司工作未滿 18 個月的員工，獲邀申請參與一項新的指導計畫，該計畫會將最多 10 位資淺員工和公司資深員工配對。目標是讓資淺員工提升職場技能、更了解公司文化，並制定更聚焦的職涯規畫。學員將嚴格依照工作任務及專業興趣分配給各導師。這一整年兩人將在彼此都方便的時間下，每個月會面三到五小時。

考慮參加此計畫，請在 7 月 1 日前填寫附件的申請表，並寄回到指導計畫主任 Tim Wrigley 的電子郵件 t.wrigley@broadsideelec.com。Wrigley 先生將在 7 月 15 日前寄出入選者通知。

指導計畫申請表

姓名：Cara Drummond　　　　　　分機：144

部門：銷售部

感興趣的專業領域：
我最感興趣的是了解我們的海外市場，並發展我對這些國際市場的銷售簡報能力。我對於一般的職涯諮詢也有興趣。

可會面的最佳工作日與時間：
除了週一之外的任何工作日早上。

Broadside 企業訊息

指導計畫見效

身為資深員工的銷售副總 Alena Russo，當人事部主管找她指導經驗不足的員工時，她就對這個去年開始的計畫很感興趣。她很高興接受這項任務。Russo 小姐說：「和 Drummond 小姐一起合作後，我對於自己的職責更加滿意了，因為我知道我幫助了一位剛起步的專業人士。我只希望早期也有人照拂我。」

Drummond 小姐解釋，她「需要如何把銷售話術做得更好的指點。」她提到現在她的業績提高了 20%；她更加理解 Broadside 電子公司提供的機會以及成為一個經理需具備的條件。「多虧 Russo 小姐，我已經可以確定我的職涯目標，而且當我每天上班時，我就是一個更快樂的人。」

現在正在組成新的指導配對，有意者請聯繫人事部門的 Tim Wrigley。

---

186. `Can locate and understand specific information in written texts`

What does the e-mail indicate about the mentoring program?

(A) It is popular industry-wide.
(B) The number of participants is limited.
(C) It is designed for staff in the sales division.
(D) Participants must attend an orientation meeting.

根據電子郵件內容，關於指導計畫，何者正確？

(A) 它在全產業界很受歡迎。
(B) 參加人數有限制。
(C) 它是為了銷售部門的員工設計的。
(D) 參與者要參加培訓會議。

正解 (B)

❶電子郵件中❶第二行到第三行提及「該計畫會將最多 10 位資淺員工和公司資深員工配對」。由此可知，參加人數是有限制的，故選項 (B) 為正解。
(A) industry-wide「全產業的」；(C) division「部門」；(D) orientation「培訓」。

💡 應試者能理解電子郵件中的資訊，即使選項改寫，也能選出正確答案。

---

187. `Can locate and understand specific information in written texts`

How will the junior employees most likely be selected?

(A) They will be chosen from a management-training group.
(B) They will undergo competitive interviews.
(C) They will be evaluated by Mr. Wrigley.
(D) They will be recommended by a local business school.

挑選資淺員工最有可能的方式是什麼？

(A) 他們將會從一個管理培訓小組中選出。
(B) 他們將會經歷競爭激烈的面試。
(C) 他們將會由 Wrigley 先生評選出來。
(D) 他們將會由本地的商學院推薦。

正解 (C)

❶電子郵件中❷第三行提到，「Wrigley 先生將在 7 月 15 日前寄出入選者通知」。由此可知，這些報名的資淺員工是由 Wrigley 先生挑選出來的，故選項 (C) 為正解。
(B) undergo「經歷」。

💡 應試者能理解電子郵件中的資訊，並選出正確答案。

188.

Can make inferences based on information in written texts

Can connect information across multiple sentences in a single written text and across texts

What is suggested about Ms. Drummond?

(A) She has worked at Broadside Electronics for less than eighteen months.

(B) She has just transferred from another department.

(C) She has received a positive annual review.

(D) She has made many successful presentations abroad.

關於 Drummond 小姐的敘述，何者正確？

(A) 她在Broadside電子公司工作不到18個月。

(B) 她剛從別的部門調過來。

(C) 她獲得了正面的年度考評。

(D) 她在海外發表過許多成功的演說。

正解 (A)

1 電子郵件中 ❶ 第一行提及，這個計畫邀請工作不到 18 個月的員工申請參加。而從 **2** 申請表中 ❶ 得知，申請人為 Drummond 小姐，由此可推斷，Drummond 小姐入職未滿 18 個月，故選項 (A) 為正解。

(B) transfer「轉換、調動」；(C) positive「正面的、積極的」。

💡 應試者能理解申請表的目的，並能針對細節做出推論。

💡 應試者能理解電子郵件的內容，並連結申請表的資訊。

189.

Can make inferences based on information in written texts

Can connect information across multiple sentences in a single written text and across texts

What is most likely true about Ms. Russo?

(A) She is planning to retire soon.

(B) She has international sales experience.

(C) She has mentored many junior employees.

(D) She recently joined the hiring team.

關於 Russo 小姐的敘述，何者最有可能為真？

(A) 她計畫即將退休。

(B) 她有國際銷售的經驗。

(C) 她指導了許多資淺員工。

(D) 她最近加入招聘團隊。

正解 (B)

3 文章中 ❶ 提到，Russo 小姐被指派指導 Drummond 小姐，**2** 申請表中 ❹ 得知，Drummond 小姐想要發展國際市場的銷售簡報能力。由此可推斷，Russo 小姐擁有國際銷售經驗，故選項 (B) 為正解。

(A) retire「退休」；(C) mentor「指導」。

💡 應試者能理解文章的內容，並能針對細節推論文章的目的。

💡 應試者能理解文章內容，並連接內文和申請表所提及的資訊。

190.

Can connect information across multiple sentences in a single written text and across texts

What benefit from the mentoring program have both Ms. Drummond and Ms. Russo enjoyed?

(A) Increased job satisfaction

(B) Quick promotions

(C) Paycheck bonuses

(D) Clearer career goals

Drummond 小姐和 Russo 小姐都喜歡指導計畫中的哪個好處？

(A) 提升工作滿意度

(B) 快速升遷

(C) 薪資獎金

(D) 更明確的職涯目標

正解 (A)

3 文章中 ❶ 第四行到第七行 Russo 小姐提到，「和 Drummond 小姐一起合作後，我對於自己的職責更加滿意了，因為我知道我幫助了一位剛起步的專業人士」。而 **3** 文章中 ❷ 第五行到第六行，Drummond 小姐也提到，「當我每天上班時，我就是一個更快樂的人」。由此可知，Drummond 小姐和 Russo 小姐都提升對於工作的滿意度，故選項 (A) 為正解。

(B) promotion「升遷」；(C) paycheck「薪資」。

💡 應試者能理解文章中的內容，並連接文章中的資訊。

Questions 191-195 refer to the following schedule, e-mail, and article.

1. 時間表

Bartowsky Manufacturing ◈
Production Trial-Run Schedule
Product: Guadiana Office Chair

Date	Activity
Sunday 8 July	• David Mateja arrives in Biłgoraj
❶ Monday 9 July	• Preproduction setup of machinery • Calibrating and adjusting equipment to designated specifications
Tuesday 10 July	• Production and assembly of parts
Wednesday 11 July	• Durability tests (weight, resistance, and material quality)
Thursday 12 July	• David Mateja departs for Bratislava

2. 電子郵件

From:	dmateja@nostilde.sk
To:	thammond@nostilde.it
Subject:	Guadiana trial run
Date:	13 July

Dear Ms. Hammond,

❶ I have an update about the Guadiana trial run at Bartowsky Manufacturing. I am happy to report that the factory is capable of manufacturing the chairs per our design specifications, and the estimated production costs suggest that this would be a viable partnership.

❷ On Monday, I supervised the calibration of the equipment, and the next day, during the trial run, I noticed that the paint that was used to coat the metal elements did not meet our specifications. They were recoated immediately with the correct paint after I pointed out the problem. There were no other issues. The chair was tested on Wednesday and passed all tests.

❸ Today, I discussed our production schedule by telephone with Martin Havranec, explaining that our distribution policy requires that the chairs be available at all retail locations on the release date. He assured me that Bartowsky Manufacturing was prepared to make a significant investment in order to meet our deadline.

David Mateja

3. 報導

Polish Firm Wins Nostilde Contract

22 July–Bartowsky Manufacturing, based in Biłgoraj, Poland, has secured a contract to produce office chairs for the international furniture brand Nostilde.

❶ Nostilde plans to deliver an estimated 200,000 chairs to all its stores in the European Union. This is the largest order in Bartowsky's history. In order to meet the demand, the company pledged to invest in additional equipment to increase the factory's production capacity.

❷ "We've been contemplating a large-scale equipment purchase for a couple of years," explained Bartowsky Manufacturing president Martin Havranec. "We have the space and an available labour pool. Once the new equipment is in place, we will be able to put many skilled applicants to work immediately."

請參考以下時間表、電子郵件及報導,回答第 191 至 195 題。

Bartowsky 製造公司 ◇◆

產品試作時間表

產品:Guadiana 辦公椅

日期	活動
7 月 8 日 週日	• David Mateja 抵達 Biłgoraj
7 月 9 日 週一	• 機器前置作業設定 • 校準及調整設備至指定的規格
7 月 10 日 週二	• 零件生產和組裝
7 月 11 日 週三	• 耐久性測試(重量、阻力和原料品質)
7 月 12 日 週四	• David Mateja 前往 Bratislava

寄件者：	dmateja@nostilde.sk
收件者：	thammond@nostilde.it
主旨：	Guadiana 試作
日期：	7 月 13 日

親愛的 Hammond 小姐，

我有一份關於 Bartowsky 製造公司的 Guadiana 試作的最新消息。我很高興地回報，該工廠有能力依照我們每一個設計規格製造椅子，而且預估的生產成本顯示這將是一個可行的合作關係。

週一我監督了設備的校準，隔天在試作時，我注意到了要用在金屬零件上的塗漆不符合我們的規格。在我指出問題後，他們立刻使用正確的塗漆重新塗刷。沒有其他的狀況。椅子在週三進行測試並且通過了所有檢驗。

今天我和 Martin Havranec 透過電話討論了我們的生產計畫，說明了我們的經銷策略要求椅子在上市日時，就要在所有零售據點準備就緒。他向我保證，Bartowsky 製造公司為了能在期限前完成，已經準備進行重大投資了。

David Mateja

波蘭公司贏得 Nostilde 合約

7 月 22 日一總部位在波蘭 Biłgoraj 的 Bartowsky 製造公司，已經獲得為國際家具品牌 Nostilde 生產辦公椅的合約。

Nostilde 計畫配送估計 200,000 張椅子到所有在歐盟境內的據點。這是 Bartowsky 有史以來最大的訂單。為了符合這需求，該公司承諾投資額外的設備以提升工廠的生產量能。

Bartowsky 製造公司總裁 Martin Havranec 說明：「這幾年我們一直在考慮大規模的設備採購。我們擁有空間及可用的勞動力資源，一旦新設備到位，我們就能立即讓許多有經驗的求職者投入工作。」

191. Can locate and understand specific information in written texts

According to the schedule, what happened on July 9?

(A) Specifications were printed.
(B) Machines were adjusted.
(C) Personnel were trained.
(D) Quality was tested.

根據時間表，7 月 9 日發生什麼事？

(A) 列印出規格說明。
(B) 調整了機器。
(C) 人員接受培訓。
(D) 品質經過測試。

重點解說

正解 (B)
1 時間表中的 ❶ 說明當天有兩件事，一件是「機器前置作業設定」，另一件是「校準及調整設備至指定的規格」，選項 (B) Machines were adjusted「調整了機器」，為最符合的答案。
(A) 文中未提及規格說明被印出；(C) 文中未提及人事訓練；(D) 文中未提及測試品質。

💡 應試者能理解時間表上提及的資訊，即使選項換句話說，也能選出正確答案。

192. Can make inferences based on information in written texts

What does Mr. Mateja suggest about production costs?

(A) They will be confirmed by Mr. Havranec.
(B) They were difficult to negotiate.
(C) They have been revised.
(D) They are acceptable.

Mateja 先生對於生產成本有什麼提議？

(A) 它們將會由 Havranec 先生確認。
(B) 它們很難協調。
(C) 它們被修正了。
(D) 它們是可接受的。

重點解說

正解 (D)
2 電子郵件中的 ❶ 第三行提及，「預估的生產成本顯示這將是一個可行的合作關係。」代表 Mateja 先生的公司是可以接收這個生產成本的，故選項 (D) 為正解。acceptable「可接受的」。
(A) confirm「確認」；(B) negotiate「協調」；(C) revise「修訂、修正」。

💡 應試者能理解電子郵件的大意，並就細節內容推論正確答案。

193. Can make inferences based on information in written texts

Can connect information across multiple sentences in a single written text and across texts

When did Mr. Mateja most likely request a change to meet specifications?

(A) On July 8
(B) On July 10
(C) On July 11
(D) On July 12

Mateja 先生最可能在哪一天要求變更以符合規格？

(A) 7 月 8 日
(B) 7 月 10 日
(C) 7 月 11 日
(D) 7 月 12 日

重點解說

正解 (B)
2 電子郵件中的 ❷ 第一行，Mateja 先生說他週一去監督工廠校準設備，接著提及隔日他發現工廠在試作時所用的塗漆不符原先規格。❷ 第三行提到，「在我指出問題後，他們立刻使用正確的塗漆重新塗刷。」由時間表可知週一為 7 月 9 日，故可推斷隔日為 7 月 10 日。

💡 應試者能理解電子郵件中的資訊，並加以推斷。

💡 應試者能將電子郵件中所提及的訊息與時間表中的資訊連結起來。

194. Can connect information across multiple sentences in a single written text and across texts

TEST 2

What was Mr. Mateja promised on July 13？

(A) That Bartowsky Manufacturing would purchase additional production equipment
(B) That expedited delivery would be available for some customers
(C) That production of the Nostilde chairs would start immediately
(D) That most materials would be sourced in Poland

Mateja 先生在 7 月 13 日承諾什麼事？

(A) Bartowsky 製造公司會採購額外的生產設備
(B) 某些客戶可以使用快速到貨服務
(C) Nostilde 椅子的生產會立即開始
(D) 大多數的原物料會在波蘭取得

重點解說

正解 (A)
2 電子郵件中 **3** 第三行至第四行提及，Bartowsky 製造公司為了在期限前完成，準備進行重大投資，而由 **3** 報導中的 **1** 第四行到第七行得知，這項投資是要採購額外設備以增加生產量能，故選項 (A) 為正解。
(B) 文章皆未提及運送方式，expedited「加速的」；(C) 7 月 13 日並未提及生產時間；(D) source「從特定來源獲得」，但文章並未提及材料來源。

💡 應試者能理解電子郵件中的資訊，即使選項換句話說，也能選出正確答案。

195. Can make inferences based on information in written texts

What does Mr. Havranec suggest about Bartowsky Manufacturing?

(A) It has produced items for Nostilde before.
(B) It designed a chair exclusively for Nostilde.
(C) It will easily find qualified workers.
(D) It will repair a section of the factory

Havranec 先生對 Bartowsky 製造公司的敘述，何者正確？

(A) 它曾經為 Nostilde 生產產品。
(B) 它專門為 Nostilde 設計了椅子。
(C) 它很容易找到合格的工人。
(D) 它將整修工廠的一個區域。

重點解說

正解 (C)
3 報導中的 **2** 第四行到第五行，Havranec 先生提到 available labour pool，這表示有很多符合資格的人員名單。而在 **2** 第五行到第七行，Havranec 先生則提到「一旦新設備到位，我們就能立即讓許多有經驗的求職者投入工作。」由此可知，工廠有更多設備後，需要有更多員工投入生產工作，故選項 (C) 為正解。qualified「合格的」。
(A) 由電子郵件及報導來看，Bartowsky 製造公司未曾幫 Nostilde 生產過任何產品；(B) 文章未提到 Bartowsky 製造公司專門為 Nostilde 設計椅子，exclusively「專門地」；(D) 日程表、電子郵件及新聞稿都未提及工廠要整修。

💡 應試者能理解報導中的資訊並就細節內容推論正確答案。

題目/中文翻譯

Questions 196-200 refer to the following e-mail, flyer, and schedule

1. 電子郵件

To:	Daniel Rodrigues Pereira
From:	Livia Romero
Subject:	Company outing
Date:	August 5

Hello Daniel,

❶ I hope you are settling in well. I'm sure you have had a busy few weeks. Around this time of year, the office manager typically begins arranging our annual company outing. I think we mentioned this during your interview in June. Previously, we have done things like going to a concert and taking a local river cruise. The outing is always great for morale, and everyone looks forward to it.

❷ This year, I think it would be a good idea to get tickets to a sporting event. I know that many staff members are fans of the San Jose Starlings baseball team. It should be an evening game when the team is playing at home. We have a budget of $600.00 this year. Looking at the ticket prices, it seems that will be just enough to get a ticket for every staff member.

❸ I'm sure Elise can assist you with this; she has often helped organize the outings. Let me know if you have any questions.

Best,

Livia Romero
Director of Administration, Loftgren Consulting

2. 傳單

Plan your next event with the San Jose Starlings!

❶ Discounted tickets are available for groups of ten or more. The more tickets you buy, the more you save —perfect for family gatherings, company outings, or charity fund-raisers! Get perks such as free tickets for the organizer, discounts on food, and your group's name displayed on the scoreboard.

❷ **Group Ticket Pricing**

10 tickets	$130.00
30 tickets	$360.00
50 tickets	$550.00
70 tickets	$700.00

❸ Contact **grouptickets@sanjosestarlings.com** or call **408-555-0101** for more information.

San Jose Starlings August Schedule

	Date	Day	Time	Opposing Team	Home or Away
❶	August 13	Sunday	1:05 P.M.	Aspen Monarchs	Home
❷	August 15	Tuesday	7:05 P.M.	Aspen Monarchs	Home
❸	August 19	Saturday	1:05 P.M.	Philipsburg Pinstripes	Away
❹	August 22	Tuesday	7:05 P.M.	Philipsburg Pinstripes	Away

❺ Purchase tickets online at **www.sanjosestarlings.com/tickets**.

請參考以下電子郵件、傳單及時程表，回答 196 至 200 題。

收件者：	Daniel Rodrigues Pereira
寄件者：	Livia Romero
主旨：	公司旅遊
日期：	8 月 5 日

你好 Daniel，

我希望你適應得很好，相信過去幾週你都很忙。每年這時候，辦公室經理通常會開始安排我們的年度公司旅遊；我想我們在 6 月面試時有提過了。以前我們做過的活動，像是去聽音樂會和乘坐當地的河輪。旅遊總是能鼓舞士氣，而且每個人都很期待。

今年，我認為買票參加運動賽事是個好主意，我知道很多同仁是 San Jose Starlings 棒球隊的球迷。當球隊在主場迎戰時，應該是一場傍晚的比賽。我們今年有 600 美元的預算。看看票價，似乎剛好足夠幫每位同仁買一張票。

我相信 Elise 可以在這方面協助你，她經常幫忙規畫旅遊。如果你有任何問題，請讓我知道。

祝一切順利

Livia Romero
Loftgren 顧問公司行政協理

與San Jose Starlings一起計畫你的下一場活動吧！

十人或十人以上的團體可享有優惠票。買越多，省越多一最適合家庭聚會，公司旅遊，或是公益募款活動！還可以獲得額外好處，例如統籌人員的免費門票、餐飲折扣，還有在計分板上顯示你的團體名稱。

團體票價

10 張門票　130 美元
30 張門票　360 美元
50 張門票　550 美元
70 張門票　700 美元

聯繫 **grouptickets@sanjosestarlings.com** 或撥打 **408-555-0101** 獲得更多資訊。

San Jose Starlings
8 月賽程

日期	星期	時間	對手	主場或客場
8 月 13 日	週日	下午 1:05	Aspen Monarchs	主場
8 月 15 日	週二	晚上 7:05	Aspen Monarchs	主場
8 月 19 日	週六	下午 1:05	Philipsburg Pinstripes	客場
8 月 22 日	週二	晚上 7:05	Philipsburg Pinstripes	客場

線上購票 www.sanjosestarlings.com/tickets.

---

196. ~~Can make inferences based on information in written texts~~

Why did Ms. Romero send the e-mail to Mr. Rodrigues Pereira?

(A) To tell him about an upcoming budget cut
(B) To invite him to a concert
(C) To introduce him to his new assistant
(D) To ask him to arrange an event

為什麼 Romero 小姐發電子郵件給 Rodrigues Pereira 先生？

(A) 告訴他即將到來的預算削減
(B) 邀請他參加音樂會
(C) 把他介紹給他的新助理
(D) 要求他安排活動

重點解說

正解 (D)
從❶電子郵件中❶第二行得知，Romero 小姐告知 Rodrigues Pereira 先生，辦公室經理通常會安排年度公司旅遊；❷說明這次員工旅遊的細節；❸提到「我相信 Elise 可以在這方面協助你，她經常幫忙規畫旅遊」。由此可知，Romero 小姐要 Rodrigues Pereira 先生規畫這次的公司旅遊，故選項 (D) 為正解。arrange「安排」。
(A) upcoming「即將到來的」，budget「預算」；(C) assistant「助理」。

💡 應試者能理解電子郵件的內容，並能從文本細節中推論出目的。

197.

Can make inferences based on information in written texts

Can connect information across multiple sentences in a single written text and across texts

What does the e-mail imply about Mr. Rodrigues Pereira?

(A) He recently attended a San Jose Starlings game.
(B) He will be leaving in a few weeks to go on vacation.
(C) He is a professional party planner.
(D) He recently began working for Loftgren Consulting.

關於 Rodrigues Pereira 先生，這封電子郵件暗示了什麼？

(A) 他最近參加了 San Jose Starlings 的比賽。
(B) 他將在幾週後離開去渡假。
(C) 他是個專業的派對策畫人。
(D) 他最近開始在 Loftgren 顧問公司工作。

重點解說

正解 (D)

1 電子郵件中 **❶** 第一行提到「我希望你適應得很好」。第一行到第二行說明公司有安排員工旅遊的傳統，第三行補充，6 月面試時就有告知 Rodrigues Pereira 先生這件事。這封信是 8 月 5 日寄的，由此可知，Rodrigues Pereira 先生剛入職兩個月，故選項 (D) 為正解。

💡 應試者能理解電子郵件中的資訊，並加以推斷。

💡 應試者能將電子郵件中所提及的資訊連結起來。

198.

Can locate and understand specific information in written texts

According to the flyer, what is a benefit of buying tickets as a group?

(A) Reduced ticket prices
(B) Free food
(C) Front-row seating
(D) T-shirts with the team's logo

根據傳單內容，購買團體票的好處是什麼？

(A) 降低票價
(B) 免費食物
(C) 前排座位
(D) 印有球隊標誌的 T 恤

重點解說

正解 (A)

2 傳單中 **❶** 第一行提到「十人或十人以上的團體可享有優惠票」，並在第一行到第二行補充，「買越多，省越多」，故選項 (A) 為正解。reduced「減少、降低」。

(B) 從 **2** 傳單中 **❶** 第四行得知，有餐飲的折扣但不是提供免費食物；(C)、(D) 傳單皆未提及。

💡 應試者能理解傳單內的資訊，即使選項以其他方式改寫，也能選出正確答案。

199.

Can connect information across multiple sentences in a single written text and across texts

How many employees does Loftgren Consulting most likely have?

(A) 10
(B) 30
(C) 50
(D) 70

Loftgren 顧問公司最有可能有多少員工？

(A) 10
(B) 30
(C) 50
(D) 70

重點解說

正解 (C)

從 **2** 傳單中 **❷** 得知，不同人數所對應的票價；**1** 電子郵件中 **❷** 第三行提到，今年有 600 美元的預算，且第四行補充，「似乎剛好足夠幫每位同仁買一張票」。藉由連結此兩個資訊，可知選項 (C) 為正解。

💡 應試者能連接電子郵件和傳單中的訊息，並能在兩個文本之間建立連結。

200. Can connect information across multiple sentences in a single written text and across texts

On what date could Loftgren Consulting employees attend a game?

(A) August 13
(B) August 15
(C) August 19
(D) August 22

Loftgren 顧問公司可以在哪一天看比賽？

(A) 8 月 13 日
(B) 8 月 15 日
(C) 8 月 19 日
(D) 8 月 22 日

重點解說

正解 (B)
❶電子郵件中❷第二行到第三行提到，「當球隊在主場迎戰時，應該是一場傍晚的比賽」；從❸時程表❷可知，8 月 15 日晚上 7:05，球隊在主場比賽。藉由連結此兩個資訊，可知選項 (B) 為正解。

💡應試者能連接電子郵件和時程表的訊息，並且能在兩個文本之間建立連結。

TOEIC® Listening and Reading Test
Official Test-Preparation Guide Vol. 8 Reading Part

TOEIC®聽力與閱讀測驗官方全真試題指南 Vol. 8 閱讀篇

發 行 人　邵作俊
作　　者　ETS®
編　　譯　TOEIC®臺灣區總代理 忠欣股份有限公司
出 版 者　TOEIC®臺灣區總代理 忠欣股份有限公司
地　　址　台北市復興南路二段 45 號 2 樓
電　　話　(02) 2701-7333
網　　址　www.toeic.com.tw

出版日期／中華民國 112 年 5 月
再版日期／中華民國 113 年 3 月
定　　價／新台幣 650 元
本書如有缺頁、破損或裝訂錯誤，請寄回更換。

閱讀測驗全真試題 (1) 練習用答案卡

劃記說明 MARKING DIRECTIONS

○ 請使用鉛筆劃記 Use only pencil
○ 圓圈請塗滿劃黑 Darken the circles completely
○ 請擦試乾淨 Erase cleanly

正確劃記 CORRECT MARK	錯誤劃記 INCORRECT MARKS

◎重要注意事項 IMPORTANT NOTICE
● 請勿劃記試題本 Marking on the test book is prohibited.
● 請勿跨區作答 Please work on the assigned section only.

1 聲明與簽名：請閱讀下方聲明文字，並全部抄寫於下方橫線中。

答案卡上記載的資料皆為我本人所親筆填寫。我同意遵守TOEIC測驗規定及違規處理規定，也不會以任何形式向他人洩漏或公開TOEIC測驗部分或全部的題目。

簽名 Signature：

測驗日期 Date：　　　/　　　/

2 准考證號碼 ADMISSION NUMBER

3 國家代碼 COUNTRY CODE

4 語言代碼 LANGUAGE CODE

5
職稱 OCCUPATION

學校／公司名稱 SCHOOL / COMPANY NAME

所在城市 CITY

6
測驗地點 TESTING LOCATION

試場 TESTING ROOM

7
試題本號碼 TEST FORM

試題本流水編碼 TEST BOOK SERIAL NUMBER

聽力測驗 LISTENING (Parts 1 - 4)

閱讀測驗 READING (Parts 5 - 7)

閱讀測驗全真試題 (2) 練習用答案卡

1 聲明與簽名：請閱讀下方聲明文字，並全部抄寫於下方橫線中。

答案卡上記載的資料皆為我本人所親筆填寫。我同意遵守TOEIC測驗規定及達規處理規定，也不會以任何形式向他人洩漏或公開TOEIC測驗部分或全部的題目。

聲明與簽名：請閱讀下方聲明文字，並全部抄寫於下方橫線中。

簽名 Signature：

測驗日期 Date： ___ / ___ / ___

2 准考證號碼 ADMISSION NUMBER

3 國家代碼 COUNTRY CODE

4 語言代碼 LANGUAGE CODE

5 職稱 OCCUPATION

學校／公司名稱 SCHOOL / COMPANY NAME

所在城市 CITY

6 測驗地點 TESTING LOCATION

試場 TESTING ROOM

7 試題本號碼 TEST FORM

試題本流水編碼 TEST BOOK SERIAL NUMBER

聽力測驗 LISTENING (Parts 1 - 4)

閱讀測驗 READING (Parts 5 - 7)